My Spectacular Bid

8 Aug 2017

Steven L. Werder

STEVEN L. WERDER

February 21, 2015

PAGE PUBLISHING, INC.
New York, NY

First originally published by Page Publishing, Inc. 2016

While some events in this story are based upon real life events, anything that resembles the truth is coincidental. No one person is a real life person but merely a combination of many people, some real and some make believe.

ISBN 978-1-68213-597-6 (Paperback)
ISBN 978-1-68213-598-3 (Digital)

Printed in the United States of America

Chapter 1

Before my life as a teenager, not much of anything happened. For the most part, I was good and rarely got into much trouble. But when my teenage years came in Callaway County, Missouri, I was pulled into another world, a world that existed only at night. Whether that world was good or bad is for you to decide. This is my story. . .

Chapter 2

The final bell rang, and school was officially out for the summer of 1977. Thankfully, it was the end of my freshman year of high school. I ran toward my best friend and yelled, "Hey, so what are we going to do this summer?"

"I heard that Jimmy was starting up his hay crew. I heard there was enough hay to buck for the entire summer, and he'll pay five cents a bail."

"Damn, I'm in on that."

"Okay then, we'll pick you up around ten or so. Be ready. . ."

I ran home and told my mom that I had already gotten a job for the summer. She was glad. She always thought I needed to be working or doing something aside from just staying at home. Until this summer, I had always mowed yards around town, mostly for the ladies from my grandmother's church. I was glad to be doing something different this summer, but little did I know just how different that something would turn out to be.

I ran upstairs to my room and turned on my AM radio. Most of the time, all you could pick up was static. I stared at a pencil drawing of Billy Jack that a friend drew for me. I loved Billy Jack; he's a real badass. But then I remembered I was on the summer baseball team and that they bucked hay at night, so I couldn't do both. I was good at all the sports, but I was the best at football, and bucking hay would build muscles for football. Plus, bucking hay would get me out of going to church camp, which I hated. Well, that settled it. I'd just not be able to play baseball that summer. While I was lying on my bed, my mind went back in time to one of those church camps. I thought about the musty smell of the old wooden chapel and how they had set out metal chairs in rows for everyone to sit in. The preacher would proudly lean against the podium and scan the group of us as we would file in. I never really felt one way or another about God, but I hated the preacher. He'd stand up, shout, and carry on like some great defense lawyer. I remember staring up at the ceiling fans as they wobbled and spun really slow. A couple of blue jays would squawk and carry on, as the preacher would speak. Then, he would slam down his fist and say, "The devil is your enemy. He's like a prowling lion just waiting to devour you."

I always worried about the prowling lion. At the end of the service, the piano lady would play, and the preacher would pray. He'd ask for all the lost souls to come forward and be spared of an eternal life in the devil's lake of fire. I was a nervous wreck and tried to go forward, but I never could. I hated that preacher for putting those images in my head, but his words have stuck with me, and even now I can feel the prowling lion following me. I figured one day I would run smack dab into the prowling lion, and we would have a showdown.

Chapter 3

Morning came quickly, and I jumped from bed with excitement. Finally, no more school and no more upperclassmen to deal with; just me and my best friend for the whole summer, doing God only knows what. I sat on our back porch waiting for them to come and pick me up. I know how to buck hay because we have our own farm, and my dad raises appaloosa horses. I was always amazed at horses because of their grace and power, and the horse, well, it ain't meant to be eaten. It's a beast of burden. Plus, I really liked the idea that engines are rated in horsepower. I heard them pull up and honk. I jumped up and hollered to my mom, "I'm going. . . . don't know when I'll be back."

I ran to meet them, and they were in a brand-new Jeep with the top off. That was the coolest thing I ever had seen. They all said, "Come on . . . get in. Let's go. . ." The driver was a senior named Walter, and his parents bought him the Jeep as a graduation present, and because he was leaving to join the Coast Guard after the summer was over. So I jumped in, and we were off. Now, the guys explained to me that we would buck hay until after dark until about ten or so, and then we would get some beer and go to a famous clay pit to swim and party.

Walter said, "Boys, if we are real lucky, we may even see some naked girls skinny dipping."

Well, now there's two things that I have never seen or did. I had never drank a beer before, and I had never seen a real-life naked girl before.

We drove to the outside of town and turned on a gravel road and then pulled up to a trailer house with a big barn. Jimmy said, "Wait here and I'll go and get the foreman." We sat and waited, and we talked of the great time we were going to have that night. While we were waiting, the back door of the trailer house opened, and the screen door slammed. We watched to see who was coming out, but it wasn't the foreman or Jimmy. Instead, it was the foreman's wife. The whole world went silent. I think even the birds stopped to look. She walked out toward the barn wearing blue jean shorts and a white t-shirt. Walter reached over and slapped me and said, "Boy, shut your mouth. You're slobbering." Then, everyone busted out laughing.

I said, "What the hell was that?" My heart was pounding in a way I had never felt. The only time I can even remember my heart pounding that hard was before a track race I was in.

She disappeared, and Jimmy came running out. He said, "Boys, you can look, but you can't touch. That guy will whip your ass in a minute."

The foreman came out and smiled at us and said, "Follow me, boys. Have I got a surprise for you." Then he busted out laughing and jumped in his new '77 Chevy Scottsdale. It was cream and maroon colored. We followed him through some trees and through a small creek to a clearing and around a corner to a giant field that had hundreds of bales of hay. Hay bales were everywhere you looked, and again, Walter slapped me to shut my mouth.

The foreman said, "Well, what do you boys think now?"

He let out a giant laugh and drove off. I guess I know why we bucked hay at night. It looked like a herd of buffalo in that field, and at night, you couldn't see the whole field.

We bucked and bucked and bucked some more until someone called "last load." We could only imagine what it would be like to have a woman like the foreman had and that was just about all the topics and conversations we had throughout that evening. We finished our last load, and Walter said, "Come on, boys. Let's go get some beer and go to the clay pit." We were as nasty as humans could get, and the thought of jumping in some water to wash off sounded good. So Walter laid towels down on the seats, and he put in an eight-track tape of Led Zeppelin's "Ramble On" and cranked it up. The night was warm, clear, and full of stars. I felt alive and free as we rode toward town. It was a different feeling of being alive, though. I think seeing the foreman's wife and images of girls skinny-dipping woke something up inside of me.

With the music cranked, all I could do was think back to when I was younger. In the early '70s, my parents would take my sister and I out to eat on Friday nights. Usually, we went to A&W or Dog 'n Suds. But I remember as we would drive through town, I would see the hippies hanging out in the vacant parking lots. They were generally sitting on top of their cars, and usually the guys would be hugging and kissing their girlfriends. It seemed as if everyone smoked cigarettes, and the intermitting glows of taking a puff looked like orange lightning bugs hovering around their cars. I was scared of them, but they also fascinated me. They had a certain appeal about them that I felt drawn to. I don't know why because the rumor that they took drugs and smoked things that would cause them to lose their minds scared me. But now as the Jeep got closer to town, I knew I wasn't riding with my parents. I was on my own and was with friends, which somehow made me part of the night people I was so scared of.

The late '60s and '70s were a rebellious period for teenagers in Callaway County. The Vietnam War was never very popular. The evening news with Walter Cronkite was on a black and white TV in our house every night at 5:30. The Beatles were always rumored to be fighting each other. Elvis tried to make a comeback but died. The answer to someone in politics was if you didn't agree with them, just kill them—like somehow that was easier. It seemed that if your last name ended with a "K," like JFK, or RFK, or MLK, they killed you. We had never recovered from those murders. Imagine a world when a Chevelle SS, Shelby Mustang, Trans AM, or Camaro Firebird was brand new. They weren't even considered a classic car. A world when rock and roll wasn't classic music but was contemporary music. This was the world I was about to enter on this Friday night after bucking hay for eight hours.

Walter fidgeted with the eight-track. Sometimes, he would have to shove a book of matches in beside it to get it to play. He said, "Boys, get ready to see a world that very few get to see." Of course, he was referring to the night people and the clay pit. We cruised slowly through town. Girls would whistle at us, and we felt cool. But our mission wasn't in town; it was the Hilltop Liquor Store. As we approached the liquor store, I felt my heart start to pound again. Walter eased into the parking lot. I noticed there were about six or seven trailer houses in the back of the liquor store. I could see a group of people down there circled around a fire, and I could hear music, but I couldn't make out any faces. They were just shadows in the night. There's no way I could ever know how my life was about to change. Maybe the prowling lion was out, but I didn't care. Walter came out carrying two boxes of beer and yelled for me to open the cooler. We iced down the beer and eased our way toward the clay pit. As he backed out and drove by, I stared down at the group of night people. I wondered who they were and what they were doing. Soon, I would discover that it was the lion's den, and I would have to face the lion at that trailer house one day.

Chapter 4

The beer was cold and tasted stout, but after a few swallows, you began to like it. So, by the time we got to the clay pit, I was buzzed, and there it was. Even at night under a bright sky, you could see the turquoise-blue, beautiful water dug deep in the ground with remnants of gray-colored clay mountains all around it. The road spiraled down to the water's edge. As our headlights shined down, people were everywhere. It was the grandest thing I had ever seen. The night opened up, and I saw a new world. People were dancing and swimming, people sitting on top of car hoods kissing and doing other things. People were drinking and smoking cigarettes and pot; some were passed out, and others were puking. I didn't recognize many of the shadow people, but I did recognize some of the upper-classmen and women and was surprised to see them at this place doing the things that people of the night did. I never really thought about it much, but they must have thought the same thing about me. However, I was still a freshman, and I doubted anyone really even knew who I was, especially any of the girls. So we got out of the Jeep with our beer in hand; you had to have a beer in your hand, or you stuck out like a sore thumb. We began to mingle. The night was full of stars, and as you got closer to people, your eyes would adjust, and it was actually quite clear. The music sounded so good. It echoed out over the water and bounced off the clay hills. Other cars would come down the hill, and you watched to see if it was someone you might know. Sometimes, the cars would go another direction from us. I always wondered who was in the cars we would see coming down the hills. I would say on that night, there must have been fifty people or more down along the water's edge. Finally, I began to feel part of the crowd. Finally, after several beers, I began to feel confident enough to be one of the group. At times, I would say to myself, my mom and dad will kill me if they knew what I was taking part in. Yet, I could not, nor would not, stop. This was too much fun. Eventually, the beer ran out, and the night was getting old, so people began to leave. One by one, I heard the loud pipes and the headlights go up the spiral road. The music faded. Yet, my friends and I stayed. I never wanted to leave. To this day, I still chase that feeling I had that night. I have never matched it, though. My friends and I just sat there listening to a Lynyrd Skynyrd eight-track we had. Finally, it was just us and a few other cars on the other side of the clay pit. You could hear their music and laughter. I'm sure they could hear ours. We didn't know them, so we stayed to ourselves. I would learn that sometimes those people weren't always just there for the party.

In the late 1970s, people of Callaway County were insulated from the trends of the current year, but eventually, the fads and fashions would make it there. The hippie generation had made its way to my town. Long hair and sideburns were in. Most of the older people really hated to see all this rebellion in its youth, and they fought it hard. I was on the football team, and our coach had a hair rule that consisted of "your ears had to be visible, and your hair could not touch your eyebrows."

Most of us hated the hair rule, even the black guys who had afros in the '70s. Being a hippie was cool, and I wanted to be one after my night at the clay pit. It was as if I had been bitten by a vampire. All I could think about was the nightlife, the parties, smoking pot and, of course, looking for girls.

I was raised well. My family didn't have a lot, but we had all we needed. My grandmother was a Baptist, and if you know anything about Baptists, they are the opposite of the nightlife people. So naturally, I had an inner war going on inside my mind. Yet, the night was going to win, for at least the next four years. I went to church on Sundays as a young boy, and I believed in God. I'm not sure why or what made me choose the nightlife, but I was all in after that first night at the clay pit. No one forced me to party or try drugs. I wanted to try them, and I was drawn to the party crowd.

So the summer began in 1977 at the clay pit and my friends and I would buck hay and go to the clay pit every night. And every night, the crowd was there. At first, my mom wouldn't say much. I guess she figured I was just being a teenager. But after a while, she began to question me, and I would get mad. But just like a vampire, I would sleep all day then run all night. Trust me when I tell you I loved it. Still to this day, I think back and wish for that feeling to come again.

Then summer was over and back to school. I was a sophomore now, and I was a veteran of the night. I hated school, I hated my coach, I hated my teachers, and I hated the cops. My mom and I would fight all the time. Now, I could only party on Friday and Saturday night, and that just wasn't enough. I needed more just like a vampire needed blood. I needed the nightlife. I had gone out so much that summer that I met new friends. A lot of them felt like I did. A lot of them needed the nightlife. Maybe we needed each other; I'm not sure. I did learn that there were other places to party, which made the night even more fun and exciting, but no other place could match the lure of the clay pit.

Chapter 5

My town is called Fulton, a small town of about ten thousand people, but it is the largest town in Callaway County, Missouri. I suppose my town is like most towns of its size. I mean not much good or bad happens that would be considered noteworthy. But my senior year of high school, which was 1980, something noteworthy was taking place. It was of the dark, evil kind. I don't mean the kind of evil that you would see in the movies, where the devil enters someone, but more of an evil that comes out when the devil works inside men and women to kill people and then kill more people to cover it up. Then, like a winter snow begins, the lies and deceit begin and usually don't stop until the storm runs its course.

Most days we would go to school, but when school ended, we would go for a ride on gravel roads and usually smoke pot and drink beer. If we weren't doing that, we were looking for someone to buy us beer and looking for a bag of pot. None of us really meant to cause any harm except the occasional siphoning of gas from a farmer's tractor, which, by the way, could get you shot at by a shotgun. No one really had a lot of money, and times were hard. Yet, we always managed to find a party, which was in the clay pit. You could climb hills in four-wheel drive or skinny-dip with friends and hope you caught a glimpse of some naked girls, which was rare, but we hoped. This was how my sophomore days were mostly spent, but. . .

Chapter 6

For some reason, I began to change, both inside and out. I felt different. I felt dark. As fall began to give into winter, we would still go out to the clay pit and party. The seasons didn't matter to us, as long as we could find a party. One clear and cool weeknight, we went out to the pit, and I could see taillights of a car on the opposite side. We wanted to go down to our spot. You always checked before you went down the road to the water; you always looked to see if anyone was in your spot. We got to our spot, rolled the windows down, popped a beer, and began to smoke a little pot and some cigarettes. The music was low, and we just relaxed. The people on the other side appeared to be doing the same. All I could think about was what they were doing. I could only see their dark shadows. Eventually, another car would come and join them. You could hear voices and music but never really make out anything clearly. I said to my friends, "Some night, we should go over there," and they all agreed.

My friends and I thought mostly the same way about life. We all loved to party and look for girls. My best friend, he always drove. He only had a dad, and his dad would get mad at us. He would say, "All you all do is run the damn streets." His dad drank and would just sit in the kitchen by himself and drink and smoke cigarettes. He would get drunk and get really mean. I felt sorry for my best friend; my family wasn't like that at all.

On Friday nights, my dad would give me ten dollars, and my friend and I would pool our money together. We'd put in gas, look for someone to buy us a case of beer and then we would be set for the night. We always saved a little for cigarettes and an after midnight snack. We had it down to a science. It would take about five dollars for gas each, which was seventy cents a gallon; two and a half dollars for beer, the kind didn't matter; fifty cents for cigarettes; and two dollars for food and ice. So with his ten dollars and my ten dollars, we would manage to get through the night.

Once we got all the beer, gas, and cigarettes, we would sit into the night. We would cruise the strip. People would be sitting in the parking lots throughout town. Usually, we'd pull up to someone sitting and ask, "Where's the party?" If we didn't find one, we just hit the gravel roads. We never really worried or talked about deep, intellectual things or politics. All we thought about were girls. None of us had been with a girl, at least all the way. We all dreamed of the day that would happen. The rumor was that the older party girls would let you have some. So we always looked for them.

There was a long gravel road called Smokey Road that would take you to the clay pit, and usually, that's what we did every weekend. We would drink and smoke as we slowly made our way to the pit. My friend said, "So and so and I heard that so and so stole a car," and that the cops were chasing them through town. I thought that was dumb. But we went on to the clay pit, and when we pulled up, red lights were flashing and bouncing off the water. They had chased the person all the way to the pit, to the spot opposite of ours. The cops had the man, and he was in handcuffs. He was tall and scroungy with long hair. It took four cops to handle him. The cops came around to everyone at the clay pit, took names, and then made everyone leave. I was mad. The cops ruined our night. The man ruined the pit. Now, the cops knew where the night people hung out.

We started up the hill to leave, the red lights bouncing off our car. I remember that the red lights were bright and clear. You could see red flashing on our faces. When we got to the top of the clay pit, I looked down and could see the cops looking into the man's car. I wondered what they found. On the ride back, my friend and I talked about how dumb it was to steal a car. We wondered why someone would even think they could get away with it.

As we entered town, people were still sitting in the vacant lots. We pulled in beside someone we knew and asked what was going on. He said that a hopped up midnight blue Chevelle SS came flying through town. It flew through every stoplight in town as if daring the cops to catch him. No one knew who was in the car or even whose car it was. We all knew what everyone drove. The rumor was that some out-of-town people who had worked at the nuclear plant came to town. They had taken some purple microdot acid and the driver had a bad trip.

Now that was new to us. Until now, we smoked some pot and drank. We never thought about the hard stuff. Plus, the hard stuff wasn't in town until they began to build the nuclear plant. As we sat in the parking lot talking, the cops began to come back through town. Then a tow truck came with the car. It was like time stopped. We just watched the infamous car being towed through town. One of our friends pulled in beside us. He had stayed at the clay pit to watch the cops. He said they had two guys and two girls in handcuffs.

All I could think about was who those people were. Why did they do such a silly thing? Even worse, I felt drawn toward them. I'm not sure, but I wanted to be as infamous as they were. They were the talk of the town. They were immortalized in a dark way, and they were bad.

Chapter 7

Winter always seemed long, but finally, spring came. Springtime in Callaway County was full of life and new beginnings. April is the best month because the days are longer and the nights are warmer. But also the wild locust trees and wild honeysuckle are in full bloom, and the whole county is filled with this heavenly sweet smell. In fact, people would say that heaven had to have locust trees because of their sweet smell. Another really cool thing that happened in the spring-time was mushroom hunting. The mushroom season was mostly compared to a modern-day gold rush. Whenever the word got out that some mushrooms were found, then we all made a mad dash to the woods to our secret spots. Some people would just as soon die and go to the grave than tell anyone of their secret spots. The arrival of the hummingbirds was also fun to witness. Most of the time, I would have to put out the sugar water feeders for my grandmother, and I would sit on the porch and watch them fight and carry on. But the best springtime spectacle was to witness the sunrise at the clay pit. The water was the bluest and clearest in the springtime. And as the sun would rise, a mist cloud would form on top just a few feet above the water. The swallows would swoop the water and feed on mosquitoes, which I was thankful for because we really enjoyed sleeping in the truck bed under the stars. And so, this is mostly why the springtime was the best time for the clay pit and for the night people. We could stay out later. It was a good time to look for girls. I know this must be the only reason we could've managed to get through the long winter. The thought of the pit and the parties there were all I could think about. I knew that I was a part of the clay pit crowd. In a way, I was entering my sophomore year at the clay pit. Since the cops had come that winter night to arrest the car thieves, we discovered there were safer places to party. This even made us more excited for the summer to come.

With summer finally there, my friends and I knew we would be free to find all the parties we could. No more hair checks from the coaches, no more homework to do. All we worried about was a summer job and going out to the clay pit. Our party routine never really changed, but with a summer job, we had more money. With more money meant more beer and cigarettes and other things. And so, this is where my life has its first encounter with the prowling lion and my first crossroad deal with the devil.

Chapter 8

One early, warm summer night, around midnight, my friend and I was driving on a backroad when a hopped up white Dodge Charger come flying up on us and tried to pass. My friend wouldn't let him get by us, but finally, the car did get by. When the car got in front of us, it stopped us in the road. Then, in front of our headlights rolled out the biggest man I had even seen. We didn't know who he was; we had never seen him before. He was a giant man with thick, long, black hair. He was heavy set, and he was coming right to the driver side of our car. In the headlights, he even cast a bigger shadow, as we could only look at him. We couldn't move or even try to get away. All we said was "Oh shit" and waited as he got to our car. I'm sure to him we were no threat. I'm sure he could see we were just kids. Then, he beat on the driver's side window. My friend rolled it down. I was wishing that I was somewhere else.

"Yes, sir?" my friend stuttered.

"Do you have some sort of problem?" the giant man yelled.

"Nope, we were just horsing around."

The giant man stood back and slammed his fist on the car hood, then yelled, "If I ever see you guys out of this car, I'm going to kick your asses. Get out of here before I decide to do it now." We didn't leave in a rush. We slowly backed up, kind of like when you are walking, and you come across a copperhead snake. We just eased back very slowly and went back toward town. My friend said, "Shit."

We just sat there. . . silent, wondering what had just happened.

As we made our way back into town, we saw our friend Larry. Larry always sat parked in the vacant lots. He would have his parking lights on, and he would just sit in his car, usually listening to Van Halen at low volume and smoking cigarettes. Larry was a true hippie. He never wore a shirt or shoes and had a turquoise necklace with an arrowhead. He had long, curly hair and a peach fuzz whiskered chin. When we pulled up to Larry, small smoke clouds were coming out of his window. A cherry red glow was beaming off his cigarette. "Hey, Larry, where's the party?" we asked.

"I don't know; I'm just sitting here."

We told Larry about the man that just about killed us. We described the guy to him, but he said he never heard of such a man, nor had he ever seen a white Charger in town. Well then, we figured maybe he was just passing through town, and we hoped we would never see him again. We were wrong; we would learn who he was a few weeks later.

Chapter 9

Summer in the '70s was a great time, especially for a teenage boy. I'm saying we didn't have a worry in the world. My friend had just bought a Pioneer cassette super tuner. No more eight-track tapes with cardboard shoved in the player to make them sound right. The car could be the biggest piece of junk, but if you had tunes; that was all that mattered. Summer had just started for us so we were as happy as we could be. The local colleges would have a short summer session, so the college kids were still in town. One early evening, my friend and I were sitting in the Hardee's parking lot, alongside Larry, when out of the evening sunset come two college guys running, but they were naked. Now, I'm not sure what would make a man even think about running through town naked, but they were, and it was quite a sight to see. We just busted out laughing as they ran on through town. You could hear cars start to honk their horns. Of course, here come the cops flying through town to catch them. That was just as funny. I don't think they ever caught them.

As we finally began to settle down, Larry said, "Would you look at that?" And as we turned our heads, we saw two girls riding horses, and yep, they were naked. This was a teenage boy's dream come true. We just stopped and watched. I'm sure our mouths were wide open. What a sight! They had to have been sent from heaven. Time seemed to stop, and we couldn't even speak. They turned the corner and headed out of sight. But that sight would stay with us all night. In fact, I can still see them in my mind forty years later. We had always heard about streakers; now we saw some.

With those simple joys fresh in our head, we decided to get some beer and go out to the clay pit. The music sounded so good; the beer was cold, and it was beginning to be night time. When we reached the pit, it was just getting dark. That was the best time to arrive. We could usually get a good spot to park, and we would smoke pot and drink and watch the cars come down the hill. As the cars started to arrive, my friend and I sat back and laughed about the men streakers. That sure was a funny sight. But we relived with great detail the visions of the naked girls on horses. We didn't laugh about the girls. We thought we were lucky to have witnessed such a heavenly sight, and most likely, God had put us at that place and time.

Most of the cars and trucks had dual exhaust, so they sounded good. In summer, when it's warm and humid, the air would be thick, and the dust from the gravel road would hover just a little higher than the trees. So when headlights from a car came to the clay pit, the light would bounce off the dust and spill out in all directions. We would watch the cars roll in one by one. We could tell this was going to be a good night to party.

However much fun we were having instantly came to a halt because we instantly recognized a car on the opposite side of the clay pit. The car was a white Charger and the giant man was leaning against it. He had a girl on each side of him. I also recognized the tall scroungy man, the man who was arrested last winter. They had a small fire going. We knew who the people on the opposite side were now. Not by name, but by faces we had seen. They were minding their own business. They didn't appear to be criminal, but they were, and we knew they were, most likely no good.

My friend and I decided maybe we needed to leave the pit for the night. So we got in our car and headed up the hill. We hoped the giant man would not recognize our car. Our encounter with the giant had been a few weeks earlier. As we got to the top of the hill, I looked back down at the water and could see the giant man. He still looked giant even from a distance. We stopped and got out. My friend said, "Maybe we shouldn't come back here for a while."

I said, "Damn, I wish we knew who the giant man was. Maybe we can get to know him and smooth things over."

My friend said, "I'm not sure he would be anyone you would want to get mixed up with."

I could only agree.

We got in the car and headed back to town. We still had beer and cigarettes. We still had gas. We decided to look for another place to party. Funny thing about us, we really didn't require much to have fun. We always found something to laugh about. We were always laughing, and I believe that was the biggest part of our lives. One time, we had bought some pork steak, bread and chips to barbecue. We had gone to our friend's trailer house. We sat the bread on the counter, played cards and just hung out. Finally, we decided to get the fire ready and cook. My friend grabbed the bread. A mouse had eaten a hole like a tunnel all the way through the center. We all just busted out laughing and ate the bread anyway. When we got the munchies from pot, we seemed to eat just about anything.

The drive back from the clay pit was slow, and we tried to figure out what to do about the giant man and his crowd. We decided to figure out what their names were and where they were from. We pulled into town, but we were nervous because we had been drinking. We saw Larry sitting in the Hardee's parking lot, so we pulled in to talk. Now, you have to understand—Larry was cool. Larry wasn't scared of anyone, and he always had a good-looking girl with him. In fact, we called him cool Larry. We pulled up beside him, and sure enough, he had a girl. They were smoking pot and listening to CCR's "Someday Never Comes" at a low volume.

My friend said, "Larry, what's going on tonight?"

Larry just kind of stared with glassy eyes and said, "Nothing that I know of. Where you guys been?"

My friend said, "We've been at the clay pit but decided to leave."

Larry and the girl were passing a joint back and forth. Larry said, "Why did you leave so early?"

Then my friend finally confessed our dilemma.

Larry said, "I'll find out who those guys are for you."

We started our car and got out of town.

We spent the night drinking and listening to music. We played a Bill Withers' song, "Use Me," and we just rode on gravel roads. We knew we had to figure out who the giant man was. I'm not sure how we got mixed up in something so serious and evil. We were just looking to have fun, maybe even get lucky and find some girls. Instead, we found trouble. It was trouble of the worst kind, trouble that you can't get away from unless something or someone helps you get away from it. My friend dropped me off at my house. I went home worried that I was getting into something I couldn't turn back from. But the night kept calling me to come out and play. My mom and dad would ask me if something was wrong. I had changed. I was darker. I stopped caring about the childhood dreams that I had. I was still really good at all the sports I played. I was still playing football. I loved to play football. Many people said I was going to play at MU one day. Yet, now the nightlife was slowly taking all that away. I only wanted to drink and party. I never thought about the future. I only thought about the present. I didn't know, but the next two years were going to be a fight, a fight for my soul. That fight for good and evil in my soul had already started.

Chapter 10

My family was good. I remember one time when I was younger; my mom told me that my dad had a surprise for us when we came home from school. I begged her to tell me, but she said I would see when I got home from school. That day, when I got off the bus, I ran inside to see what my dad had gotten for us. It was a color TV. I felt like I was the luckiest person alive. Now we could watch Gunsmoke in color. My mom and dad always tried to do something fun for my sister and I. Mostly, we would go out to eat. But sometimes they would take us to the movies. We saw *Gone with the Wind*, *The Poseidon Adventure*, *Butch Cassidy and the Sundance Kid*, *Jaws*, *True Grit*, and *Rocky*. I loved all those movies. I still remember them to this day. I remember how innocent I felt back then, just being with my mom, my dad, and my sister. I know we didn't have a lot of money growing up, but I know now that it didn't take a lot of money back then either. My grandmother had a color TV before we did. We would go to her house on Sunday after church and have dinner.

I remember my grandmother always asking me about church. I would get really uncomfortable. Sometimes, we would have to watch Billy Graham specials at her house. I really hated to watch him. In fact, he scared me. Yet, I knew that he was talking about good and evil. I'd always be hungry for those Sunday dinners. But when I started to hang out and party, I'd have a hangover on Sunday and could hardly even look at food. Everyone would ask me if I was sick. I'd say I just wasn't hungry.

To understand my inner struggle, you need to understand my grandmother. She was a small lady. She grew up in the Great Depression. She was a kind person who usually found good in all people or things. My grandfather died when I was nine or ten. So I was to become the man around her house. My sister and I would stay with her every Friday night. We would watch *Sanford and Son*, *All in the Family*, and then *The Waltons*. *The Waltons* would best describe my family and their beliefs. *The Waltons* had the same innocent children and lifestyle that my sister and I had. I believe that's why I struggled so hard with myself because I really enjoyed the nightlife parties and people. It was so much the opposite of what I had been taught.

Chapter 11

The weekdays of summer were much the same as the weekends. It didn't matter to my friend and I. We would stay up almost every night all night long. After all, to buck hay, you never started until after lunch. Plus, most of the time you were bucking hay you felt miserable anyway. So it's hard to say if it was a hangover or just the hayfields. But by the time we finished for the night, the hangover was gone, and we would simply repeat the previous night's routine.

We finally figured why the liquor store outside of town was called Hill Top Liquors. It was strategically located on top of a hill and near the clay pit. So I bought a fake ID and could pass as twenty-one at Hill Top Liquor. There is no way I looked twenty-one. The store manager knew it, but he didn't care. My ID said I was twenty-one, and that's all he needed. The Hill Top Liquor store was as rundown of a place as there could be. It had a multicolored metal roof. It was weathered on the outside with chipped white paint, and a lot of rotten boards around the windows with crooked, dusty mini blinds. There was a cowbell above the door that struck the top of the door when you opened it. It was always thick with cigarette smoke. It smelled moldy, and the beer coolers made a buzzing sound. Also, it had a junky garage beside it. Car parts would be strung all around the garage. Country music played inside of the garage. Behind the liquor store was a rundown trailer park. That's where six or seven trailers were parked in a parallel pattern and where I noticed the night people were partying. Unleashed dogs walked around, sniffing for food or just lying under the small front porches.

We pulled up to the liquor store. We could taste the cold beer so well that if we drank water, it would have tasted like beer. My friend stayed in the car. I opened the front door. The cowbell rang. A heavy-set balding man came from a room behind the counter. Beads were hanging over a doorway to the backroom, and the low volume of the TV was coming from behind the counter. The man wasn't friendly. In fact, he was really mean-looking. I'm sure he had seen his share of outlaws and bums. With a mean look, he said, "What do ya need?"

I said, "A twelve pack of the cheapest cold beer you got."

He said, "It's all cold, but PBR is on sale. That'll be the cheapest."

"I'll take it then," I said.

My friend honked his horn and the man and I both looked. "That'll be two bucks" and put his fat hand down with his palm up.

I turned and stopped, "Oh, I need some ice."

"That'll be fifty cents."

I gave him the change and headed out the door. I instantly knew why my friend had honked his horn. The white Charger and the giant had pulled through and went back around the old garage. I hurriedly got in the car, and we eased over to the clay pit.

Now, I'm telling you, I was getting really tired of seeing that white Charger. We didn't even want to look in the direction of the old garage. But we couldn't help but take a glance toward the old garage as we slowly eased our way to the highway. I did see another man with the giant as they both were getting out to go into the garage. He was dressed in a baby blue leisure suit. But it was just a weeknight. And why would anyone be wearing a leisure suit going into a junky garage?

As we made our way to the gravel road, we popped a beer top and lit a cigarette. We had some Bob Seger "Night Moves" playing on the super tuner. I said to my friend, "I wonder who that man wearing a light blue leisure suit was."

He said, "I don't know." He appeared to be mad at me.

I said, "Something just doesn't seem right. I don't know what it is, but something just ain't right." I can't say that because the man was wearing a blue leisure suit I thought he was evil. I just thought that was odd and out of place.

We made our way to the gravel road that took us to the clay pit. When we turned onto the road, I said to my friend, "What's wrong with you?"

He said, "Man, I'm getting a bad feeling about the giant."

"What do you mean?" I said.

"Well, first of all, who is the son of a bitch and why is he here?" My friend had a sense of urgency in his voice.

He said, "I think those guys are up to no good."

"So how are we going to find out without the giant finding us out?" I said.

"I don't know, but it's time we did," he said, then lit a cigarette and took a drink of beer. He was digging through the cassettes and found some Aerosmith to put in the super tuner. "Sweet Emotions" came on, and we just sat back and listened at a low volume to the song. It sounded good. We began to relax, and for a moment, we forgot about the giant. As the beer began to work my friend and I, we dreamed of the naked girls on horseback, and we wondered if the girls had boyfriends. There was something about the pit that relaxed us, something magical that I can't explain. We were the only people there this night. The night was clear and full of stars. I thought about the times my mom and dad would take my sister and I to see a movie at the local drive-in theater. It had to be a clear night to go to the drive-in theater.

Then I remembered the movie *True Grit*, the part when the girl got knocked down a hole, and it was full of rattlesnakes. She tried to stay calm and not move, but she still got bitten. I knew that's what was about to happen to my friend and I, only we didn't have Rooster Cogburn to fight with us. It was our fight.

My friend and I planned to lay low for a while. We finally found a card game at a buddy's trailer house where we could drink beer, and smoke pot and cigarettes, where we could listen to music and enjoy the company of friends and not worry about running into the giant. While we were playing cards, someone said they heard of a big party that was going to happen at the clay pit at the end of the summer. They said that a local band was going to play live music. That sounded cool to us because when a band played that meant a lot of single girls would be there. Usually, that meant girls would get drunk enough to go skinny-dipping.

Chapter 12

Most of what was left of the summer, my friend and I spent bucking hay and exploring gravel roads. If you were to get on an airplane and fly over Callaway County, the gravel roads would look like blood vessels in a body. All the gravel roads would lead to a town. We discovered a small town in North Callaway County called Auxvasse and a small town to our south called Mokane, which was located right along the banks of the Missouri River. One of our favorite gravel roads to take was called Dark Hollow. It was the grandest of gravel roads, cut into limestone rock hills with a lazy creek that ran alongside the road. The hills went up on both sides, and a canopy of oak and hickory trees would wrap around the road so that you felt like you were wrapped up in a cocoon made of leaves. Sometimes, the creek and road would cross. But I have often wondered if when a creek and a gravel road cross, maybe that's God's crossroad because you still can only go one way and there really ain't much temptation to go into the creek. Then you either drive through the creek water or you turn around and go back to where you came from. A lot of the times we would stop along the road and get out of the car. We would lean on the car hood and drink and smoke and listen to music. Most of the time in the summer just before sunset, you can hear the crickets, locusts, and whippoorwills sound off. Then, when it would begin to get dark, the lightning bugs would fill the air around you.

So while driving down Dark Hollow, my friend and I began to try to make sense of the trouble we were feeling that we were about to become mixed up in. He said, "I don't know what to do about the giant, but I'm going to figure us a way out of this mess."

I just looked at him. He had a wide open-eyed look, kind of like the look your mom would give you when she meant she was serious.

I said, "I think we need to talk to the giant and tell him we meant no harm."

He said, "Nope. These guys are bad, and I do not want to have anything to do with him or his group."

Well, that settled it for me. I could tell my friend was serious. We drove down the gravel, put in some Van Morrison, "Wild Night," and made our way to the small town of Mokane.

Mokane was located in South Callaway County near the banks of the Missouri River. It is about twenty miles from Jefferson City. We discovered this town because every year on Labor Day they had a fair. Just about anyone could buy beer there after sunset. There would be a band and a lot of girls. It had a park and a guy who had this huge set of speakers and this stereo that he would set up in the park. All the hippies would come to listen to this famous guy and his music. My friend and I would always ask if anyone knew where the guy with the stereo was playing. Mokane had about two hundred people in the town itself, but it was surrounded by a lot of country people. It had a bar, post office, a gas station, and three churches. About every five or six years, the whole town would flood, and you would swear you were looking at the ocean. In Mokane, you could party all night long. It had no cops so the night people had their own method of justice. Not all the time, but sometimes, a fistfight would break out. I have seen some good ones. All in all, it was a fun time to watch the sun rise while sitting along the streets of the town.

The Missouri river access ramp was a quarter mile from the streets of Mokane. A lot of people would party right on the river. The Missouri River was real muddy, and I always wished it was clear because I wanted to see the bottom, and I wanted to see all the giant catfish that they said could be big enough to swallow a man. The river at the access ramp was probably about four to five football fields across to the other bank. The other side of the river bank was nothing but trees. Some trees were about to fall into the river because they were too close to the bank. The river fishermen used the tree limbs to catch catfish with what they would call limb lines. The river looked like it was running slowly and calmly, but it was full of whirlpools. Mostly fishing and boating happened on the river. They didn't swim in it much. Located along the river were sandbars that people would ride their boats to and then party on them. The river could also be the perfect place to hide a body if one were to commit murder.

Chapter 13

The summer of '78 was coming to an end. I hated the fact of school beginning to start. My friend and I didn't cut our hair for three months. We started to grow some peach fuzz on our chins. It didn't look good, but we wanted to be hippies. We wanted to look like the guys on the album cover of Lynyrd Skynyrd. The one bright spot to the end of summer was the upcoming band and party at the clay pit. We were mostly nervous to go because we figured the giant would be there, but there was no way we would miss it. There was not a chance in hell that the giant or even the devil himself was stopping us from going to the clay pit that night. The news of the party was spread by word of mouth, no written invites or anything like that. I always wondered who got all the parties started. It's not like there was a promoter or something. Regardless, I was glad that somehow the party was organized.

A few weeks earlier, my friend's dad had bought a new Ford truck with a camper shell. So we moved the super tuner into the new truck. My friend had said, "The giant won't know who we are, and I doubt he remembers what we looked like." I felt relief. My friend figured out a way for us to avoid the giant. We set out on the town. It was the Friday night before the band party. The party at the clay pit would start early on Saturday and, of course, last all night. The town was buzzing. The night people were parked in just about every vacant parking lot. The Hardee's parking lot was so full the manager would come out and asked us to move off the lot. Because my friend and I knew the manager, we got to stay. Larry got to stay as well. We were parked by Larry. He was smoking a cigarette; his windows were down. I could hear the song "Love Me Tonight" by Head East playing on his radio at a low volume. He had a girl with him, but this girl was black, and she was very pretty. We knew her; we just had never seen her out with Larry.

My friend said, "Larry, you going out to the clay pit Saturday night?"

He said, "Yeah."

We waited for him to say more, but he didn't. He just smoked his cigarette. I got the impression he was in some kind of deep thought. But then I thought about him and figured he was just stoned. While we were sitting and watching, the white Charger came purring by us.

Then Larry said, "Hey, I forgot to tell you guys. I found out something about the man in that white Charger." We turned down our music and looked at him.

He said, "That man has been in prison for the last five years. He and some guy got caught stealing cars." He puffed on his cigarette, blew the smoke out, and said, "Yep, the cops even shot him with a shotgun while he tried to resist arrest. The man is a real life gangster."

My friend and I just stared at Larry while he talked. One reason we just stared at Larry was because he didn't really talk a lot. The other was that we were hoping he was going to give us some kind of stoned hippie advice. But after he spoke about the giant, he just shut up. Then he started to mumble something to the girl. Man, she was pretty. I didn't blame Larry for having divided interest between her and us. My friend and I could believe the giant was a real badass, but I'm saying the part about being a real gangster; well, let me just say that was a little hard to believe. I guess if you thought really hard about where our town was located, downtown Chicago is about three hundred or so miles north. Then you can understand why we had doubts about the gangster ties. Funny thing about Larry, he was a stoned hippie, and he didn't talk much. But as we would discover later that night, he was right about the giant.

My friend started the truck. We both lifted our heads and showed peace signs to Larry and drove off onto the street. I was searching for a cassette to pop in the super tuner. I settled on BTO's "Taking Care of Business." We turned it up to about mid-volume, lit a cigarette, and headed to Hill Top Liquor. My friend and I didn't talk all the way to the liquor store. We just sat and listened to the music, and it sounded good. We pulled in really slowly, and I got out to go into the rundown liquor store. My friend turned the music down and lit another cigarette. While I was going in, I glanced into the trailer park to see if I could see the white Charger. Sure enough, it was down at the end trailer along with a few other cars. One must think, why would you go out of your way to get so close to danger? Why push it? I can only say that my friend and I never really believed we were in that much danger. We had gained some street smarts, kind of like when you know, a mean dog is on a chain, and as long as you stay outside of the chain, you were safe. I went in, and I heard the familiar cowbell hit the door. The owner came through the beads. He knew me by now, but he was never nice.

"What are you looking for?" he snapped.

"What's on sale?" I said in a way that meant you know what I'm looking for.

He said, "PBR, same as last time you were here."

"Okay, I'll take a twelve pack and a bag of ice." The place may have been a dump, but man did it have cold beer, which was a must for us. It didn't matter what kind of beer it was; it just had to be ice cold. While my back was turned and I focused on the cash register, the door opened, and the cowbell rang. I didn't look. I stayed focused on the change I had coming. I heard the door shut. I got my change, turned, and there was the giant and the suit man, each of them had a good-looking woman with them. They went over to the beer cooler and started to look at the beer. I made eye contact with the giant and just nodded my head in a "What's up?" manner. My heart was thumping. I could hear it. I felt my pulse raising. I could feel the veins in my neck moving in and out. As I made my way toward the door, the women looked at me. I looked right at them, right into their eyes. Funny thing, you can tell a whole lot about a person just by looking in their eyes. And the women had the most heavenly eyes

I had seen. I could only imagine what good times a young boy like myself could have with one of those girls.

One of the girls said, "Hey, do we know you?"

I said with the most nervous voice a person could have, "I don't think so." I reached around the girls, and one of them brushed next to me and smiled really nicely and softly laughed while I got my ice and slowly and calmly walked out and got in the truck. I looked in the window, and the girl who brushed next to me was watching me from inside. I could see her eyes, and we made eye contact. She never blinked, but I did. I will never forget her eyes. I thought she was an angel, that somehow God had sent an angel to watch over us, and she was it.

When I jumped in the truck, he started it at the same time. He put it in reverse and slowly backed up. When we got far enough away, I yelled, "Shit, shit, shit," and slammed my fist on the dash. My heart was thumping so loud and fast that I thought it was going to explode. Then I yelled, "Shit, shit, shit" again. We turned down on the gravel road, and we popped a beer top. My friend lit a cigarette and turned up the super tuner. It was ZZ Top, "Blue Jean Blues" and it sounded good. As we got closer to the clay pit, my heartbeat slowed down, and for some reason, I looked over at my friend and we both just busted out laughing. Why were we laughing? I couldn't tell you, but it felt good to laugh; sometimes, laughing was our best mental defense.

Chapter 14

The night was humid. You could see heat lightning far off high in the sky. We stopped at the top of the clay pit and looked down toward our spot. It was clear. We knew some of the cars down there. You could hear music and laughter. They had a fire. We slowly went down the hill, pulled up to the small crowd, got out, and began to drink and mingle. Everyone was excited about the band on Saturday. We all knew it was going to be a night to remember. We sat around on the car hoods and tailgates smoking pot, just enjoying the music and the night. It was around 11:30 or midnight. I thought I could hear the faint sound of a car with loud pipes coming toward the pit. And then I could see headlights in the night sky. They were jiggling as if the bumps in the road were making them loose. The car pulled to the top of the clay pit and stopped. The headlights shined over the top of the pit. A figure got out of the car, walking in front of the headlights. A large shadow eclipsed the headlights, and a shadowy figure, about thirty feet tall, reflected off the clay hills. I knew who it was, and so did my friend. None of the other people acted as if there was anything to be worried about. The car started up with a loud "whap" and then headed down the hill toward us. As the white Charger idled down the hill, dust from the road began to boil up in front of the car. As it came to a stop next to our cars, the cloud of dust rushed toward us. We just turned our heads and closed our eyes. I could hear music coming from the car, and the girls were laughing. The giant and his crew sat in the car until the dust finally settled.

The door opened with a squeaky sound and a pop. Then, as before, out rolled the big burly man. This time, I could look him over. Part of me hoped that I had made him bigger in my mind. But my mind was right, and he was big. He had long, thick, black curly hair. He was taller than I was, and I'm six feet tall. He wasn't ugly to look at; he was just big. He looked like an NFL lineman. When he walked, he had kind of a slow step, but you could tell he wasn't afraid to move fast if the situation called for it.

The man in the suit got out of the passenger side. The door squeaked and popped. I started to size up the suit man as well. He was bigger than me too. He had blond hair with a blondish beard. He wore a leisure suit. I'll never forget or understand why he was wearing a suit. But he had a reason, which we were all wondering about but never did find out. He wasn't ugly either. He also had kind of a slow, "I'm a badass" walk. The girls, which I vividly remembered, got out. They stumbled out and around—drunk. They laughed a lot.

The giant walked up to us and said, "Hey, it looks like you're having a party here. Hope you don't care if we join you."

None of us openly objected. Our small fire was crackling and popping. Other than music, the fire was the only noise. The suit man said, "Are you guys over here a lot? Because we've been on the other side mostly when we come here." We all just looked at each other to see who was going to talk to them. My friend said, "Yeah, we come here all the time. We see you over there. Are you guys from here?" There was a moment of silence. The giant said, "I'm from here, but I've been in prison the last five years. I just got out last winter." The giant didn't mind telling us that he had been in prison. In fact, he seemed to enjoy telling us. The suit man said with a tension-breaking laugh, "But we aren't looking for trouble. We're just looking for people to party with." I was silent. I just looked at them, almost as if to study them. But mostly, I kept looking at the girl, the one I had looked at in the liquor store. I wanted her to come near me and talk, but I also knew I would be beaten for it. So I just made eye contact with her. She made eye contact with me as well. With all the small talk, the cassette had stopped. My friend opened his truck and began to fumble through the cassettes. In a premeditated way, he popped it in and out came The Rolling Stones' "Sympathy for the Devil." I just looked over at him. The girls danced around slowly, and we kind of began to relax. Tensions relaxed, and we began to drink and smoke cigarettes.

The suit man asked, "Do you all like pills?"

I said, "What kind of pills?"

He reached into his pocket and pulled out a bag of pinkish looking pills. "We call these pills soapers," he said with a salesman-like tone. A funny thing was starting to happen. The giant and suit man weren't half bad. They didn't seem mean or bad. They just acted about as normal as us. They liked music. They certainly liked women, and they liked to party. I found myself reevaluating my opinion of them. Maybe they weren't so bad after all.

I said to the suit man, "What do they do to you?"

In a typical sales-like fashion, he said, "Well, if you like to get drunk, this pill equals about a case of beer."

That got my interest. I said, "How much do they cost?"

"Well, normally, I can get ten dollars a pill, but seeing how we just met, I'll take five dollars for two pills." Then he stopped talking and just stared right at me. I looked over at the girls and wondered if that was why they were acting so drunk. Then the suit man said, "Tell you what. Go ahead and take four of them off my hands tonight. Try one, then if you like them, you can pay me the next time you see me." Now, if I was a fish, I just got hooked. Really, even before I said anything, the suit man was standing right beside me getting four pills out of the bag. I began to think *What the hell?* and told him with a nod and shrug, "Okay." I looked over at my friend thinking he'd be mad at me, but surprisingly, he just gave the same nod to me. The giant took a big swig of beer and threw it in the fire. "Come on, girls, let's get out of here." They loaded in the white Charger and started up the car. It made a loud "whap." It sounded good. My friend and I loved the sound of good pipes.

As the giant and his crew headed up the hill, the headlights jiggled and shined up into the dark sky. Then, slowly, the sound of the pipes and the headlights faded. It was just us, and I looked at the pills as I unfolded my hand. The giant and suit man were only with us for an hour or so. We never really worried about time. A lot of times, we stayed up all night.

My friend said, "Well, let's try one of those pills."

"Okay."

So we ate one pill each, lit a cigarette, and got a beer. Four or five other friends were standing around the fire with us. My friend went over to the super tuner and found a radio station we liked out of St. Louis, "KSHE95." The heat lightning was still visible high in the sky but seemed quite a way off. The pill didn't have an instant effect. Yet, you could gradually feel it doing something. All my friends stood next to the fire. It was a small fire, mainly for the light it put off. One of the guys was sipping his beer and asked if anyone wanted to smoke some pot. We all nodded and shrugged our shoulders in a "Why not?" sort of way. The music was sounding good even at a low volume. I felt my head start to tingle, and my legs were feeling numb. I started to smile and looked over at my friend. He was looking down at the ground. Then he looked up at me and smiled. I knew then we were about to take a "trip." The guy passed the joint around, and we all took hits off it. I didn't believe it was going to make any difference on how I was feeling. The suit man had just hooked some fish, and by now, I'd say he was smiling.

My friend smiled and said to the guys around the fire, "Hey, man, guess what happened to us last weekend?"

Everyone slowly turned their heads toward my friend. One of the guys spoke and said, "What?"

"Well, SL (that's me) and I decided to go to 7-Eleven before we went home." I could hear Dunny's voice (that's my best friend), but it was fading like he was walking away from me and getting farther away. While he was telling the story to our campfire friends, my mind could only think about this pill I had taken. Man, it was kickin' in high gear now. I felt like—well, that's just it. I had no feelings. I was completely numb, and I thought if I took a step, I would fall on my butt. Then Dunny's voice began to come back toward me. The way you would turn the volume back up on the radio. I picked up with the story.

"SL goes over to the cooler and gets a burrito and sticks it in the microwave. Then, puts it on high for about five minutes. The lady at the cash register was helping other people check out. So SL got another burrito real fast and put it in the microwave. So the lady would think he was still heating up the one. We got our sodas and chips. The first burrito that was done he slid it beside the microwave and the lady never really looked at him. The microwave dinged when it was done. So while the lady wasn't looking, he slid one of them inside his pants, and we went to check out. While we were standing in line, the one in his pants slipped down and was now resting beside his balls. I checked out and turned and looked over at SL, and I could tell he had a funny look on his face. SL then checked out. The lady seemed to know what he had done. She began to act real slow and took her time at counting back the change. SL finally made it to the truck and pulled out the steaming hot burrito. He had a blister on his balls and leg.

The funny thing is, the cash register lady came out to the truck and said with a smile, "Next time, don't cook it so long." We all just busted out laughing, and so did the lady." We all knew the lady at the 7-Eleven. We had been there a lot. We figured she never even thought we were stealing food. It turns out, she knew all along but never really said anything. I don't think she was afraid of us. I think she just knew we were kids, and she didn't want us to get in trouble. While everyone was laughing, the volume in my head began to fade away again. I just knew that I was going to fall over. I decided to ease my way over to the tailgate on the truck. My head was spinning so fast. Sure enough, I took one step, and down I went. The volume turned up in my head, and I heard everyone burst out laughing. I tried to laugh, but all I could do was see everything spinning. This may seem funny to most people, but I was having fun. Most of the time when I got this out of it, I was about to puke. I didn't have a feeling to puke; that's just it. I was drunk without drinking. All the guys at the campfire wanted one of those pills. Then, I knew what the suit man was doing. He knew we would like the "soapers." He knew we would want more.

Dunny and I knew we couldn't drive, mainly because we couldn't even walk. I pulled myself into the bed of the truck, and that's the last I remember of the night. When I woke up, it was just about time for the sun to come up. I looked around. I could see the smoldering fire and the faint smoke it was putting off. Dunny was passed out in the front of the truck. The radio was hissing and static. It was just him and me. The clay pit was silent. I could hear blue jays going on and some turtledoves hooting, but no other birds; it was silent. The silence was actually loud, and I looked over at an orange flower, we called butterfly weed, and it was covered with so many butterflies that I could hear their wings moving. I pulled myself out of the truck bed. I expected to feel like hell, but I didn't. I didn't feel bad at all. Only like I just had the best night's sleep I could imagine. I pushed on Dunny to get him up. He rubbed his head and eyes and said, "Damn, what the hell was in those pills?"

We both laughed and just said, "Damn."

I walked around for a while to make sure I was back to normal. I smoked a cigarette. I realized that I was not scared of the giant anymore. In fact, I knew we were going to be seeing him and suit man even more.

We got in the truck and headed toward town. Dunny and I couldn't believe that we had come face-to-face with the giant and lived to talk about it. We felt so much relief. Now, we felt maybe the storm had passed us. We were wrong. The storm we were about to be a part of was long from over. In fact, the worst was on its way. Dunny pulled in my driveway.

I said, "Wait here. I'm just going to get some clean clothes." When I went in, my mom was waiting for me. She never said much to me except when I didn't come home. When she woke up and looked in my room, she would get real worried if I wasn't in bed.

She said, "Where have you been?" in a sharp and mad tone.

"I stayed at Dunny's house. It got late, so I just slept on the couch."

"I think you should stay home tonight."

"Not tonight I ain't."

"You better not be mixed up in any trouble."

"I ain't. Come on, give me a break."

I went up the steps to my room. My room was my spot. No one really messed with it. My mom wouldn't even go in it. She'd just throw my clean clothes on my bed. I was supposed to put them away, but I never did. I figured, why put them away? I would just have to get them back out. My room had posters of Rocky leaning on his pull-up bar, Rooster Cogburn in *True Grit*, plus my Billy Jack picture and every teenage boy's dream—a poster of Farah Fawcett in a swimsuit. I hurriedly started to change my clothes before my mom had more time to question me about my plans. I turned to hit the light switch. For some reason, I looked right at an embroidered picture of the words "God Loves You" that my grandma had made for me when I was younger. I stopped and thought about how innocent I felt back then. I knew inside that God did love me, but I knew that I wanted to live in the dangerous world of the night people. I just wanted to party. It was fun. Yet, I also knew it had a price. To lose your innocence, to stray from the path that God wanted you to take, is costly—a high cost that I learned would take all I had to pay back. In fact, even forty years later, I still see the consequences of my actions in those rebellious teenage years.

I turned away from my room and ran down the steps. I ran into my sister. She wasn't a teenager yet. She was with my mom, and they were talking and eating breakfast. My mom said, "Are you coming home tonight?"

"No, I'm going to stay at Dunny's house." Well, that's what Huck Finn would call a "stretcher." Basically, it was true. I was staying with Dunny, just not at his house.

I said, "Bye" and ran out of the house. I was so pumped about the band at the clay pit. I was visualizing how great the night was going to turn out. I jumped in the truck and smiled really big at Dunny. He smiled back then lit a cigarette. It was only mid-morning, and we needed to get some rest. We went to Dunny's house. You have to understand that we weren't unhappy and hateful teens. We loved life and wanted to live and not miss a moment of fun. The only fears we had were with the giant. Luckily, he must not have recognized us. We did look a little different. Our hair was longer, and we drove a different vehicle. So we knew that the night was going to be long, and we wanted to be rested for all that was to happen. Dunny's dad wasn't so nice. As soon as we walked in the door, he let us have it.

"Oh yes, there's my two dumbasses."

We called him Junior. I said, "Ah, Junior, how's it going?"

He would shrug his shoulders, throw his hand up, and say, "Ah shit. All I do is sit here by myself. All you shitheads do is run the damn streets."

Then his face got red, and he would yell at us, "You shitheads are gonna wind up dead if you ain't careful." Dunny just went to take a shower and left me to argue with his dad. Junior smoked unfiltered Lucky Strikes.

"Junior, let me bum one of those cigarettes."

He smiled and said, "Shit, you better grow up before you smoke one of these." He always liked it when I sat with him and smoked. All he really wanted was some company. He was really skinny and sickly. He would cough and gag then spit in the trash can by his feet. Dunny got out of the shower and came into the kitchen. He started to cook lunch. Dunny was a really good cook. We never did get any rest because Junior wanted me to go and get him a twelve-pack, cigarettes, and a fifth of whiskey. I said, "Let's get a case and we will drink a few with you."

He smiled and said, "Get my wallet."

About that time, the phone rang. It was one of our best friends, Tee Bone. Now Tee Bone was calling to see about going to the clay pit with us. Most of the time, Tee Bone was with his girlfriend. He was one of the lucky ones who had a regular girlfriend. But I guess his girlfriend didn't want him to be hanging out with Dunny and I. Well, this night, Tee Bone was going to hang with us, and Dunny and I were glad. For the most part, the three of us had been hanging out since fifth grade. Dunny and I had missed his company. Tee Bone was one of the good guys. He always stayed out of trouble and had a good head on his shoulders. Maybe it was because his dad was a city cop. Tee Bone was a big guy, about six feet three. In fact, we all were six feet tall and by no means would one consider us to be small. He was clean, but he had shoulder-length hair.

He would always say, "My hair is the best part about me" and then laugh really loudly. Tee was his real name. He got the bone part of the name one day while we were at a friend's trailer house playing cards. We all decided to get pork steaks and barbecue. Tee decided he was going to get a T-bone steak. Tee always had money. So we started the fire, and Tee kept on mouthing about how good his T-bone steak was going to taste. He insisted that his T-bone be put on the grill first. He put it on; then we put our pork steaks around the T-bone. He pulled his off after just a little while and disappeared into the kitchen of the trailer. Dunny, another friend and I stood outside to cook our pork steaks. We were drinking and smoking cigarettes. All of a sudden, the door swung open, and Tee came out holding his plate in one hand and his throat with the contrary. I was standing next to him and wasn't exactly sure if he was just joking with us. When I decided he was choking, I hauled off with all my might and punched him in the back with my fist. When I hit him, a big chunk of meat shot out of his mouth along with the T-bone that was on his plate. There were two old porch dogs on the deck. As soon as the T-bone hit the ground, the dogs jumped up and scarfed it down. Tee had a fist bruise mark on his back. But he was so thankful. He said I saved his life. We all just busted out laughing. Now we call him Tee Bone.

Chapter 15

Dunny and I got some money from his dad and set out to get Tee Bone. Then got some beer, whiskey, and cigarettes. It was just a little past noon, and we never did get any rest. We just figured we'd get the night started by drinking with his dad. We pulled in front of Tee Bone's house and honked the horn. He came out running and was smiling from ear to ear. Sure enough, his hair did look good. I got out of the truck and said, "I get by the door, you're gonna have to ride bitch."

Ride bitch is what we called anyone who had to ride in the middle of two guys. We always laughed when we said, "You have to ride bitch." Tee Bone jumped in the middle, and we headed to Hilltop Liquor. Dunny and I filled Tee Bone in about the events of summer. Mostly, we laughed and elbowed each other, but we did tell him of our several near-death experiences with the giant and suit man. I'm not sure how much Tee Bone believed us; later on, he became a believer.

We slowly pulled into the Hilltop Liquor store. I scanned the trailer park for the white Charger. Sure enough, it was parked down at the last trailer. I said to Dunny, "When I come out, take me down there. I want to pay them for those pills. I don't want to owe them anything." I opened the door, and the cowbell rang. Here came the manager. He had that same pissed off snarl on his face. I tried to loosen him up on every occasion I could. I'd smile and joke with him, but he wasn't' interested in being friendly. He'd just say, "What are you looking for?"

I'd say the same thing I always said, "What deals do you have today?"

He caught me off guard this time. "I got a new shipment of Old Milwaukee if you want it. I'd sell for two dollars fifty cents a twelve-pack."

I said, "Okay, I'll take two twelve-packs and two bags of ice."

"That's six bucks," he said as he banged his hand down on the counter with his palm side up. I paid him, grabbed my beer and ice, and headed out the door. I looked out at the truck, and Tee Bone had a smile that covered his whole face. He got out and helped me put the ice and beer in the cooler.

I said, "Dunny, I forgot to get the whiskey." I turned and ran back inside the liquor store. I opened the door in a hurry, and the cowbell made a violent ring. The manager came out from the back room and gave me a "What's up?" look.

"I need a fifth of whiskey." I never bought whiskey, so I didn't know what kind to ask for.

"What kind?"

I scanned the back shelf and hurriedly picked one. "Southern Comfort," I said.

"That's going to be four bucks," he said with little to no emotion. I was reaching for the bottle while he put it in a brown sack. I turned around to head out the door, and the man said, "Hey."

I stopped with a skid, feeling like someone was calling me out like a Western duel in the streets. I slowly turned, and the man said, "I know that's a fake ID you have. I don't give a shit, but if you get caught by the cops and they come here." Then he just stopped and looked at me and said, "Well, you'll find out. You understand?"

I acted tough and said, "My ID ain't fake. You don't need to worry about me."

Then he said, "You think you're tough, but I'm tougher. I can promise you that."

"No problem, man, I'm not looking for any trouble." I started back toward the door, and the man said, "Hey."

I stopped again and turned around. "Let's just see how tough you think you are." I swallowed but remained calm. I was wishing Tee Bone, and Dunny were in there with me. I said, "What do you mean?"

"Come back here with me."

I didn't want to go back there, but I moved slowly toward the back. I studied the back room the way you look for a mean dog in someone's yard. I was anxious, but I was drawn toward the room. I always wondered what was back there. When we got past the beads on the doorway, the man was standing there. He was holding a Mason jar with what looked like water. He said, "Here, take a drink of this." I took it and smelled it at the same time it was on my lips. It had an apple scent to it, so I drank some. It was like I drank fire. I coughed and snorted.

The man just busted out laughing. "See, you're not as tough as you think."

He grabbed the jar, screwed the lid on, and said, "Here take it. I call it apple crisp." I did take it, and I was relieved because I figured the man was going to put a gun to my head. In a way, I guess he did. . . The gun was moonshine.

I told him "Thanks" and hurried out the door. Dunny and Tee Bone were in the truck waiting for me. When I jumped in the truck, they said, "What the hell took you so long?" I showed them the moonshine the man gave me.

"Wow, is that moonshine?" They both grabbed it to take a sniff. Tee Bone took a little sip and coughed and gagged something fierce. I busted out laughing, just the way the man did at me. Tee Bone said, "Holy shit, that tastes like paint thinner."

Dunny eased the truck out of the driveway. I glanced down at the trailer house and said to stop. "Take me down there. I'm going to pay those guys." Dunny put the truck in forward and eased toward the trailer house. My heart started to beat faster, and I was getting nervous. I thought sooner or later the giant was going to remember us.

We pulled up to the trailer, and an old dog was sitting on the porch. It didn't even bark; it just wagged its tail. I suppose it was used to people coming and going. It was silent around the trailer. I got out of the truck and headed up the porch to the door. The dog came up to me and sniffed then went and laid down. Still no noise from inside of the trailer, I knocked on the door, kind of softly. Finally, out of the corner of my eye, a curtain pulled back slightly. A voice said, "Yeah, what do you want?"

I said, "I just came to settle up with you."

The voice said, "Just a minute." I heard the trailer squeak and felt it move. It was definitely the giant. The giant came to the door. He opened it and said, "Come on in." His hair was messy, and his eyes were halfway open. "Settle up with me on what?"

I said, "The soapers."

"Oh, I forgot all about that. You were at the clay pit last night."

I said, "Yeah, well he said two bucks a piece. We got four, so here's eight bucks."

"Well, did you like them?"

"Yeah, they kicked our ass."

He busted out laughing. Almost the same way the liquor store man laughed when I took that swig of moonshine. I thought to myself, *Now I know why he doesn't remember us. He was taking those soapers, and they did make you forgetful.*

About that time, the suit man came out of the back room; only, this time, he was in his birthday suit. That was a sight I didn't need to see. Then his girlfriend, the one that I thought was an angel, came out with barely anything on but a smile. That was a sight I did need to see. The worst and best part about seeing her was she saw me looking at her, and she smiled at me, and I saw her beautiful eyes as I dropped my head really fast before the suit man caught us looking at each other. I told the giant, "I'll catch you later" and headed out of the trailer.

I jumped in the truck and lit a cigarette. Dunny leaned over Tee Bone and said, "Well, did anything happen?" I smiled and said, "No." Then I said, "Well, that is if you count seeing a naked woman as nothing happening." They both looked at me with their eyes wide open and said at the same time, "What?" Then I described to them in great detail what she looked like. I could tell they envied me. Dunny eased the truck on out of the trailer court. Tee Bone said, "How did you manage to buy beer at that liquor store?" I told him I bought a fake ID. Tee Bone was impressed but insisted on knowing more.

"I ain't real sure. I just gave Larry some money, and he came up with it."

Tee Bone told Dunny, "Come on, let's go! I want to get the night started."

The only problem was, it was only one o'clock in the afternoon. Dunny and I knew we would need to pace ourselves. We knew we were going to stay up all night. We headed back to Dunny's house to hang out with Dunny's dad.

Chapter 16

Junior was waiting in the kitchen when we came inside the house. He had a small radio on a country music station. It was playing Crystal Gayle "Don't It Make My Brown Eyes Blue," and it sounded good. He was smoking a Lucky Strike cigarette, and he was moving his feet to the song. He said, "About time you shitheads got back." He was smiling. I knew he was excited to have some company for a while. I sat the whiskey down and then I showed him the moonshine.

He said, "Get us a glass." He reached over and turned the radio up. It was Hank Williams's "There's a Tear in My Beer." He'd always say how this was good music. It seemed that all the grown-ups hated rock and roll. I took a few glasses out of the cabinet and pulled out my chair next to Junior. Tee Bone and Dunny were standing behind me by the kitchen sink. They were not sure that wanted to start drinking. Dunny never did drink a whole lot if he knew he was going to drive. I decided that I would drink a little with Junior. I opened the moonshine jar and poured him a shot and I a shot. He just reached over and grabbed the shot glass and tipped it right into his mouth. He made a little grimace and looked at me. He said, "Your turn."

Trying to show I was a man, even though I was only sixteen, I grabbed the shot and slammed it back. I knew it was going to burn. Sure enough, I just about gagged. Then I heard him take to laughing nonstop. I'm not sure why, but all I could think of was, *That's the third time this day someone has laughed at me.* I'm not sure that it meant anything profound. Yet, it seemed to stick in my mind. Junior said, "Now that's a shot," then smiled and lit a cigarette.

I knew that I could not just drink one after another, so I said, "You all want to play some cards?" Everyone nodded their heads yes and pulled up a chair. Junior was happier than I had seen him in a long time. He just sat alone so much. I felt sorry for him. We settled on a game of pitch, a really fun game with a partner involved. We sat and played. Junior drank a lot. I drank some and Tee Bone, and Dunny drank iced tea. We laughed, told stories, and smoked a lot of cigarettes. The house was full of smoke. Junior and I finally got Tee Bone and Dunny to take a shot of the moonshine. They gagged so bad, and I laughed so hard. Now I understand why everyone laughed so hard at me when I took a shot. It's sort of a rite of passage thing or an odd form of hazing. The memories of that afternoon card game, the sounds of us laughing, the sounds of staticky AM country music, the thick, smoke-filled room—I'll never forget. It's odd how certain times in your life you never forget. Why do we remember sometimes and forget others? It's not like you say to yourself, "I'll never forget this moment." It's just for some reason that special time gets branded in your memory.

The afternoon quickly went by, and I could tell Junior was not wanting us to go. The only problem we had was that the event of the summer was about to take place at the clay pit. Looking back at the moment, I think, *Would I rather have one more day with Junior or the memory of the clay pit party?* The answer is I want both. Junior wasn't going to live much longer. Plus, I hated the fact of him just sitting around all alone. Dunny said, "We got to go, Dad." I could see the disappointment on Junior's face.

He put on his tough man face and said, "Ah, get out. You don't need to be hanging around with an old man."

I said, "Junior, let's take one more shot of moonshine."

He smiled, lit a cigarette, and said, "Pour one. What are you waiting for?" We all poured a shot glass and gave a toast to good friends and good times. Dunny went to his room and got a clean shirt. Tee Bone, he was clean enough. Me, well, I never wore a shirt. I only kept one in the truck just in case I had to go buy beer. Most places of business had a sign, "No shoes, no shirt, no service."

Chapter 17

Finally, the night was about to be upon us. It was around 5:30 in the afternoon. We were feeling good. We paced ourselves playing cards, maybe a shot an hour. But Junior sure had fun, and he could drink. Tee Bone jumped in the middle; Dunny got in and started the truck. Before Dunny put it in reverse, he had to put a tape in the super tuner. He settled on The Eagles' "Take it Easy." He backed out slowly, and a hissing noise came across the speakers. He was waiting until we got to the highway to push play. It was still hot—at least in the ninety-degree range. The sun was still high in the sky. It wouldn't get dark out until at least 9:00 p.m. When we hit the highway, Dunny pushed play and cranked the volume. The song came on, and we sang out loud with every note. We smiled and laughed as we made our way toward town. When the song ended, we were in town at the four-way stop sign. Dunny turned down the volume.

He said, "Let's see who's in town, then we'll hit the gravel roads." Tee Bone and I nodded our heads yes.

The streets seemed to be a buzz with people. The night people were already coming out and cruising around. Almost all the friends we talked to knew of the band party at the clay pit. All of them had the same feeling that it was going to be a good night for a party. We came around the corner and saw Larry sitting in the Hardee's parking lot. We wouldn't be able to sit there long because it was busy with people getting their evening food. We pulled in beside Larry. You could see the familiar cloud of cigarette smoke coming out of his window. Larry was cleaner looking that usual, which is hard to do when you don't wear a shirt. His hair was still wet like he just got out of a shower. It was odd, though; he didn't have a girl with him.

We asked, "Why are you by yourself?"

He slowly turned to us and said, "I got to pick up Ruby at seven o'clock tonight."

We looked at him just in case he was going to say more, but he just turned his head toward his stereo and changed the radio station. While we were sitting in Hardee's lot, a car pulled next to us and parked. It was a family—a mom, a dad, a boy, and a girl. A funny thing happened. I looked over at them, and they acted scared of us. I looked at the little boy, and he just stared at me. Then I remembered I was that same little boy not too long ago. That was my family not too long ago. I wondered, *Did I look like that little boy?* I felt confused because I wished for the little boy to do good and not do what I did. I wished for him and his family not to be scared of us. I knew we weren't bad people; all we were doing was having fun. I was serious for a moment, and it bothered me to see the look on that little boy's face. It bothered me that someone would be afraid of us. But as they say, "Birds of a feather flock together." Then I thought maybe I was bad; maybe I've turned into something I wouldn't recognize. Finally, I slowly came back to the here and now. I could hear Dunny and Tee Bone talking about getting something to eat.

They were asking me, "What about Sonic?"

"Huh? Yeah, that sounds good."

Sonic was a good place to eat. We could be drunk, and we could eat in the truck. I didn't have to put on a shirt. We could listen to music and relax while we ate. We would play a game of see how many bites someone could eat a foot-long chili dog in. Of course, Tee Bone held the record of eating the foot-long chili dog in two bites. That record still stands to this day. We made our order. We smoked a cigarette until the girl roller skated out to us. Depending on who the girl was, we would tease and flirt with her. Then we would wait until she turned and skated back so we could watch her butt. A lot of the times they would turn back around and catch us looking. We would just burst out laughing when she caught us looking. While we were eating, Tee Bone asked, "Do you think we'll run into the giant out at the clay pit?"

Dunny said, "Oh yeah."

Dunny still had his doubts about whether the giant knew who we were. But I was pretty relieved to think he didn't know who we were. Those soapers really wiped out your memory. Dunny said, "We'll just steer clear of him and his bunch."

Tee Bone said, "That's fine by me." We finished our meal, lit up a cigarette, and watched the cars go by. It was about 6:30 p.m. and the sun had begun falling in the sky, but it was still hot.

Tee Bone said, "Come on. Let's hit the gravel roads."

Dunny straightened up to start the truck. "Give me your trash," he said with his cigarette in his mouth. We passed all the trash to him. We eased out of Sonic and turned to the nearest gravel road.

I'm sure it may sound odd to some people, our obsessions with being on gravel roads. That's just what we did for fun. It was the safest place to be and not get in trouble with the cops. We would drive really slowly and drink and smoke pot. We would stop a lot of times and get out and relax on the tailgate. Mostly, we felt free from the city lights and just enjoyed the clear and clean outdoors. Dunny, Tee Bone, and I had spent so much time together. We'd laugh and drink. We'd dream about girls. We'd solve all our problems while driving on gravel roads. There was a whole network of gravel roads that we had discovered. We could just about go from one end of the county to the other and not hit any pavement—a feat we were proud of, I might add. Tonight, though, the gravel roads we needed to take would lead us right to the clay pit. Dunny figured on an hour of graveling, then stop at Hilltop Liquor to get more ice and cigarettes.

Our beer was ice cold, and it tasted good. We still knew we had to pace ourselves. It was hard not to slam the beer because of the heat. Yet, we managed to do a good job of sipping on them. Tee Bone wondered how many girls would be at the clay pit. I said, "Hundreds."

In reality, there would only be about twenty or so. We wondered if any of the girls would go crazy and skinny dip. Maybe what I mean to say is we wished some girls would go crazy and skinny dip.

Dunny said, "Most of the girls there will be with someone." We all figured that would be the case. The closer we got to the Y in the road, we noticed a giant cloud of dust boiling into the evening sunset.

Dunny said, "Damn, there must be a hundred cars going toward the clay pit."

I said, "Damn, is this looking good or not?"

Tee Bone said, "Do you think we have enough beer?"

Dunny stopped the truck, so I could take a quick count. One thing was for sure; we did not want to run out of beer on this night. I slammed down the tailgate and opened our cooler. It would hold a case. I looked in and quickly counted. We had fifteen by my count. I jumped back into the truck and told them, "We got fifteen beers."

Dunny said, "Well, we better get two more bags of ice and one more twelve pack."

Tee Bone and I agreed. One part of the Y in the road took you straight to the clay pit. The other part took you to the blacktop. It was risky getting on the blacktop after dark and after you have been drinking. But Dunny was the best driver on the planet. We got on the blacktop, and Dunny did the speed limit all the way to Hilltop Liquor. That's one key to never being pulled over; always do the speed limit. We never could understand why people would break the law while driving and drinking, even though drinking and driving were breaking the law. We just figured if you didn't give them a reason to pull you over then they would leave you alone. I still follow that rule today and can count on one hand the number of times I have been pulled over.

We finally made it to Hilltop Liquor. I looked down at the trailer for the giant. The white Charger was there, and that blue Chevelle was there too, the one we had seen being towed through town last winter. There was a black Z-28 Trans Am and a custom painted Cutlass Supreme. The giant was standing in the front of the trailer shouting at the scroungy tall man that drove the blue Chevelle. Dunny pulled up to the front of the liquor store. You couldn't see the giant's trailer when we pulled all the way up to the front of the store. I jumped out. I could hear the arguing all the way up at the store. I couldn't make out any clear words because I was moving kind of fast to get in and out. I hit the door hard and rang the cowbell good. Sure enough, here came the manager. And yep, he had that same joyful glow about him.

"Boy, I'm going to knock you in the head if you break my cowbell."

"I'm sorry, sir, I was just in a hurry."

"Slow down. If you're in that big of a hurry, you should have left earlier. What do you want now?"

I explained my circumstances, and he pointed me to the Old Milwaukee beer. I paid him, and he just shook his head. Off I went, and *bang,* I hit that door and the cowbell clanged really loudly. But this time, I reached up and touched it to make it stop ringing. The man said, "Boy," then he turned around and disappeared into his backroom. When I came out, I still heard shouting. But I couldn't see anything until we backed out of the liquor store parking lot. I ran around the back of the truck and put our beer and ice in the cooler, then jumped into the truck and told Dunny, "Okay, let's go so we can get a good spot at the clay pit." He sat up, straightened up, and started the truck. Tee Bone said, "What's all that hollering about?"

As we backed up and looked down the trailer park, we could see the suit man. He was holding a gun to the tall guy's head. Now, Tee Bone figured out that we weren't kidding about the danger we had managed to be messing with. We were shocked to the bone. Suit man was saying to the guy, "You best keep your mouth shut, or no one will be able to find you when I'm finished with you." The tall man didn't move. He just stood there staring at the gun in his face. The girls were on the porch, not making a sound. They were motionless. They all had cigarettes in their hands. The suit man's girl looked up toward our truck and looked at me. Later on that night, she would find me, and I would learn more about the suit man. The giant and all the people at the trailer knew we saw him. We weren't really sure if we were going to get in any trouble because of what we witnessed. Dunny said, "See, I told you those guys are no good." Tee Bone said, "Come on. Let's go. Stay out of this mess." Dunny pulled out of the liquor store driveway, and we headed to the pit. Tee Bone said, "Damn, it's about damn time."

Chapter 18

We pulled onto the gravel road. The dust was thick and high in the air. I would say that it looked like a cattle stampede. It was nearly 7:30 p.m., and it was time to be relaxed at the clay pit. We followed the cloud of dust all the way to the entrance of the pit. Dunny pulled over to the top the way we always did. The three of us got out to look down. As we looked down, we saw cars parked everywhere. We saw people everywhere. It looked like a who's who party for hippies and night people. Backed up into a gray colored hill of clay were the band and its homemade stage. The band was facing the water's edge, and people were all around the stage. I'd say there were one hundred people or more, girls everywhere, most of them in blue jean shorts and skimpy tops or their swimsuit tops. There was every kind of car and truck you could think of; it was like a car show and a party mixed up into one event. We looked at each other and grinned. We knew we were about to have one great time. We hoped we would hook up with some girls.

Tee Bone said, "Come on, let's go" for the hundredth time. We ran and jumped into the truck. Dunny slowly went down the hill. We found a place toward the back of the clay pit, and Dunny backed it up to the edge of the clay hill, about fifty feet tall. That way, we could just sleep in the truck if we slept at all. The night had finally come; we were fit to be tied. The three of us had waited our whole lives for this night. All sixteen or seventeen years of our lives came down to this night—at least that's how we felt. We could hear music over the band's speakers, and you could see the band members tinkering with some homemade lights. There wasn't electricity, so they had to use a generator that sounded like a lawn mower running. It was a bigger generator, and they had it parked way off in a wooded area. I guess the band had done this sort of thing before. We got ourselves a beer and headed toward the crowd. Tee Bone was smiling so big. Dunny was smoking a cigarette and nursing his beer. I was staring at everyone but mostly the girls. I could only imagine who the lucky guys were to be with such heavenly creatures. I knew that the churchgoers would say that this night was the devil, but I sure thought I was in heaven. The sights, the sounds, even the taste of that night still to this day is indented in my mind. It's the kind of memory that I have chased after for my whole life.

We mingled with the crowd. We saw many people we knew. We saw many people we didn't know. I know some guys had to be at least fifty years old. I know the alcohol had to be working on my brain because I didn't see one girl that I thought was ugly. In fact, I figured my future wife had to be somewhere in this crowd. When we reached the edge of the water, the band was doing a sound check. We were surrounded by people. Pot smoking was all over. You could smell it in the air. I was buzzing. We had a saying when we were all drunk or stoned or both. We would ask, "Are you full?" That meant that you couldn't stand to take another drink or puff. We were nowhere near full, even though we had been at it all day long. While I was scanning the crowd, I noticed a guy with shoulder-length, blondish hair. He wasn't wearing a shirt, and he was wearing blue jean shorts and had sandals for shoes. He was mingling like he knew some people, but he wasn't drinking or smoking. He had a girl I knew following him, and they were holding hands. The girl was my age. She was the prettiest girl in our class. She was a good girl. *Why is she here?* He somehow got close to me. I could hear him talking to a friend.

He said, "Man, I quit drinking and smoking. I quit all that stuff."

His friend said, "Why did you go and do that for?" We later named him Preacher.

Preacher said, "God saved me. I went forward at church and gave my life to God's service." The man took a drink of beer and said, "Well, good luck with that," and he quickly got away. Then Preacher looked right at me. He saw I was looking at him. He made his way toward me with his girlfriend. I was tongue tied to be so close to his beautiful girlfriend. She said "hey" to me. The fact that she said anything to me meant that I had just witnessed a miracle. Preacher said, "Hey, man, how's it going? Are you having a good time?"

I said, "Yeah. I've been waiting most of this summer for this party." I was really buzzing by now. Preacher said, "You know the things of this earth are only temporary. Now is the time for us to store up riches in heaven." I thought if God would let me have a girlfriend like he's got, I'd be spreading the word of God as well, and it surely would be considered a miracle. Then he said, "This may seem like the cool thing to do, but really it's the devil's den." Then he said, "Why don't you come to church in the morning?"

I said, "Man, I doubt that I even go to bed tonight. Maybe some other time."

Preacher said, "I go to the First Baptist Church."

My heart nearly skipped a beat. That was my grandmother's church. I didn't want the man to know that my grandmother went to his church. So I changed the subject to "Well, I got to use the bathroom. I'll see you around." I looked at his girlfriend, and she just smiled at me. That was the second miracle. I told Dunny I was going to the truck to get a beer and take a leak. Dunny and Tee Bone said, "We'll stay here. Can you bring us back a beer?"

I nodded my head yes and staggered off toward the truck. I could not stop thinking about Preacher and his words. But I didn't want to be bothered with thoughts of church. I just wanted to have fun.

Chapter 19

I bumped and bounced my way to the truck. It was 9:00 p.m. It was dark. I could hear the band start. They started right into Santana's "Black Magic Women." Now let me tell you, no words can explain the sound that guitar made. It bounced off the water, hitting the clay hills. It was a perfect spot for music. It was so clear and so pure. I stopped dead in my tracks. I couldn't move. I could only relish that moment. People just stood in awe as the band played. Everyone that was at this party knew they were about to witness to a night never to be forgotten. I promise you, even today, forty-plus years later, anyone that was there that night can tell you they remember that night. I wasn't in a hurry anymore. The first song just ended, so I went around the truck and went to the bathroom. I was looking up at the stars and the moon. It wasn't full, but it was bright. I turned to get myself and the guys a beer and suit man's girlfriend was standing in front of me. I wasn't sure if maybe this was a sign, first the preacher, and now this girl that I thought for sure was an angel. I looked around to see the suit man and the giant, but I didn't see them.

She said, "Hey."

I said, "Hey," but I wasn't nervous. I guess once you see someone naked, the nervousness must go away.

She said, "I need to talk to you."

I was confused. "What about? I'm not sure I should be talking to you. Your boyfriend will kill me if he sees us alone."

She said, "He won't find out. They left us girls here while they went off to Auxvasse for a while. They won't be back for a while."

"Oh, yeah."

"I've been watching you look at me."

Now I was nervous. I said, "Oh yeah, I'm sorry. I didn't mean—"

She reached up and kissed me really softly. Now, I was not sure what the heck just happened. She said, "How old are you?"

"Sixteen, but I'll be seventeen really soon."

"My name is Lisa."

Man, I was just about to explode. I had never been much past first base with any girl. But I was getting the feeling that was about to change. If this wasn't the forbidden apple, I don't know what it could have been. She kept getting closer to me. Feebly, I tried to stop her. She said, "You don't want to get mixed up with those guys. They are bad people. They have killed people. They take them to the Lake of the Ozarks and dump them with weight on them."

"Why are you mixed up with them then?"

"They get you hooked on drugs and money, and you can't get away."

I said, "Damn." I did suspect as much, but this sort of thing didn't happen there. She kissed me again. She ran her fingers through my hair. I could hear a song in the background, but I couldn't think of anything but her.

She said, "You sure are tanned."

I couldn't say anything. I was just about to die. Finally, I got my strength up and said, "I need to go back to my friends."

She kissed me some more. I just knew I would get caught if I stayed with her. She said, "You can have me if you want."

I said, "I better go," and I walked off toward the band. I looked back, but she wasn't there. I'd kick myself in the ass if I could. I kept telling myself, "You're a dumbass," as I walked up to Dunny and Tee Bone. They were jamming and loving it.

Dunny said, "Did you puke or something? You look like you've seen a ghost."

I said, "I saw a ghost all right." Really, I still thought I saw an angel.

The band started into another song. It was ZZ Top's "El Diablo." While I had been back at the truck, the band had played a few songs, but I didn't remember them playing. Everyone was having fun. They were dancing and grooving to the music. I could hear laughing and clapping. In between songs, I could hear loud pipes on cars as people would show off to the crowd when the band wasn't playing. The three of us just kicked back and enjoyed that moment.

Dunny said, "Let's go back to the truck and get a beer." We all staggered back through the people. Girls were everywhere I looked. We felt as though every girl in the world must be here. I could tell everyone was getting drunk. By now, it must have been 11:00 p.m. The night was still young. We'd say, "What's up?" as we made our way to the truck. The band was going to take a thirty-minute break, so we opened up the tailgate and sat down.

Tee Bone said, "I wonder where those outlaws are."

Dunny said, "I don't want to know. You can bet they're up to no good."

I didn't say anything. I knew they'd be there sooner or later. We started to talk about how many girls we were seeing. We would discuss the ones that were exceptionally hot. Man, for teenage boys, an event like this was almost torture. How could we be having the time of our lives, and yet, at the same time feel like we were being tortured? I'll leave that to the smart people to figure out. My torture was even more enhanced by my encounter with Lisa. My almost heavenly encounter I would later that night confess to Dunny and Tee Bone. We sat on the tailgate and laughed and joked around. Sometimes, a few friends we knew would stop by and talk with us. Then I remembered we hadn't seen Larry yet.

Dunny said, "I doubt Larry makes it."

I said, "Why?"

"Well, Ruby's black, and she might feel out of place here."

"I don't blame him. If I had the chance to be with Ruby, I'd take it."

Tee Bone nodded his head yes. Then I realized we were doing all this just to meet girls. It all boiled down to that basic need. Whether it was good or bad, it was no doubt normal and basic. I felt comfortable in my rationale. Dunny said, "Come on, let's go back. I'm not seeing any girls come to our truck."

While we were making our way back to the band area, I looked over at the spot across the clay pit, and I could see the white Charger. Sure enough, it was them, along with other cars that had managed to arrive. They had a small fire. They were all holding on to their girlfriends. I could see suit man and Lisa holding on to each other. I was a little confused. *Does she really like him?* Just a few hours ago, she had kissed me. We kept walking. I'm not sure Dunny or Tee Bone saw them. We finally got to the band area.

Dunny said to someone, "Why aren't they playing?" They said the bass player passed out. He found some pills, and they knocked him on his ass. Dunny looked at me, and we both thought *Soapers*. That's what happened. It was too much of a coincidence. The suit man was here, and now people began to pass out. It's really hard to drink enough beer to pass out. Usually, you just get numb from beer, but you didn't pass out.

A band member came on the mic, "Does anyone here know how to play the bass?"

A couple of people said they did. So while the new base player came up, they put on a radio station. It was KSHE95. Some good rock and roll, the song "Crystal Ball" by STYX, was on the radio. That seemed to please the crowd. I scanned the crowd. I could tell, or maybe I could feel, that several people had taken the soapers. People were really acting out of it. I saw girls that were dancing; now they could barely even walk. I saw girls helping their guys walk and guys helping their girls walk. Not everyone was on soapers but several were, that was no mistake.

I looked across the clay pit. I could see the small fire, but I didn't see the giant or anyone else. I looked in the direction they would come from to walk over to the party. I found them walking in pairs toward the band area. They knew a lot of people because they stopped and talked a lot as they made their way over. The tall scroungy man had his arm around a girl. There was another man with him, and he had a girl too. *Oh great, now four of them to deal with.* I elbow nudged Dunny and nodded him to look. Dunny looked, and I could see his disappointment. I could tell he was about tired of running into the giant and his crew. I remembered that Lisa had told me that the suit man had gone to Auxvasse.

Auxvasse, a small town in North Callaway County, was small, maybe two hundred people, but it was a larger farming community. It's good flat land for crops and hay fields. We would go there and hang out in the parking lots at night. It had a four-way stop sign that the city cop would sit and watch. We had friends in Auxvasse, but they were known to dabble in harder drugs. Not that we judged them to be any worse than we were, it's just the harder drugs cost more money. In a very good way, our lack of money is what most likely saved us from the worst part of drugs. Dunny and I liked to get drunk because it was cheaper. The only thing I couldn't figure out was why the giant and the suit man would be going to Auxvasse. I knew that I was going to need to get Lisa to tell me a little more about the Auxvasse connection. Later that winter, I heard that a veterinarian was being blackmailed.

About the same time that we looked over at the giant, the band started to play. The lead guitarist struck a note that I'd say is still going to this day. He rocked back, grimaced and struck the guitar again. It was a Molly Hatchet song, "Gator Country," and man, it sounded good. Some girls came up to us and asked us to dance.

We said, "Why not." We got in the middle of the crowd and began to dance. We had our hands in the air and were clapping to the beat. The song came to an end, and Dunny and I went back to the water's edge. The band went into another song by Led Zeppelin, "Stairway to Heaven." If anyone had a girlfriend, they would dance to that song. While I was standing and watching, a girl came up from behind and put her hands over my eyes and said, "Let's dance."

I didn't know who it was and said, "Sure." When I turned around, it was Lisa. It was too late to say no. I said, "Are you trying to get me killed?"

She said, "He doesn't care. Besides, he is married."

Now I was really confused. I said, "I thought he was your boyfriend."

She said, "He thinks I'm his girlfriend, but he's not my boyfriend."

I gave up trying to make sense of the situation. We danced close together, closer than I'd ever been with a girl. I liked it even more than I'd ever imagined. I knew I was going to be in a bad spot if the suit man saw us. The only problem I was having was that I couldn't let go of her. I was thinking about how good she smelled. She didn't have a lot of perfume on. In fact, it was a small amount. But we were sweating, or maybe I was just sweating, and her perfume got on me. I could smell her on me the rest of the night. We just danced, not saying anything, just dancing. I didn't want the dance to end. It did end, and she just drifted away into the crowd of people. When I let go of her, it was like on the river when two boats that were tied together turned loose of each other and drifted apart. I walked back to the water's edge, but I didn't see Dunny or Tee Bone.

The band was getting ready to play another song when I looked up on stage, and there was Dunny. Dunny had a really good voice. He knew the words to just about all of our favorite songs. The band started to play "They Call Me the Breeze" by Lynyrd Skynyrd. Dunny had a smile that would fill up a room. He was singing, and girls were dancing, and he was loving it. Tee Bone came up to me, and we both just busted out laughing. I was very happy for Dunny. I think the band letting him sing was the highlight of his life. Some girls would blow kisses at him while he was singing. When he finished the song, some people yelled "More, more, and more." So Dunny bowed like a King Arthur knight and looked over at the band. They signaled with a "one more" finger. He went over to the band talked for a little while why the guitarist struck a chord. It was "Hey, Baby" by Ted Nugent. The girls started to scream and dance and sing out loud. It was so much fun. *How come this night has to end? How could I ever top this feeling of grandeur that I was feeling?* While Dunny was singing, I looked over at the giant and suit man's spot where they were parked. All I could see was taillights of the white Charger going up the hill. Then I could see the other cars in the giant's crew following him on up. Dunny was about to finish his last song. I knew I was not going to encounter Lisa anymore this night. I turned around, ran, and jumped into the water. I was thinking a cool dip in the water would help cool off the fire I felt inside by body. Next thing you know, everyone was jumping in the water. The girls were jumping like they were jumping overboard of a sinking ship. I was impressed. I figured at least some of the girls would take off their tops. Sure enough, their tops came off. So much for putting out the fire I had inside me. Dunny jumped down and ran into the water. We swam around, of course. We looked and tried to memorize every girl we could see. No way could this night have gotten any better. The band turned off their lights and turned off the generator. It was quiet. The only noises I could hear were people talking and laughing. One by one, cars would start and head up the hill to leave the clay pit. The dust began to get thick as everyone was leaving. Tee Bone, Dunny, and I weren't going anywhere. We knew we were staying there all night. Pretty soon, the pit was empty, and it was us and a few scattered cars with people sitting on them. Tee Bone and I walked over to the truck and started to look for firewood. We weren't cold, but it was nice to have a little fire to hang out by. Tee Bone was going on about seeing all the girls in the water. He was describing how good so and so looked. I listened to his voice, but my mind wandered off to the dance I had with Lisa. I couldn't get her off my mind. I could hear Tee Bone's voice. He was asking me, "Do you think those girls know what they do to a guy when they are skinny dipping like that?"

I said, "I'd guess they do. I know if I was a girl, I'd think it sure would be easy to get a guy. All I'd have to do was show my boobs."

Then we just laughed and laughed. But still, all my mind would do was flash back to Lisa kissing me and us slow dancing.

Lisa wasn't real tall. She had long brownish hair down to her belt buckle. It had some blond streaks in it, but mostly, it was brown. She wasn't at all strung out looking. In fact, she was very pretty and clean cut. She had tiny braids woven in her hair that was tied back and woven throughout with colored beads on the ends of the braids. She had a pretty smile and nice white teeth and emerald green eyes. She had a really cool laugh and a soft voice. She was tanned and a little thin, but all and all, I'd say she was just about as perfect as any girl I'd ever seen. She was the only girl I'd ever seen naked. I'm sure that added to my idea of her perfection. I just couldn't figure out who she was or where she was from. We'd never seen her around before. Of course, Dunny and Tee Bone still didn't know anything about my latest encounter. But before the night was through, I would tell them everything. I was confused about why she was hanging out with the suit man. It seemed to me she could have any guy she wanted. Plus, why was she messing with me? Later, that fall and winter, I would try to get some answers to my questions. Most of the answers I wouldn't like, but nevertheless, I got answers.

Tee Bone's voice faded back into my mind, and he and Dunny were still going on about the skinny dipping. We all figured tonight's events wouldn't come along that often. The fact is, a night like that night never happened again. We laughed and joked about Dunny singing. We said, "Damn, Dunny, you need to sing more often."

He said, "I think I'm going to take up the base guitar." We thought that'd be a good idea. The fire was crackling and popping. We had plenty of beer, and we had some weed. So we decided to kick back and finish off the night. Dunny brought up the time when we were at this party and how I drank a bunch and decided I was John Travolta in "Saturday Night Fever." I thought I was a dancing machine, and some dude got so mad I was dancing with his wife. That man chased me around every car at the party, but he never could catch me. Finally, Dunny started the truck while the man was chasing me and I ran and jumped on the bumper and Dunny sped away. The man was hollering "I'm going to kill you" while running after us. When we got far enough off, Dunny stopped, and I got in and played, "Gimme Three Steps" by Lynyrd Skynyrd. Funny how life sometimes imitates art, but really, I'd say it's the other way around, because, without life, there wouldn't be any art. Tee Bone and Dunny just laughed their heads off. I thought it was funny now, but not at the time. Man, we had so many stories for guys so young. I still can hear them laughing. Most of our young lives were spent getting in and out of jams. This fall and winter would become the worst kind of jam to get in, and it would prove to be nearly impossible to get out of that one.

We decided we wouldn't sleep until all the beer was gone. We turned on the radio to KSHE95, just enjoying each other's company. I thought *Tomorrow is Sunday.* Then, I remembered Preacher telling me to come to church. *Ain't no way I'm making it to church.* I thought about Lisa, and I thought about the devil tempting Eve with the apple. *If Lisa was that apple, I would bite the apple just like Eve.* I wondered why God would let such a powerful temptation happen to anyone. My mind was made up. The next time I saw Lisa, I was not going to stop her. I didn't care if the suit man killed me or not. Funny thing about a fire being started in a young man's soul because I'm not sure a young man can think clearly when the desire for a woman gets that strong. And my desire wasn't about to go out, even after a cool dip in the clay pit. We guzzled the last beer down. It was about 3:30 or four o'clock in the morning. The fire was going out, so we curled up in the truck bed and passed out.

Chapter 20

I woke up to the warm sunlight on my face. My head hurt, but not too bad. The birds were singing and carrying on. The clay pit was blue and calm. Dunny and Tee Bone were still passed out. I got up and lit a cigarette. I was dreading the day. I knew it would be a long day filled with memories of the party. *Man, I don't want to go back to school. I don't want to study. I don't want to get a haircut. I'm not in any shape to practice football.* I knew that all the structure of school and sports were going to pin me up, like a young stud, thoroughbred horse. I needed to run and be free. Dunny and Tee Bone began to stir around in the truck. I said, "Get up, you deadbeats. Let's go to Gaspers Truck Stop and eat breakfast."

Tee Bone said, "Damn good idea." Dunny got in and started the truck. I got in the middle, and Tee Bone hopped in, slamming the door. We all looked at each other and laughed and punched each other. So with our hair sticking up everywhere and our teeth dirty from all the dust, we jumped in and headed toward Gaspers Truck Stop.

Tee Bone said, "You was going to tell us about suit man's woman, but you never did."

"I'll tell you after we make our breakfast order." I lit a cigarette.

Tee Bone gave me a curious look. "Come on, tell us now."

"I will, just not now."

Tee Bone was disappointed in me. Dunny was curious as well. When we were pulling into the truck stop, Dunny said, "How much money do we have? I need to get some gas."

We managed to come up with ten dollars between us. That left us with five dollars apiece to eat on. Dunny pulled up to the gas pump and got out. Tee Bone said, "You hooked up with that girl. That's why you were gone for so long that one time you went to get beer."

"Well…" Before I could say anything else, Tee Bone slapped me on the shoulder and said, "You dog."

I said, "No, it wasn't like that."

Tee Bone said, "Don't lie to me. When you came back, you looked like you had seen a ghost. So was it good? What was she like? I bet she was wild."

I can say I know now why you don't forget your first love because I didn't want to say anything. I wanted that to be private and only for me to know. Dunny looked in the truck and smiled at both of us. I said, "What?"

"I'm parking, and you're going to tell us all about what you did."

The funny thing is, I only wished I did half as much as they thought I did. Maybe I should just lie and make up a story for ages. Even if I thought Lisa wasn't an angel, I wasn't going to tell a story on her. I liked her too much to tell lies about her. In my mind, I could see her smiling at me as she gave me a kiss. Wow, now I'm really kicking myself in the ass. I'll probably never get that chance again. Dunny parked, and we headed into the truck stop to eat. We saw a few people that had been at the clay pit party.

Everyone said, "Damn, that was a great party." Tee Bone would punch me and say, "It sure was." Then I'd punch him back. We always horsed around like that with each other. He and Dunny are the best friends I could ask for. They were all excited to sit down. When we finally did, they both said, "All right, tell us all the details."

Then I proceeded to tell them most of all the details. They didn't believe me on most of the details. Plus, they said I was "holding back." I wasn't holding back; it's just that nothing happened. They'd say, "Yeah, right." We laughed and laughed and ate our meals. We still talked about the skinny dipping. We felt sorry for our friends like Larry who missed the party.

Dunny said, "Let's go. I need to get home."

Chapter 20

I woke up to the warm sunlight on my face. My head hurt, but not too bad. The birds were singing and carrying on. The clay pit was blue and calm. Dunny and Tee Bone were still passed out. I got up and lit a cigarette. I was dreading the day. I knew it would be a long day filled with memories of the party. *Man, I don't want to go back to school. I don't want to study. I don't want to get a haircut. I'm not in any shape to practice football.* I knew that all the structure of school and sports were going to pin me up, like a young stud, thoroughbred horse. I needed to run and be free. Dunny and Tee Bone began to stir around in the truck. I said, "Get up, you deadbeats. Let's go to Gaspers Truck Stop and eat breakfast."

Tee Bone said, "Damn good idea." Dunny got in and started the truck. I got in the middle, and Tee Bone hopped in, slamming the door. We all looked at each other and laughed and punched each other. So with our hair sticking up everywhere and our teeth dirty from all the dust, we jumped in and headed toward Gaspers Truck Stop.

Tee Bone said, "You was going to tell us about suit man's woman, but you never did."

"I'll tell you after we make our breakfast order." I lit a cigarette.

Tee Bone gave me a curious look. "Come on, tell us now."

"I will, just not now."

Tee Bone was disappointed in me. Dunny was curious as well. When we were pulling into the truck stop, Dunny said, "How much money do we have? I need to get some gas."

We managed to come up with ten dollars between us. That left us with five dollars apiece to eat on. Dunny pulled up to the gas pump and got out. Tee Bone said, "You hooked up with that girl. That's why you were gone for so long that one time you went to get beer."

"Well . . ." Before I could say anything else, Tee Bone slapped me on the shoulder and said, "You dog."

I said, "No, it wasn't like that."

Tee Bone said, "Don't lie to me. When you came back, you looked like you had seen a ghost. So was it good? What was she like? I bet she was wild."

I can say I know now why you don't forget your first love because I didn't want to say anything. I wanted that to be private and only for me to know. Dunny looked in the truck and smiled at both of us. I said, "What?"

"I'm parking, and you're going to tell us all about what you did."

The funny thing is, I only wished I did half as much as they thought I did. Maybe I should just lie and make up a story for ages. Even if I thought Lisa wasn't an angel, I wasn't going to tell a story on her. I liked her too much to tell lies about her. In my mind, I could see her smiling at me as she gave me a kiss. Wow, now I'm really kicking myself in the ass. I'll probably never get that chance again. Dunny parked, and we headed into the truck stop to eat. We saw a few people that had been at the clay pit party.

Everyone said, "Damn, that was a great party." Tee Bone would punch me and say, "It sure was." Then I'd punch him back. We always horsed around like that with each other. He and Dunny are the best friends I could ask for. They were all excited to sit down. When we finally did, they both said, "All right, tell us all the details."

Then I proceeded to tell them most of all the details. They didn't believe me on most of the details. Plus, they said I was "holding back." I wasn't holding back; it's just that nothing happened. They'd say, "Yeah, right." We laughed and laughed and ate our meals.

We still talked about the skinny dipping. We felt sorry for our friends like Larry who missed the party.

Dunny said, "Let's go. I need to get home."

Chapter 21

We headed home, but we wished our summer would never end. Dunny dropped me off at my house. I went in, and my mom and sister were eating breakfast. My mom said, "Well, look who's here. It's a stranger."

"Come on, Mom." I went to my room.

My mom and dad are the best parents anyone could ask for. In fact, my whole family is the best. My mom was about seventeen when I was born. So I'm thinking she understood what being young and wild was all about. Most of my young life, my parents would give me the slack I needed to be free. It's just that teenage boys aren't always thinking with their brains. My dad would take me with him everywhere he went. Mostly, I went with him to feed his horses. That Sunday, he wanted me to go and help him fix the barn. Earlier this spring, the stud horse had kicked down his wooden gate and got into the field with the mares. So he asked me to go with him, which I did. We rode together to our farm. It was about thirty minutes away in North Callaway County. He usually had the same country station on that Junior listened to. I didn't really mind. I just enjoyed spending time with my dad when I could. I asked him why the stud horse kicked the door down. He said, "When they stay pinned up all winter, they can't take it when spring comes because the mares would go into heat."

Then he said, "I guess he couldn't take it anymore and kicked the door down." I just thought of myself. Damn, I know how that stud horse felt. He told me about how I don't need to be getting in any trouble. He said, "Sometimes, trouble seems to find you when you don't even look for it."

I thought he must be spying on me. Sometimes, trouble seems to find you even when you don't look for it. We fixed the gate, and I looked at the stud horse. I felt sorry for him for having to be pinned up. It didn't seem normal to do that to any animal. When we were on the way home, my dad told me he would try to get me something to drive.

"You're kidding me."

"We'll try."

Most of the time, my dad would do what he said. My dad and mom always tried to give my sister and I what they could. I knew that if I had a car of my own, I would be able to find out the truth about the giant and his crew. More importantly, I might be able to find Lisa and get her to tell me about the suit man and her. While we were on our way back to my house, I began to reflect on the events of the past few days. In one weekend, I had met a group of very bad people and I just about went all the way with a girl I didn't even know, who, by the way, was with a bunch of drug dealing, car stealing, and murdering thugs. Now, *Were my dad's words coming from God "Trouble seems to find us"*? What if I was being played for a fool? What if I was the mark? I just couldn't believe Lisa could be playing me. All I know was I was going to find out, and I hoped I'd live to tell the story. My life could be compared to a river exploration. Most of the river was calm and peaceful, yet when you could finally see around the bend, and a bunch of dangerous rapids appeared, your heart began to pound. But you knew it was too late, and you couldn't steer away from the rapids and their danger. You knew you have to go head on right through it. Many times while in the rapids, you had to paddle your way through them, and if you didn't, the rapids would send you into a spin. Well, my junior year of high school was the rapids, and it would take all my will and strength to paddle through it. When we pulled into our driveway, my mom was watching for us. I came inside, and my mom said, "Dunny called and needs you to call him when you get home."

Chapter 22

I went up to my room and gave Dunny a call.

"Dunny, what's up?"

"When I got home this morning, Junior was not feeling well, so I took him to the hospital."

"Damn, is he going to be okay?"

In a shaken up voice, he said, "Yeah, but he has to stay the night. Do you want to hit some gravel roads, then stay here with me?"

"Yeah, come and get me," I said. I ran into the bathroom and took a washrag bath and changed my clothes. I put on a clean t-shirt and blue jeans and went to sit on the porch.

While waiting, my mom came outside and said, "Listen to me. You need to be thinking about school starting. Summer break is over. I know you had fun, but you have to get ready for school."

"I know, Mom, but I'm just not interested in school right now."

"We all have to do things we don't always like or want to do."

"I know."

Then she just went inside. The thing she was referring to was school. The thing I was referring to was taking on the suit man. Dunny pulled in, and I could hear his stereo playing a song we liked. Pink Floyd's "Have a Cigar." I hollered inside to my mom, "I'm going now. I'm staying at Dunny's house."

She yelled back those famous words that parents say, "Okay, be careful."

Dunny lit a cigarette and waited for me to get in the truck. I jumped in and said, "Let's go. . . So how's Junior?"

"He's okay. Let's go get some moonshine." We headed out toward Hilltop Liquors. We listened to the radio station down low. I was thinking that we might run into the giant and his crew. When we got to the liquor store, I looked down at the trailer house, but no cars were parked down there. My heart was pumping so hard I could feel it moving my t-shirt. When I didn't see anyone down at the trailer, I was disappointed. I wanted to see Lisa. I went into the liquor store, but this time, I didn't bang the door cowbell as hard. Here came the manager.

"What? We don't serve beer on Sundays."

"I know. I want some of your apple crisp."

He just smiled and showed his yellow teeth. "Come on back," the man said. He was the most excited I had ever seen him be, toward me anyway. Because he sold other things, he could be open on Sundays, but really, I didn't see what the other things were he was selling.

"Tell your buddy to come in. We'll turn the sign to closed."

I went to the door and flagged Dunny to come inside. He gave me a confused look, but he came in. I said, "Follow me." Dunny put his head down and stayed close behind me. The old man was sitting at a little table that was tight against one wall. He poured us a shot of the apple crisp and reached over to his AM radio. Patsy Kline's "Crazy" was playing.

"Pull up a chair, boys. Let's drink." He smiled. This was one side of the old man I had not seen before.

I said, "Why not?" I grabbed a shot and tipped it back as fast as I could. I knew the fire was going to hit me. I knew the old man was going to bust out and laugh at me. "Wow!" I slapped my chest and coughed. Dunny slammed his shot and had the same trouble I did.

"So," the old man said, "what's the deal with you boys?"

I said, "What do you mean?"

"You boys are in here every other night. I know you're still in school. Don't your parents watch you, boys?"

We acted all tough and said, "They don't care what we do. Besides, we're twenty-one."

"Bullshit," the old man said. "But I don't give a shit how old you are, just don't tell them I sold you anything." Even though the closed sign was on the door, I heard someone pounding on the door.

"Wait a minute."

Dunny and I sat there and tried to listen to who the person was. Our eyes lit up. It was the suit man and the giant. I heard the giant's voice say, "Hey, Uncle Charlie, we need some bread and chips." While the giant and suit man were talking to Uncle Charlie, I looked out the window toward the trailer. I could see Lisa and three other girls on the porch smoking cigarettes. I wanted to see her so bad, but I knew that was reasonably impossible.

Dunny said, "What are you looking at?" in a whisper.

I put up my finger to say, "Shhh."

The girls and the two scroungy guys were talking and milling around. I heard the giant say, "Come on down and eat with us, Uncle Charlie."

Then the wood floor squeaked, and the giant popped his head in the backroom and said to us, "And you guys can come too." Then he laughed real loud because he knew he had caught us off guard.

I said, "Sure, why not?"

Then I heard the door open, and the cowbell rang loud as the giant and suit man left. The old man they called Uncle Charlie came through the beads and slowly sat in his chair.

"Let's take our shot. Then we can go down to their trailer."

We all three slammed our shot of apple crisp. Then he said, "Let me tell you two something. You'll need to stay away from that bunch down there. That's my nephew, but they're no good, and it's no good to be hanging around them." Dunny looked at me with an "I told you so look."

Then Uncle Charlie said, "You two seem like good enough boys. I know what it is like to want to have fun, to drink, to chase girls." Dunny and I listened to old Uncle Charlie as he gave us some advice. The funny thing is, the advice was the same we had heard. Preacher had told us, my parents had told us, Junior had told us, even

Larry had told us that trouble seems to find you and that you need to be on guard to see the trouble and stop it before it's too late. Maybe God did use people to speak to me, but I still had to find out about the suit man and Lisa. I wasn't so dumb to think that I couldn't get into trouble. It's just that for a sixteen-year-old boy filled with desires that can't be put out, it's hard to listen to any advice that doesn't line up with my own thoughts. Well, like my dad's stud colt, sometimes, you just have to kick down the door of the pen you're in and get out in the world to be free and find out what's out there. Hopefully, you don't meet up with the stud horse. I remember my dad saying that the two stud horses could kill each other. Dunny and I got up from the table and headed toward the door. We said, "See you later," and rang the cowbell as we left. We got in the truck, and Dunny said, "Man, I don't want to go down there."

"I only want to because I need to find out about those guys."

"Yeah and you want to see that girl down there too."

"Yep, that too."

I told Dunny we just about had to go because they would be expecting us to come down. If we didn't, I thought they would be expecting us to be some sort of spies or something. Sometimes, a guy just can't win no matter what he decides to do. Dunny started the truck and slowly backed up then slowly went toward the trailer. The closer we got, everyone began to stop what they were doing and began to look at us.

We rolled into a spot next to the white Charger. Finally, I made eye contact with Lisa. She was smoking a cigarette. She locked her eyes on me. Dunny and I slowly got out of the truck. I tried not to look at Lisa, but I just couldn't take my eyes off her. I would look over at suit man to see if he was catching Lisa and I looking at each other. If they were playing me, they were good at it. Suit man was talking to someone on the telephone, and he never really paid much attention toward Dunny and me.

The giant said, "Come on down, boys. Let's have a drink and a smoke. You boys smoke pot?"

We said, "Yeah" and walked closer to the group.

The giant said, "Pull up a chair." We were all standing in the little front lawn. "So I never did get you boys' names." The giant looked at us. I knew Dunny didn't want to say his, but I spoke for us.

I said, "He's Dunny, and my name is SL."

He said while everyone but suit man was standing and watching us, "Well, it's good to know you, boys. Let's see, the young lady here is Debbie, and she's Kathy, and she's Missy—she's mine—and this here is Lisa."

I looked at everyone one at a time and nodded to them with a head nod. But when he introduced Lisa, I looked then dropped my head. I could not make myself look at her as if we were friends. Dunny nodded his head to each girl. Lisa looked at me really calmly and coolly, and I could feel her looking at me. The giant said, "These dudes, that's Randy, and that's Terry. I'm Jesse, and that's DW," pointing to the suit man. Finally, I could put a name to a face. The whole time Jesse was talking to us, the suit man, or DW, was on the phone. He would pace back and forth talking and smoking a cigarette. We pulled up a lawn chair, and one of the girls gave me a beer. I looked at her, but tried not to stare and nodded my head. She gave one to Dunny. Then she went into the trailer and came back out with a joint and lit it. I could hear it pop and sizzle as she put a flame to it. About every other minute, I peeked over at Lisa to see what she was doing. But she was as cold and cool as ice. She would look at me and smile then look away. Someone turned up the radio that was in the window of the trailer. It was AC/DC's "It's a Long Way to the Top." It sounded good. It wasn't really loud, but I could hear all the words. Finally, DW hung up the phone and came down the steps toward me. He put his hand out, and we did the hippie's version of a handshake. He nodded his head at Dunny, and Dunny nodded back at him. He said, "So glad you boys could join us." Then he went over to Lisa and put his arm around her. I wanted to fight him right on the spot. But I knew I would get killed. She didn't hesitate and put her arm around him. He said, "I'm going to go to Auxvasse." Then he looked over at the giant.

The giant said, "I'll take you."

Here's my chance. I'm going to find out something when they leave.

Dunny said, "Let's go then."

The giant told him, "No, you guys stay. We'll bring something back for you."

Dunny gave me that look of disappointment that he always would give me. The giant and suit man got in the white Charger and eased on out of the driveway. The two other guys, they stayed with us, and the four girls stayed too. I'm not sure if the other two girls were with the two guys or if they were just friends. Before the white Charger got too far away, Missy jumped up and yelled, "Jesse, stop. I want to go." So the giant stopped and let her in the back. Now, I was thinking my chances were getting better to get Lisa alone to talk to her. Dunny sat there and swigged his beer. I could tell he was nervous and wanted to leave. One of the girls came over to Dunny and started to talk to him. I was glad she did that. The two guys and the other girl went into the trailer. I could hear them talking about someone's checkbook.

Now, I know I only had about an hour, and they would be back from Auxvasse. Auxvasse was only about ten minutes from their trailer. I said, "I got to take a leak" and made eye contact with Lisa. I wasn't sure if she would pick up on my clue. I went over to the edge of the woods and looked up in the night sky. My heart was about to pound out of my chest.

I finished taking a leak, and someone put their hands over my eyes and said, "Guess who?" I knew this time who it was. My heart was beating so hard. I turned, and there she was. She smiled and laughed. She had that same smell. She was just as calm as anyone could be.

I said, "Man, I got to know more about you. Are you in any danger?"

Before I could say anything else, she put her hand over my mouth and said, "Shhh, be quiet." One of the guys had stepped out on the back porch to take a leak. She kept her hand on my mouth and smiled at me. We just looked into each other's eyes. The scroungy guy went back inside the trailer. Lisa lowered her hand to my face and then she kissed me. She said, "You guys have got to get away from here. When DW and Jesse come back, just tell them you have to work tomorrow and thank them and leave."

I heard her voice but didn't hear a word she said. I was in a trance. She said, "Hey, did you hear me?"

I said, "Yeah, but I can't leave. I can't take being away from you, and I can't take it that you're here with this bad guy."

She put her hand over my mouth again. Then she said, "It's not what it looks like. I'll find you, and I'll tell you everything." She smiled at me and said, "I meant what I said to you at the clay pit."

Now my heart was pounding in a way I hadn't felt. I didn't know what to say except "Okay, but—"

And before I could say anything else, one of the girls hollered, "Anyone seen Lisa?" When I turned around, she was gone. She circled around and came out by one of the cars. Lisa said, "I'm here. I had to pee."

Chapter 23

So I walked back toward Dunny. When I got closer to him, the other girl was still talking to him. They looked like they were into each other. The door on the trailer opened up, and the two guys and a girl came out. They were drinking and smoking a cigarette. One guy, I think his name was Randy, sat down on one of the steps of the porch and said, "So what exactly do you boys do for a living?"

I said, "Odd jobs mostly. Right now we buck hay."

Randy said, "Damn, boy, that's hard work. You need to come with us one night. We'll show you how to make some easy money."

One of the girls said, "Shut up, Randy." I looked over at Lisa, and she smiled, but she was calm. *There is just no way she's playing me.* If she was playing me, she needed to be in Hollywood.

The other girl said, "Dunny, you want another beer?"

"Why not?"

Then we all sat in silence until the other guy Terry said, "Randy, come here for a minute." They went and looked inside of his custom Cutlass. They were looking at the driver's side corner dash. They were whispering. I couldn't really figure out what they were whispering about, but it was something with the serial number. While they were occupied and Dunny was occupied with the girl they called Kathy, Dunny, myself, and the girl were talking and laughing up a storm. Debbie was somewhere in the trailer putting on some music. I eased up from my chair and walked back to the backyard to go to the bathroom. I knew that the giant and the suit man would be back any time now. I looked to see if Lisa was still over by the porch, but she was gone. I heard her inside telling Debbie she wanted to put on Tom Petty's song, "Breakdown."

Debbie said, "I'll find it."

So I heard the screen door open and shut. I stayed around back standing in the shadows of the dark woods. Then around the side of the trailer, I could see her shadow. She was walking slowly, almost silently, toward me. She came up to me and said, "Hey there" and just smiled. I can only say that I thought she was the most perfect girl God could have made. I'm not sure if she was the one I would be with forever, but I was sure she was the one I wanted to be with for now. And as far as I was concerned, now was forever. She put her arms around me and said, "Listen, I'll find you, and I'll explain everything, but you need to get away from me. When I said 'He doesn't,' I meant if I dance with someone. But he doesn't think twice about beating someone and even killing someone. He's as bad a man as they make." The first time I met Lisa, I was scared of the suit man. Now, I wanted to kill him. Then, I decided I was going to play these guys. I was going to paddle through the rapids. I wasn't going to let them play me but was going to let them think they were playing me.

I said, "You'll have to let me know more. It's killing me thinking about you." At that time, the song she requested came on. The guitar rift filled the humid air. As the words slowly came out, she whispered them in my ear. The lyrics went through me like an arrow. As the song played, she kept singing the words to me. I could only just listen to her sing and hold me. We slowly danced in the shadows. She squeezed me really tightly, and I squeezed her tighter. I could smell her perfume, and I held her as tight as I could, like the next minute, the next tick of the clock, I was going to explode. I think I could feel her heart beating. I know she could feel mine. The second verse started to play. But then we saw headlights turn to the driveway. The headlights circled across the sky, the yard, the trailer, and even briefly caught Lisa and I holding on to each other. I didn't think they saw us. I hoped they didn't see us. It was dark again, and Lisa kissed me and drifted back into the night. She never was anything but calm. I saw her go up on the porch and go inside the trailer. The song was interrupted. I wanted to finish it holding on to her. I was so frustrated. But I knew now I was in a different game. Not a Friday night high school football game, but a game that was about life and death. I became the player, and I wasn't going to let anyone know. I walked back from the woods and acted as if I had just taken a leak. It's like when you break from the huddle to run a play. You run up to the line of scrimmage, and you run the play. I knew if Lisa could play it calm, then I had to do the same. After all, she had been in the game for a good while, and I had just entered the game.

Chapter 24

The Charger rumbled to a stop. The dust from the road came boiling up in a cloud with the Charger. It boiled high up into the night sky. I was next to Dunny and Kathy. They were pretty well lit. I was drunk, but it wasn't from anything I had drank or smoked. I was afraid for Dunny. He was a good driver, but he was enjoying himself. The suit man and the giant walked up to us. I was watching them come toward us. The suit man had a clear bag full of pills. I knew what they were as soon as he got next to me. Out of the corner of my eye, I looked up at the window in the trailer and could see Lisa looking out. She was washing dishes. I could tell she was calm, and she was fully aware of everything going on around us. The giant said, "Look here, boys. Let's play," and then he laughed really loudly. He called everyone over to take a soaper. "Let's all go on a trip," he said as he gave everyone a pill. Dunny looked worried. I was worried, but I wasn't about to show it. I took mine and slammed it with a guzzle of beer. Dunny took his the same way.

I watched everyone take one, or at least I thought they all took one. Lisa had been inside putting on some music. She came out, and suit man said, "Here, babe," and handed it to her. She didn't even hesitate. She calmly took it and swallowed it. She smiled at suit man, but not the same smile as when she smiled at me.

I knew it was only a matter of time, and I'd be out of it. Not just me, but everyone would be knocked on their ass. I listened to the music. It was Heart's "Barracuda," and I just sat down and began to feel my body tingling. I looked around, and Dunny was laying his head in Kathy's lap. She was laying her head down on his back. I jumped up and said, "Dunny, let's get in the truck."

The giant said, "No, man. Just go inside." My head was spinning. I was only minutes away from going out. The giant and suit man were laughing at us. Yet, to me, they didn't seem to be out of it at all. Kathy helped me lay Dunny in a chair. Dunny passed out cold. I sat down in the chair beside him. I went out.

Chapter 25

I woke up. I wasn't sure what time it was. The birds were singing and carrying on. The windows on the trailer were open. I looked over and shook Dunny. He tried to stir, but it was taking him awhile. On the couch was Debbie and Kathy. They were covered up with a quilt. I got up and looked outside, and all the cars were gone except our truck. Lisa and Missy were gone, and all the guys were gone too. I shook Dunny again. "Dunny, get up. Let's get out of here."

He stirred around but finally began to come out of it. Dunny said, "Damn, what the hell happened? I don't remember anything once I took that damn soaper."

"You went down faster than a bag of rocks."

"I guess I did." We got up to head out, and Dunny said, "What time is it?"

"I don't know. I'll look for a clock." I found one, and it was eleven o'clock in the morning. I told him.

"Damn, I got to go. I need to pick up Junior from the hospital."

"Okay, I'll go with you. Come on, let's get out of here," I said.

We started to go to the truck. I was worried about where everyone else had gone. Kathy woke up and said to Dunny, "Hey, can I see you again?"

Dunny perked up. "Of course. I'll catch up with you again."

I said to Kathy, "Where is everybody?"

She said without any hesitation, "They went to Hampton, Tennessee, and then Greensboro, North Carolina. They won't be back for a few weeks."

"How come they went there? I was wanting to talk to them about making some of that easy money."

"They are from there, except for Jesse, Debbie, and I."

"Where the hell is Hampton, Tennessee?"

"It's way up in the mountains next to the North Carolina border."

How did they all get here?

"Why did they up and go now?"

"Well, they found someone in Greensboro to buy their cars."

"Why would you sell your car?"

"There are more cars. There are always more cars. Just hang around, you'll see."

Dunny was outside in the truck. He didn't want anything to do with this bunch. I did think he liked Kathy though.

I told Kathy I'd be back in a few weeks. We were about to pull out when Debbie came out and flagged us to stop. Dunny stopped. She came up to my side and put her head up inside to me. She said, "Hey, that stuff Kathy told you. Well, you better not say anything to anyone. These guys will kill you and anyone who you know. They won't think a thing about making you all disappear."

I said, "Why would I say anything? You tell them I want in."

"Don't be messing around with these guys. You boys seem like good guys."

"I am a good guy, but I want to make some easy money. You just tell them I want in."

She backed away from the truck and lit a cigarette.

Dunny backed up and said, "What the hell are you all talking about?"

"Ah, nothing. I'm going to sell some of those soapers for the suit man. She's just trying to scare me."

"She's doing a pretty good job of scaring me."

Now, my plan was starting to take shape. Now, my dance with the prowling lion was about to take place, and it was going to be another one of those meetings at the crossroad.

We drove off and away from the trailer. Dunny said, "I don't know what's in those soapers or what they are even really meant for, but damn, they will flat kick your ass. There ain't no way you should sell those damn things to anyone."

"Relax, I got this under control."

Dunny always would tell me how I was lucky and good at everything I did. He hoped I was good at this game I was playing with the suit man and the giant. Believe me; I hoped I was good at it too. I really didn't have experience being a criminal. I would soon learn, though.

Chapter 26

We went to the hospital to pick up Junior. He was all right because he lit into cussing us as soon as he saw us. Dunny wheeled him up to the truck, and I got out and helped him in. Junior was skin and bones. He looked like a POW. Dunny went back to give the hospital the wheelchair. Junior and I talked. He said, "Give me a cigarette." I did. There was no arguing with him. I smoked one with him.

"So where have you two shitheads been?"

"Ah, we've been out running the damn streets." Then I smiled at him.

"I don't doubt it." Dunny jumped in the truck, and we headed home. We knew school was going to start the following week, so we planned to hit it hard every night until it started.

Junior said, "Let's drink some of that moonshine and play some cards."

"Sure, why not. I'll give Tee Bone a call when we get to your house."

That made Junior's day. We pulled into Dunny's driveway and parked close to the door. I got out, and Junior grabbed my arm. I helped him into the house. I grabbed up the telephone and called Tee Bone. Tee Bone said he would come over about four o'clock. Dunny and I pulled up a chair at the kitchen table and started to shuffle cards. We all lit a cigarette at the same time.

Junior said, "Five card stud, jokers are wild."

My mind wondered when he said, "Jokers are wild." I wondered why the joker was always wild in our card game. I was wondering how I was going to play the suit man and the giant. I needed a game plan, and I needed to draw a joker. I needed to hatch a plan and have it all played out in my head; I needed to think through as many combinations of hands everyone could be holding. I needed to be sure of myself, and most of all, I needed to be calm. Suddenly, in my mind, I realized the high stakes game I was in. The suit man held the one ace, and that was Lisa, but Lisa held the wild card joker, and that was me. But no one at the table knew that I held an ace and a joker. Or did they know? I knew that in a card game, everyone is studying each other and that the slightest motion could send a signal, and they would pick up on me in a minute. Now, I realized they were playing me. They were sizing me up. I was young enough to be trained. But I was playing them as well. Then I realized that, at some point, they would test me. My mind came back to the real card game with Dunny and Tee. Junior said to me, "Let's drink some of that moonshine, boys."

Dunny got us all a glass. Then he poured us all a shot. I grabbed mine and slammed it. Fire went plum down to my belly button. Junior laughed really loudly. *I guess someone is laughing when one takes a shot is always going to be funny?* We heard a knock at the door. It was Tee. He came in and smiled from ear to ear.

"What's going on, fellas?"

We all nodded at the moonshine. Dunny poured him a glass. He slammed it, and yes, we all laughed. I was looking around, and I was thankful for such good friends. They were the best friends in the whole world. We laughed and played. We heard an old country song by Waylon Jennings, "Are You Sure Hank Done It This Way." It seemed that cards and country music went hand in hand. Plus, a good cigarette didn't hurt.

We played until about six o'clock, and Junior said, "Boys, I've had enough. I need to eat and lay down." So we cleaned up our mess, and Tee said, "Dunny, can you just come by my house and pick me up?"

"Okay."

Dunny made Junior a sandwich, and I went outside and smoked. I still needed a plan. I knew that juniors in high school could take a class called COE. I didn't have any idea what the initials stood for, but the class was where you got out of school and worked a half a day. I thought that would work for me. The only problem was I would need to quit the football team to take the class. Dunny came outside and got in the truck. I told him that I was going to be quitting the team. He just said, "Why? You're good enough to go play at MU."

"I just want to work. I hate school."

"Well, whatever. I ain't your dad."

Then we drove off to get Tee. We got to Tee's house and honked. He came running out. He was still smiling from ear to ear. I said, "Tee, why you so happy?"

"Man, me and my girl just broke up. So now I can go with you boys every weekend."

It's funny, but Dunny and I were happy. Tee was fun to be around.

We cruised through town and the night people were starting to gather in the vacant lots. We knew a lot of them by now. We'd honk and flash the peace sign at most of them. We came to Hardee's, and sure enough, there was Larry with his parking lights on. We pulled in, and no one said anything. Everyone gave an "I'm cool" head nod. Larry had a girl we couldn't see until we got closer to him. It was Debbie. Neither Debbie nor the three of us acted like we knew each other. Larry never was the type to introduce his girlfriends. I just looked at Debbie, and she looked back at me. She smiled a small smile and nodded to me. They were smoking a joint. They had music on but down low.

Larry said, "I heard it was one hell of a time at the clay pit last weekend."

Dunny said, "Yep, man, it was something else."

Tee said, "We got to see—" then stopped himself because Debbie was listening. I was afraid he was going to say something about Lisa and me, so I made sure to change the subject. I'm not sure Debbie was as friendly as Kathy. I'm thinking she would tell on me for sure if she was pushed hard enough. We told Larry that Dunny sang two songs, and he tried to play the base guitar. Larry laughed a little.

Larry said, "I knew Dunny could sing. Dunny, that should be all you need to do to get some girls." We told him that some girls threw their tops at him. He laughed again.

"I should have been there." Then that was all the conversation we had. We sat and watched a few cars, and Tee said, "Let's hit some gravel roads." We nodded at Larry and started the truck. I looked at Debbie. She waved goodbye, and we waved back at her.

Of course, the first stop we had to make was back to Hilltop Liquor. Tee said, "Let's get a twelve-pack. I'll buy." Dunny was fooling with the radio and driving. Finally, he settled on a station. It seemed to me that we were always buzzed that summer. It seemed like we drank all the time—maybe because we did drink all the time. We didn't drink because we had to; we drank because we wanted to. It felt good. Tee kept looking at me like he wanted to ask me something.

"What?"

He smiled and said, "You hooked up with that girl yet?"

"No."

Then Dunny leaned over and said, "Well, you did have a chance to talk to her last night."

I lied and said, "When did I have a chance to?"

Dunny said, "I thought I saw you two in the woods when the suit man pulled up."

"No. That was just me taking a leak."

"Oh."

Ted Nugent's "Strangle Hold" came on the radio. We cranked it up and sang the words. It felt good just to sing and not think.

Dunny pulled into the driveway of the liquor store. I looked down at the trailer house. It was empty—not a car in sight. I wondered what on earth they were up to. I was worried for Lisa, but I figured she got this far without me helping her. I still had a little doubt that she was real. I jumped out of the truck, and this time, I eased the door, so it barely rang the cowbell. Old Uncle Charlie came around from the backroom.

I said, "Hey."

He smiled. That was the first time he ever smiled at me when I came into the store. "What's up with you, boy? You didn't about tear down my door when you came in."

I said, "Ah, just thought I'd trip you up and make you wonder who it was."

He said, "You boys want to take a few shots of apple crisp?"

I said, "Sure, I'll get them." Tee and Dunny didn't want to come in, but they did. We went to the backroom, and Old Uncle Charlie had already poured us the shots. He'd never met Tee, so he had to get another glass. I sat down and just grabbed mine up and slammed it back. This time, I fought off the fire and tried to act like it didn't burn. Old Uncle Charlie slammed his and said, "Damn, boy, you act like you've drunk this before." Then he busted out laughing and poured us another one. I have to admit; it did seem like I was getting used to it. We slammed back another. I asked Uncle Charlie where everyone got off to. He said, "Oh, they won't be back for a while. Hell, they may not ever come back. That would be fine with me."

"Why's that?"

"Well, they go back to Tennessee, way up in the mountains almost next to North Carolina. You won't hear from them for months at a time. One time, I didn't hear from them because they were in prison. They got caught stealing cars. Then they'll just show up here all of them driving different cars. They work on them back here in the garage, painting them and stuff. They'll get the car all cleaned up and purring like a cat. Then they'll disappear and go sell them."

"Damn, that must be some good money."

"Yep, until you get caught or killed," he said while pouring us another shot. You see, I figured out how to talk to people. If you want to get information from people, you have to get them to trust you. They have to feel comfortable around you. The best way I found was around a kitchen table drinking moonshine. So I learned my first play in this game—trust.

I figured that I better get as close to Uncle Charlie as I could. That was going to be my best shot at getting into the operation. I said, "Uncle Charlie, we got to go. We need to hook up with some friends down the road." He stood up and said, "Oh well, I know you'll be back. Hell, you're in here about every night."

"Hey, do you play cards?"

"I ain't in a while. I used to play all the time."

"How about we play some cards this coming Saturday or Sunday?"

"I'll play Saturday after lunch. It's not that busy until it gets dark."

"Okay, we'll see you then."

Now, Dunny and Tee weren't really sure about hooking up with the old man, but really they didn't care as long as we could drink for free. I liked Uncle Charlie, and I wasn't going to get him into any trouble. Let me explain. He hated the cops. We hated the cops more than the bad guys. So the information I was seeking was to try to free Lisa. Who knows? Maybe Lisa didn't want to be or was free. I just knew that the suit man was bad, and I was going to take him down for her, not for the law. I wanted to take him down for us. Even though I thought I was really tough on the inside, I was really scared of getting killed by the suit man.

Chapter 27

We got in the truck and headed to the clay pit. We were buzzing like bees. Tee said, "Let's smoke a joint."

Dunny had pre-rolled some, so he said, "Get it out of the glove-box." We got to the top of the pit and looked down. No one was there. We headed down to our spot along the water, turned off the truck and got out. Dunny put the radio on KSHE95. Aerosmith came on, "Sweet Emotions." It sounded good. The guitar echoed off the water and bounced off the clay hills, and we bounced our heads to the beat. Those famous words "Talk about things and nobody cares." The lyrics came through crystal clear. I always thought those words summed up our teenage conversations. We smoked the joint and listened to the song.

Dunny said, "Why are you trying to get close to all those guys, man?"

"I don't know. I just like meeting up with new friends."

"Yeah, but they ain't no good."

"Ah, they want you to think they're tough."

"They got me fooled if they ain't."

I tried to change the subject. "What about Kathy? You didn't seem to mind her last night."

Tee perked up and said, "What are you all talking about?"

"Ask Dunny."

Tee looked over at Dunny and said, "Well?"

"She's nice. I could take some of that."

Tee and I busted out laughing. Tee had a girl, and they had been all the way, but Dunny and I hadn't been past a kiss. It was almost a quest to get all the way with a girl. Sometimes, it's a quest that eats you alive. Needless to say, it's a quest on your mind 24-7. Dunny laughed with us. We stayed out there at the clay pit drinking and cutting up. We made a fire. Then we decided we had too much to drink, so we slept in the back of the truck again. It was nothing to pull the truck over and sleep it off. While we were lying in the truck, they went to sleep, but I couldn't yet. I got up and smoked a cigarette. I thought about the giant and suit man. *How do you steal a car? Do you just walk up to someone and take their car? What was Lisa's role in all this? When would they come back? Would things be different?* I wondered what she would think about me. So much stuff ran through my mind. I decided to calm myself. Remember, you're in a game. Remain calm. I relaxed and crawled into the truck and went to sleep.

The sleep was good. I needed some sleep. Sometimes, it takes sleeping to put things in order. I woke up, and I could hear the birds singing and felt the warm sun on my face. I elbowed Dunny and Tee. They began to stir. I got out of the truck and kicked the small smoldering fire. I lit a cigarette. Dunny and Tee rolled out of the truck bed.

Dunny said, "Damn, I'm not sure that I have ever slept this good in my whole life."

Tee said, "Man, I felt like I was in a dream." I'm not sure why we slept so good. I think maybe God was looking after us. I'm sure God was aware of our lives. It's just that I couldn't think about church and the idea of not being able to party. I knew I was dancing with the devil. I knew trouble was all around me. I was choosing to find out how much trouble was out there. I told Dunny I needed to go home for a while. I needed to go to my room. I felt safe in my room. I felt safe at home. My mom would ask me, "Is something wrong?"

I'd just say, "No." But I'm sure a mom can sense when their child is in danger. I stayed mostly at home that week. I did stuff with my dad. I got ready for school. I was thinking about the summer and the fun Dunny and I had. Friday night came, and Dunny called me. "Hey, man, you ready to go?"

"Yep, come and get me."

I had taken some time to develop a game plan. I was ready to pick up my cards and see what kind of hand I had been dealt. I was going to do whatever it took to put an end to the suit man's grip on Lisa and on us. Dunny honked the horn. I ran down the steps and yelled to mom, "I'm leaving. I'll be staying at Dunny's tonight."

She said, "Okay, don't stay out all night," as I ran out the door.

Dunny was waiting. He was smoking a cigarette. I jumped in the truck and said, "Hey, what's up?"

He nodded and said, "Not much, getting ready for school." He slowly backed up and headed out the driveway.

I said, "Where are we going tonight?"

"I heard that there was a bonfire for the end-of-summer party out at the old archery range."

"Yeah that sounds good. You think some girls will be there?"

"Yep, I'd say that a lot of people will be out there."

I thought this sounded like a change of routine. Maybe even Dunny sensed we should try to break our old patterns. One pattern we couldn't break was how we got our beer. We both knew that we would need to go to Hilltop Liquor.

Dunny said, "Let's spin through town and see who's out."

Chapter 28

We drove through town, and Dunny punched in a tape, Grand Funk Railroad's "We're an American Band." It sounded good. We smoked a cigarette and just enjoyed the ride. I began to wonder about the night we slept so deeply. It's as if something changed our course. Dunny seemed different. I seemed different. I went home after that night, and so did Dunny. I know now it was the calm before the storm. The storm had arrived. You know how when you look to the west, and you can see the black and grayish green cloud coming, you can tell it's going to be a bad one. You can see lightning and hear the thunder. But, even though it's dangerous, you can't help but watch it bare down on you. Well, that's the same feeling I was having when I thought about the suit man and the giant and even Lisa.

Dunny saw Larry and pulled in beside him. This time, he had both Debbie and Kathy, who was in the back seat. One of our good friends we called Cee was in the front with him. They were smoking a joint and passing it around. We all nodded our "I'm cool" nod and said, "What's up, man?"

Larry said, "Nothing, just sitting here." Dunny and I both looked at the girls. They smiled and waved at us. I'm not sure, but I don't think Larry knew that we knew both the girls. Then Larry said, "Hey, you all ever heard of soapers?"

Dunny and I just swallowed our tongues. I looked at the girls, and they looked back at us. Larry went on to say, "These pills are so badass. We are going out to the archery range tonight. We got fifty of these pills, and we're going to sell them." Then Larry said, "You all want one of these? They are five bucks each."

Dunny and I both said, "Nah, we're low on money right now," which was the truth. The girls looked at us funny; it was just last weekend that we had all taken the soapers while out at the giant's trailer. Dunny said, "We got to go" and started his truck. "We'll see you at the archery range." Then we drove off. Dunny looked terrified.

I said, "What's wrong?"

"Man, if Larry takes soapers out to that party, it's not going to be pretty."

"Yeah, I know."

We were headed toward the liquor store, and Dunny turned up the radio. The song was "Hurry Sundown" by the Outlaws. I knew the storm had begun. This pill had made it to the streets. It was going to spread like a virus throughout the hippies and night people. One thing about the night people that I knew; we'd try anything at least once.

Dunny pulled into the driveway of Hilltop Liquor. I jumped out and ran inside, but I hit the door softly. Old Uncle Charlie came through the beads and said, "I knew you'd be here. We still playing cards on Saturday?"

"Yep."

I was wanting to see if I could learn any more about the suit man and the giant's whereabouts and plans. But for now, we needed to go to the archery range. I said, "I'll just get a twelve-pack, some ice, and two packs of Marlboros for tonight."

"That'll be five bucks for you today."

I looked up at him because I knew he had cut me a break. Then he said, "Go on, get out of here before I change my mind." Those words struck a chord and a memory of when the giant had spoken those very same words to us not too long ago. I hurried and got all my stuff, paid him, and then pulled on the door hard. The door hit the cowbell and banged it really loudly. I turned and looked back, and he gave me that look. I reached up and stopped the cowbell from ringing. He shook his head and went back to his kitchen. I got to the truck, and Dunny was waiting. He said, "Come on, let's get out of here." I put the beer in the cooler with the ice and jumped in the truck.

"Okay, let's go."

Dunny backed up then tried to get out quickly. He knew I'd want to look down at the trailer. Even so, I did look, but it was empty. My mind wandered back to Lisa. I couldn't get her off my mind. I reflected back to seeing her in the liquor store for the first time. No way could I tell she was in danger. She was as calm a person as I could think of. In most every sport I had ever played, the one thing you were taught was to stay calm. Put yourself in that one moment. Slow everything down and remain calm. I had heard this advice over and over. It took seeing Lisa in real life for me to realize how important that advice would be. She had perfected the art of calmness. If she could do it when her life depended on it, then I could do it for myself.

I said to Dunny, "Hey, man, don't be worried. We are going to get through all this mess."

"Man, I liked it better when we just drank some beer and hung around, maybe even stay up all night. Now, if you take one soaper, you go out and don't remember anything." I took a deep breath and started to reflect on the times Dunny and I had laughed so hard, and when we saw those streakers. I'm sure that we were going to have a lot more fun times. It was just hard to get past these uncertain moments. It was anything but the fun we were used to having. It was as if the prowling lion was lurking and stalking us for the right time to pounce.

We found a gravel road that would take us right to the archery range. Dunny and I talked and even laughed our way down a less familiar gravel road. Even now we managed to laugh and to find humor in our lives. The night was clear and full of stars. Mostly, we listened to music and would stop on occasion and smoke a joint. Dunny loved to smoke pot. I liked it too. I would tease him about getting hooked up with that Kathy chick. We thought it would be nice to finally get to go all the way with some chick. It was pretty much to a point that any girl would do. I told him again that I was not going to play football this year. I know I had said that several times throughout the summer. I guess he never believed me. I told him I was going to take COE and that I had a job lined up at Louie's Auto Body. He said, "I never knew you wanted a job at an auto body shop."

"I didn't know myself. I just figured I needed a job." The truth was, I figured if I got interested in cars, that would give me a reason to get on the inside of the giant and the suit man's operation. We slowly rolled into the archery range. We could see the fire. Cars were backed up for at least a football field long. We stopped the truck and parked. We got a beer and headed toward the fire. It was only about 9:30 or so. We walked by cars; some people would be sitting on the hoods. Some people were hugging and kissing. We tried to see if we knew anyone as we walked by. Every once in a while, someone would say, "Hey, what's up?" After a while, you'd begin to notice the same cars and same people at all these parties. We finally got near the front and came across Larry's car. It was funny to see his car and not him in it. When we got up to the fire, I'd say there was about twenty-five to thirty-five people drinking and smoking cigarettes. The music was coming from a stereo in someone's car. It sounded good. You must understand that in the '70s, a stereo mattered as much as the car itself. Dunny noticed some new younger chicks and pointed them out to me. We thought the night was looking good. I surveyed the crowd. I kept hoping to see Lisa in every girl or group that would walk up to the fire. I wondered if I would see her again. A group of girls came up to us and talked and flirted with Dunny and I. It felt good for girls to flirt with us. They'd tease Dunny and say how good he was singing at the clay pit party. I felt like I was with a celebrity. We laughed and stared and carried on about all the girls in shorts and wished we might get lucky with one of them. Mostly, we laughed and for a moment, it seemed like old times, that is, if sixteen- and seventeen-year-old boys were even old enough to have "old times."

It's strange we didn't feel like teenagers. We both felt older than we were. I told Dunny I was going to take a leak. This time, no girl followed me. I wished Lisa would have somehow been there. I looked back toward Dunny and Larry, and his friends were standing next to Dunny. I knew those girls would be somewhere close. Sure enough, they came from the keg that was in the back of someone's truck. Dunny was smoking a cigarette, and so were Larry and the girls.

I walked to them and said, "Hey, Larry."

"Hey."

Both Debbie and Kathy were really friendly to me. They would dance around and hug and kiss on me. They were drunk, but I have to admit, I liked it. Kathy was really drunk and kissing Dunny a lot. Dunny didn't mind it. We were having fun.

Dunny said, "I got to go take a leak." He walked over behind a car in the dark. I knew where he went, but I couldn't see him. Debbie was carrying on with Larry, then me. Larry didn't care. He had more women than anyone I knew. Dunny came back, and I turned and looked at him. His face and eye were swollen. I said, "Damn, man, did you fall or what?"

"No, this big bodybuilding-looking dude grabbed my arm and pulled it behind my back. He told me I thought I was cool because I sang at the clay pit. Then he spun me around and hit me."

I was pissed. Neither Dunny nor I were fighters, but we never got messed with much except by the seniors and juniors when we were freshmen.

I said, "Who was he?" But Dunny didn't know, plus it was dark.

"Let's get out of here."

"No, I'm going to find out who hit you."

It was getting close to midnight. Next thing you know, this guy was grabbing another guy by his arm and just slinging him around like a ragdoll. The crowd started to gather around the guys fighting. Dunny said, "That's the dude who hit me."

He was a big guy that was eaten up on steroids. He was fighting everyone, and no one could do anything about him. He grabbed the man he was slinging around and got on top of him and started to hit him. I couldn't stand it, so another one of my friends and I ran up and kicked the man right square in the mouth. Blood went all over the place. Then, Dunny hauled off and hit him right square in the mouth. Then he jumped up, all bloody, and just growled at us. He wasn't human. He started toward Dunny. I tripped him, and he fell. Then Larry hauled off and kicked him right in the throat. The man grabbed his throat and acted like he was choking. We didn't care. We wanted to kill him. And then another guy kicked the man square in the ass. The man finally laid out on the ground. The crowd began to cheer, and some guys grabbed the man up and threw him in the bed of a truck. He just laid there and moaned. We didn't care how bad he felt. Finally, the guys in the truck left with the man still in the back. My heart was pounding. We had just tasted blood. It felt good. I had never hit someone before, at least outside of football. Everyone there was pumped up. Larry said, "I got something to calm this crowd." He left for a minute then came back. He had the bag of soapers. People had heard of soapers, so when word got out that someone had some, it was all over. The funny thing is, the soapers were needed to calm the crowd. I thought when Larry said "calm the crowd," I knew exactly what he meant. The crowd was in mob mode. It was anything but calm.

Larry said, "You guys want one?"

Dunny and I said, "No." Debbie and Kathy were passed out in Larry's car. I'd say they already had one. Larry took one; then some other people bought some from him. Dunny and I sat back and watched. Then I realized that's what suit man and the giant did. They never really took the drugs. They just sold them. I really think that Lisa never really took them either. She was calm without them. Soon, people began to stagger around, and even Larry began to stagger. It was not a party anymore. Dunny and I decided we better leave. As we left to head home, we took a slow ride on the gravel road. We still had some beer to drink; one thing you never wanted to do is leave a cold beer in a cooler. It was a ritual to drink all the beer that we had. I looked over at Dunny. Even with one eye, he could drive and smoke a cigarette and find a tape to put in the super tuner. I could only wish to be so talented. With the familiar hissing and my buzzed anticipation, the song came on. It was Atlanta Rhythm Section "So into You." Man, it sounded good. I sat back and drank as we sang that song and enjoyed the guitar and beat of that song. I immediately pictured Lisa, and I wanted to hold her again, but I wasn't sure if that was ever going to happen.

Chapter 29

The next morning, I woke up on Dunny's couch. I could smell bacon and eggs. My hand was swollen but not nearly as swollen as Dunny's eye. Junior was standing over me smiling. He said, "What's the other guy look like?"

"I don't know, but I hope that son of a bitch is dead. But I doubt we could get so lucky."

"Dead? Better hope he didn't die."

"Why not? It was self-defense."

"I don't give a shit if it was self-defense or not. They'll throw you two in the jail just the same."

"Well, he ain't dead. He was still moving when they drove off. I'm sure that won't be the last time we run into him."

Dunny came around the corner, and his eye looked really bad. I said, "You better stay home the rest of this weekend." We ate breakfast, and Dunny gave me a ride home.

When I got home, I went and asked my dad if I could use his truck. I told him Dunny got hit in the eye and was staying home. I told him I'd be home early, but I needed to do something. That something was to go to Hilltop Liquor and hang out with Uncle Charlie. I needed to get more answers. I was going to need to drink to get answers, and that meant drinking and driving if I was going to come home. I decided to tell my dad I was just going to stay at a friend's house and not drive. He agreed, but he said we shouldn't tell my mom about the drinking part. She was cool, but she was still a mom. It was getting near noon, and I figured Uncle Charlie would be expecting us. So my dad gave me his truck and said, "Look here. If you drink, you stay where you're at because I don't have enough money to get you out of jail."

The funny thing is, I believed him. I may have been a wild teenager, but I knew I didn't have the right to get in trouble and expect my mom and dad to get me out of it. I backed out of the driveway. I was wishing Dunny was with me. Then I thought of Lisa and how calm she was, so I stopped in my driveway and took a deep breath. I calmed myself down. I slowed down everything in my mind. I knew I needed to be calm. Again, I wondered, have you ever been standing outside when a storm is coming at you? First, you see it in the form of a dark cloud, then everything stops—for a moment silence. From the straight line winds, the trees start to make a noise like a train is coming. Then you see the trees bending and leaves blowing around. You can hear the rain hitting the trees. Thunder and lightning following with the wind and rain. Well, this is what I saw in my mind as I drove to Uncle Charlie's liquor store. I pulled in and turned off the engine. I wasn't scared, but I was anxious. I wished I could see Lisa, but no one was down at the trailer. It was as if they were ghosts. I opened the door and rang the cowbell. Old Uncle Charlie came out, and he said, "Turn that sign to 'closed.'" I turned the sign and went back to the kitchen.

"Hey, Uncle Charlie, what's up?"

"Look here, I got us a shot ready."

"Damn, was you expecting me?"

"Yeah, I've been waiting all day for you boys to get here."

"Well, I'm by myself. My buddy took a punch in the eye last night." He didn't say or ask for any details. I guess he must have seen his share of fights.

He said, "Well, I guess it's just you and me then." Then he grinned and laughed really loudly.

I pulled up a chair and sat down. Uncle Charlie pulled up a chair opposite of me. He said, "Well, let's have a drink."

I grabbed mine and slammed it back. The fire went right down to my belly button. My eyes watered as I put the shot glass down on the table. I knew Uncle Charlie was going to need to have a few drinks before he began to talk about anything that was personal. He had his old country AM station, KFAL, turned down low. It was Merle Haggard's "The Fightin' Side of Me." Some great classic country music was coming across the airwaves. A small fan was blowing the stale, humid air in our faces. The kitchen window was open. You could hear noises from the garage in the back. Someone was always fixing a tire or working on their truck or car in the garage. I could hear people and cars coming and going from the trailer park. No one was at Jesse's trailer. But I couldn't tell.

Every once in a while, a dog would bark at an unfamiliar car. It seemed that a lot of cars would pull in and then circle out. It was like they were looking to see if Jesse was home. I didn't really recognize any of the vehicles, but there was a steady stream of them coming in and then leaving. Uncle Charlie kept a handkerchief to wipe the sweat off his head. It was really hot outside, even hotter inside that kitchen.

He spoke up and said, "So you and your buddy got in a fight last night?"

"I guess you could call it that."

He picked up the bottle and poured another shot.

"Some big son of a bitch came up to the crowd and just went off on anyone around. He hit my friend while he was taking a piss."

"Damnedest things. People can't drink and enjoy themselves. There always seems to be someone wanting to fight."

"Well, he got a fight then. I'm not so sure he likes to fight now, though."

"Oh, what makes you think that?"

"A whole bunch of us stomped his ass and then sent him down the road."

We both took our shot glass and slammed it back. The conversation stopped for a minute. Then he said, "Yeah, my nephew Jesse, he's a real badass."

Here we go. I'm going to get to hear about the giant.

"Man, Jesse was always fighting when he was a kid. He never really was a bully or looked for a fight. But he never really steered clear of trouble either. He went to Vietnam when he was eighteen years old. I guess he was in some real shit. He came back with bullet holes in his leg and one in the shoulder. I don't think he was ever right in the head when he came back. He never had a job he could keep. He liked cars—hopped up and badass cars. He'd work on them back here in the back of my garage. I'd say it was about five years ago he and some guys started to steal cars. When they got caught, the guys he was with, they gave him up to save their own asses. Well, that didn't sit too well with Jesse, and he went to whip their asses for them. Jesse ain't scared of anything. He found them outside of town hiding in an old trailer house one night. They got to fighting, and someone called the cops. The cops pulled a gun on him, a twelve-gauge shotgun. Jesse tried to get away, and as he was running, they shot him in the back. He was a good way off when they shot at him. But he was hurt and as he tried to get to his car to get his gun, that's when the cops finally got him arrested and sent him to prison. I'd say everyone knows prison only makes you a better criminal.

While in prison, he met a bunch of car thieves. And he discovered a whole chain of car thieves spread all over the states. When he got out, he came here to my trailer court and lived back at the end. I guess he's been here a year or two now. I kind of hoped he might get a job, but he still liked cars. It wasn't too long after he got out that DW and those two girls showed up here and stayed in the trailer with him. DW always had a roll of money on him and so they'd bring a car here and then fix it. Then they'd be gone for a while. Still doing that same thing today."

He stopped for a minute, then he said, "Well, let's have another shot."

I guess he figured I'd say yes because he poured mine first. Now, it may seem to someone who doesn't drink that at sixteen, I did drink a lot. But I'm not sure back then that I thought about how much I drank as much as I thought about how I felt when I drank. Three shots of moonshine would get you in a relaxed state of mind. I liked that feeling.

"Uncle Charlie, you been to any wars?"

"Yeah, I was in the Korean War, along with my brother, Jesse's dad. He got killed over there. I came back and been right here ever since."

I found myself starting to like Uncle Charlie. I even started to like Jesse. I realized that we were the ones that caused the trouble for him when he pulled us over that night awhile back. He wasn't all that bad as much as bad things around him made him be bad, a path that I was heading down myself. I looked out of the window, and I saw Larry's car come in and go down to Jesse's trailer. It stopped, and two girls got out of the car. It was Debbie and Kathy. They went inside, and Larry drove off.

"So you going to open back up? It's getting on in the afternoon."

"Yes. Let's have one more for the road."

We slammed a shot, and I said, "I guess I better go."

"Well, you'll be back. Go on and get out of here." He let out a really big laugh.

I stood up, and my head was buzzing, like a bunch of bees were in it. There was no way I should drive. I got to my truck and started out. Then I decided to drive down to the trailer and hang out with Debbie and Kathy. I figured I could go there and let some of the moonshine wear off.

I started my truck and turned on the radio. One of my favorite songs of all times came on. Dunny and I would crank it and sing along, The Eagles' "One of These Nights." I just put my head down on the steering wheel and listened. My head was spinning as fast as a top. I was only thinking of one thing, and that was Lisa. That seemed to slow down the spinning. But nothing seemed to fill that strange feeling I had for her. I wished I'd go in that trailer, and she'd be standing there smiling.

I wondered if she could feel me thinking of her. I sure knew I was thinking of her. I just wasn't sure what she was doing. I wasn't sure what her point was in all this mixed up stuff. The song ended, and I came back to reality, and I looked into the window, and I saw Uncle Charlie staring out the window at me. The whole earth was spinning. I could see Uncle Charlie smiling, and I'm sure laughing really loudly. But I gathered myself, and I drove on down to the trailer. I figured I would try to get some more answers from Debbie and Kathy. I needed to find out about Lisa. As I pulled up, I could see the curtain pull back just a little. Because there were no cars at the trailer, I figured the girls didn't want anyone to know they were inside. I stopped and got out. I walked slowly to the door of the trailer. I knocked really lightly. Someone said, "Who is it? Jesse ain't here."

I said, "It's me." Then the door opened.

She said, "Come in. Hurry. No one is supposed to know we are here."

I hurried inside and shut the door. They had the stereo on really softly. Kathy was in the shower; I could hear the water running. Debbie said, "Hey cutie, what's up?"

Then, I said, "I've been up to the liquor store when I saw Larry drop you girls off." I didn't want her to know that meant Uncle Charlie and I were drinking buddies. She said, "I love old Charlie. He's a good guy."

"So I thought I would hang here for a while. My buddy got hit in the eye last night."

She said, while lighting a cigarette, "Yeah, I heard there was a big fight and that some dude got the shit kicked out of him."

I was glad that the word was out about the dude getting his ass kicked. About that time, the bathroom door opened, and Kathy came out naked except for a towel on her head. She looked right at me and didn't even flinch. She said, "Hey, baby, what's up?"

I couldn't understand how these girls could be so comfortable when they were naked in front of me. *Damn, she looks good.* She just went on into the room. I could hear her opening drawers. Then I heard a hairdryer. Debbie just looked at me and busted out laughing. She said, "Boy, how old are you?"

In a tough way, I said, "I'm twenty-one, why?"

She said, "You're the first twenty-one-year-old man that I've ever seen turn as red as a cherry at the sight of a naked woman. How many naked women have you seen?"

Still in my tough guy manor, I said, "I've seen my share."

She laughed and said, "You could have fooled me. You look like you've seen a ghost more than a naked woman." Then Kathy started to laugh, and they both laughed.

Kathy said, "Wait until I tell Lisa that she might have a virgin on her hands." I stopped any expression I had and looked at Kathy.

She said, "Yeah, I know you two been sweet on each other."

Damn, I was hoping that it was a secret. "She told me that she loved you and that I was supposed to keep my hands off of you." Man, when I heard that, I almost fell down. My head was still spinning a hundred miles an hour. My legs got so weak. Man, I wanted her now more than ever, and I didn't think that was ever possible.

Debbie said, "I don't care how tough, how old, or how much of a past someone has. When the love bug bites, you can see it written all over one's face. And boy, right now I can see a whole book on your face." Then, Debbie and Kathy busted out laughing some more. Then Debbie said, "There's only one problem with you two's way. That'd be DW." I knew that's what she was going to say.

She said, "We better smoke a joint, don't you all think?"

I was in no shape to smoke pot but, I couldn't mess up a chance to get more information, so I shrugged my shoulders and said, "Why not?"

Kathy said, "I thought you'd never ask." Kathy went over to a coffee can and got a small bag of weed. She took an album cover and separated the seeds out of the weed. When she lifted the pot on top of the album, the seeds would roll down on the table, and the weed would stay at the top. Then she rolled a joint and lit it and passed it to Debbie. They would take a puff, let smoke come out of their mouths about six inches, and then hurry and suck it back in and hold it. I just smoked it.

Chapter 30

Debbie said, "Boy, let me tell you a little bit about DW. He's one smooth-talking and good looking conman. He was in the Vietnam War. He and Jesse were in the same company. They both saw some bad shit. They both killed plenty of people. DW, Lisa, and Missy are from Hampton, Tennessee, way up in the mountains near North Carolina. They are poor as hell up there. They ain't got no jobs that's good and especially no jobs that pay anything. While in Vietnam, Jesse and DW came up with the idea of stealing cars in Greensboro, bringing them here, chopping them up, then building something new to sell. There's plenty of cars and plenty of people who will pay a lot of money for a badass car."

Kathy said, "There's always plenty of cars."

Debbie continued, "So when Jesse and DW got back from the war, Jesse came and set up the garage. DW went to Hampton and started to steal some, but he got caught. Some dudes narked on him, which wasn't a good thing to do. Anyways, DW went to prison for five years and got out in 1975 or so. Meanwhile, Jesse got into his own trouble here, and he went to prison for, you guessed it, five years. Now, I guess while they were both in prison, they came into the whole underworld of stolen cars. The mob and all kinds of badass people were involved in stolen cars. So now, Jesse and DW are out, and that's where we are at right now." I'm not sure if it was the joint or the moonshine; I'd say both. I couldn't even talk. All I could do was listen. Debbie stopped and said, "Damn, I'm going to need a drink before I go on."

She got up from the kitchen table and poured a shot of moonshine they had in the icebox freezer; moonshine won't freeze, and it's best cold as you can get it. She said, "You'll need one of these so I can finish the story." We all three took our shot and slammed it back. Kathy slapped her leg and said, "Wow, that's some kickass stuff!" Then she laughed and lit a cigarette. Then Debbie lit one and gave it to me, while she lit another one for herself. Then she got up and went over to the stereo and put on an record. It was Fleetwood Mac "Rumors" album. She came back over to the table and sat down. Never really missing a beat, she said, "Oh, so Jesse got out of prison, and then DW came here. DW married somebody from around Mokane. But I think that was part of his con to look legit. When DW got out of prison, right before he came here, the guy that had rolled on him came up missing. Well, that guy was Lisa's older brother and Missy's cousin. No one ever found his body, but everyone says DW sank it in a big lake near Hampton. Lisa told me that DW had told her he would sink her and all her kin in that lake if she ever breathed a word of her brother's death to the cops. The funny thing is, that's why she's here with him. It's so he can keep his eye on her. Now, Missy, she doesn't know all the details, but I'm sure she has a good idea. Plus, Missy really likes Jesse, so I'm saying there ain't much she won't do for him." I just sat back in my chair. It was all I could do to keep my head from flying off my shoulders. I went from having no answers to being overloaded with answers. My head was hurting. I didn't want to think for a while. But then I had to say one thing, "I don't see how you could be around someone that killed your brother." Kathy stood up and said, "She ain't got no choice. DW said he'd kill everyone she cared about if she didn't come here and drive these cars as they steal them. DW is a bad man. I think he likes killing people. He's a smooth-talking, nice-dressing man, but he'd just as soon kill you than look at you. And now, Lisa's gone and fell in love with you."

Debbie said, "Now are you sure you want to get involved in all this?"
I said, "Get involved? It looks like I'm already involved."

Chapter 31

I looked out of the window in the kitchen, and the sun was about to set. The girls said they were just going to stay at the trailer and sell soapers if anyone needed some. Man, I thought soapers and DW were one and the same. Both of them could kill you if you weren't careful. They said, "Why don't you just stay with us tonight? We won't hurt you." Then they'd laugh and giggle.

I said, "Hell, why not?" trying to be tough as I could. I thought I might go up and hang with Uncle Charlie for a while.

They said, "Oh, he won't close until midnight or so." So we decided to play cards, get drunk, and smoke pot until we passed out. Debbie said, "Put some music on. I got to take a shower." Kathy and I sat at the table while Debbie was in the shower. Kathy was getting drunk.

"That Lisa sure is sweet on you. I know why now. What I could do with you would make the devil blush."

I just looked at her. All I could think about was, man, how come this is happening to me? Two weeks ago, I would have dreamed of this, and now all I wanted to do is wait for my first time to be with Lisa. *That is the dumbest thing you've said to yourself.* Kathy was very nice looking. She had blond hair that was braided and weaved into a ponytail. She had a great body, was kind of tall, but not taller than me. She smiled all the time. She had blue eyes, and she wore a peace symbol necklace. *No way should I let this pass.* While I was looking at Kathy, the water shut off and here came Debbie out of the shower.

Of course, naked as she could be and just walked by me to get to her room. The girls busted out laughing at me. All I could think about was eve and the apple. Why would God even feel the need to let man be tempted? What was the point of showing something so tempting that there was no way possible to turn it down? I knew I wasn't married or even sure that the night I was waiting for with Lisa would even happen. It seemed that what was going on here was a sure thing. *Let me change the subject with the girls for a few more minutes.* Then, maybe I will lose my willpower and just dive in with both of them. I said, "So if no one knows you are here, how are you going to sell soapers?"

Kathy said, "DW will call and let us know. There's a veterinarian in Auxvasse he gets them from. All we got to do is go there and get them."

"You don't have any here?"

Kathy said, "Yeah, we got some, but Larry took most of them with him."

It's getting kind of late and I ain't taking my dad's truck to Auxvasse to get pills, which is what I figured was going to happen if I stayed. "Hey, girls, how about we take some soapers right now?" It was about eleven o'clock. I had begun to kind of sober up with all the talking, but I was still buzzing from the weed.

The girls said, "Hey, why not?" They opened up the icebox, and there was a small bag of them in the butter tray of the side door. Debbie poured a shot of moonshine for each of us, and we took the soaper with the shot. We sat back down at the kitchen table. Debbie looked good to me. Her hair was wet. She had a t-shirt on but no bra. I could see them move when she did. She would just smile at me when she caught me looking at them. These women liked to see me fidget around. They put on the album "The J. Geils Band," Whammer Jammer. It sounded good. My head was spinning so much now. All I could think of was keeping it together. They got up from the table and started to kiss all over my face. I liked it, but I was completely numb. I couldn't feel anything. They girls were laughing, and they took off their shirts. I remember them dancing with each other, then pulling me up out of the chair to dance with them. We were falling about the trailer until we all three fell on the couch. And that was it. We all went out like the lights.

I woke up with two women; neither had a shirt on, and they both were curled up next to me. *There's no way any of my friends can find out about this.* I'd never hear the end of it. I really ain't so sure I believed it myself. It was still pretty early in the morning. I had to stop and take as long of a look as I could before I had to leave. Debbie was dark complicated, almost looked like an Indian. She had black hair and always kept it in a ponytail. She was short but built just right. She had brown eyes and always wore a t-shirt that had some saying on it like "On the eighth day, God created me." I liked her a lot. I liked both of them a lot. I took a quilt and covered them up. I shook Debbie and said, "Can I get a rain check on you two? You all passed out on me."

She smiled and said, "No problem," then she went back to sleep. I figured I better leave while it was early. So I grabbed my shirt and headed out the door. I drove home thinking that in a matter of two weeks, I had the chance to go all the way with three women. But instead, nothing. In baseball terms, that's called "wearing a collar." A zero batting average. I drove off wondering, *Was that good luck or bad luck?* Ask any sixteen-year-old boy, and he'd say that was definitely bad luck. I got home even before anyone was awake at my house. I went to my room and fell asleep. I was too tired to dream. I woke up, and it was almost 3:00 in the afternoon. *Damn,* I thought. . . *What just happened?* There's something about sleeping in your bed. I felt refreshed, and I even felt calm. I went down the steps to our kitchen, and my mom was fixing dinner. We always ate well on Sunday. She was adding to some food my grandmother had made. Then I felt bad. I hadn't thought about my grandmother for a while.

My mom said, "You need to go by and spend time with your grandmother."

"Yep, I'll go now for a while. Can I take your car?"

I drove off to see my grandmother. I knew she was going to give me heck about going to church. But I loved her, so I just listened when she would preach at me. I got there and went hollering for her.

She was making a quilt. She always quilted. I have three of them still to this day.

"Who's here? Do I know you?"

"Come on, Grandma, you know who I am."

"Why you sound like my grandson, but you don't look like him."

I guess I had changed maybe and didn't know. I didn't cut my hair anymore, but other than my hair, I didn't think I looked all that different.

"Come in. Sit down and talk to me. What have you been doing this summer?"

I told her I was busy hauling hay every day it didn't rain.

"I was hoping I would look up at church and see you there. You know it's important to go to church. God says we need to be saved and confess our sins."

"I know, Grandma."

"There's been this young man about your age that has been speaking at church sometimes. He'd been messed up with the wrong crowd, but Jesus saved him, and now he's going to school to be a preacher."

I knew exactly who it was. It was the guy at the clay pit.

"He's going to speak tonight at church. You want to go with me tonight?"

"Nah, Grandma, I need to get ready for school. It starts tomorrow."

"Oh yeah. What grade will you be in?"

She knew I'd be a junior but I said, "Junior. Well, Grandma, I got to go, but I'll come by and see you when I can."

"You need to know that the devil loves to see God's children live in sin and his soul mission is to look for lost souls and to keep them on the path of sin."

"I know, Grandma. I love you. I'll be back to see you."

I kissed her and hugged her goodbye. When I got in the car, I let out a deep breath and said to myself, *Whoa, I got that over with* then started the car and went home. As I was driving home, I said to myself, *I'm not too sure how much of my soul the devil is worried about.*

So far, I've had three chances to get lucky and got nothing to show for it. I think the devil has bigger fish to catch than me. The way I saw it, I messed things up on my own. I didn't need the devil's help.

Chapter 32

The first day of school as a junior was, I have to admit, a day I did look forward to. Finally, I was considered an upperclassman. My freshman and sophomore years were not easy. Usually, I would get picked on, or I had to do things for the upperclassmen. I guess it was a rite of passage sort of thing. I warned everyone I wasn't going to play football. So I went to the guidance counselor and signed up for the COE class. That meant that I would come to school in the morning, and then leave and work in the afternoon. I liked the idea of getting out of school to work. I just hated school, and I'm not really sure why. The only good reason I could come up with was I just wanted to work. My high school was old, and it was located in the middle of town. If you had a car or truck, you could drive yourself to school. I didn't have a car or truck at first so Dunny would come by and pick me up. We could not smoke cigarettes on school property, so we would stand on the edge of the property and smoke there. We dared anyone to stop us from smoking. As I got ready to enter the school as a junior, Finally, I'm an upperclassman. When I walked into the front door, the hallway was full of new student freshmen. I had several freshman girls flirt with me. *Well, this may not be so bad.* I wasn't really used to girls coming up to me. I made it to my home-room. My homeroom teacher was also my coach. He stopped me and asked why I wasn't going to play football this year. I said, "I'm going to work this year."

He said, "Boy, you'll have your whole life to work, but now is the best time of your whole life."

The best time? I'm having the best time and it's not because of football. My homeroom teacher was a great guy, and he seemed to understand teenage boys. It's just that my interest was girls and partying. I went to my classes, and I could only dream about the summer I had. It was as carefree and interesting of a summer as I could ask for. I was absolutely bored out of my mind. I could only count down the days until Friday and the weekends. My auto body job was working out; it was just slow. I wanted to hurry up and learn all I could. I also took a night job at a gas station pumping gas. I loved working and making money, a lot of times, when I got off at the gas station, usually around nine o'clock, Dunny would come by, and we would go for a ride and smoke some pot. But the days turned into weeks and then months. I'd go to Hill Top Liquor, and there would be no sign of the giant or suit man or anyone. Even Kathy and Debbie had disappeared. The only one around was old Uncle Charlie. I'd hang out with him, and we would take our usual two to three shots of his brew. But when I would ask about Jesse, he'd say, "We're better off not knowing anything." I just figured they were in jail or dead. I just quit going to school. I didn't drop out. I just quit going. The funny thing was, no one ever really said anything to me. One time, Dunny went every day to Algebra and slept every day. He would sign his name on the test and turn it in. The teacher passed him. A lot of times, the classes would be set up to pass if you just came to class. Soon, it was fall and no word or sight of the giant and suit man. Plus, no word from Lisa. I thought maybe I had been played after all. Dunny and I would party and ride gravel roads. We even went to the clay pit. Sometimes, people were there, and we'd talk about the fun we had when the band was there. The band party night was infamous. It was our mini version of Woodstock. I never told Dunny or Tee about my evening with two half-naked older women. I was ready to kick my own ass over that night. Finally, Christmas came, and I had really begun to forget and even give up on the idea of a hookup with Lisa. It helped to forget her because some girls would want to party with us. I never could get past third base, though. Because the suit man and his crew had gone, the soapers dried up. People weren't having car wrecks and passing out all over the place. It seemed that our wave of corruption had passed. We were partying as much, just for the most part, we could remember them. My grandmother never would let up on me about church. We even ran into Preacher at several parties. I would talk to him. He was easy to talk to. But I still had my doubts about going to church. I really believed that God was real, but I never could get past the fact of giving up drinking and the nightlife at such an early age. I felt that most of all people had wild sides to them, whether they wanted to admit it or not. I couldn't imagine my life as being on the straight and narrow path. I knew I was dancing with the devil. The bigger problem for me wasn't knowing that I was flirting with the devil; my problem was, I liked it. I wanted everything that the devil had to offer or, at least, I thought I did. Later that year, I would see an uglier side of what the devil had in store for me.

My mom, and for that fact, everyone who cared about me would gripe at me about not going to school. I just hated it, and I just wanted to work and become good with cars. I still thought that one day the giant and the suit man would come back to town. I wasn't sure if Lisa or any of the girls would show up with them. I just figured I needed to give her a little more time. I was not ready to give up on her promise to me. Sometimes, a young man confuses love with lust, but I'm saying from my point of view, they were the same thing. I'm sure that any other girl could have taken Lisa's place in my heart, but no girl ever did; I was left with a vision in my mind of her dancing with me in the dark, the feeling of her breathing on my shoulder and hugging me like she knew I was something good for her. No matter how hard I tried, I couldn't erase those brief moments I had with her. I would continually look for her wherever I went. Every time I'd tell Dunny at a party, "I got to go take a leak," I'd look around for her. Surely, this was hell because I thought being with her would be heaven. Maybe that's the devil's game to dangle the forbidden apple; let me see it, smell it, and even touch it, then get me so worked up that I'd sell him my soul at some crossroad. Well, the truth is, if that was his game, it was working. I could feel the prowling lion in the shadows, and I knew deep down inside that the lion and I were going to have it out.

Chapter 33

The winters in Missouri are usually back and forth. One day, it might give you a little taste of spring and then the next day it could be below zero. To me, this winter seemed extra-cold and extra-long. A lot of my buddies had four-wheel drive trucks. We would wait until a big snow came and all the streets would be empty. We had the run of the town. The cops only had cars, and if it was really bad, they would put chains on their tires. We knew they couldn't even catch us.

One snowy, wintery weeknight, I had borrowed my dad's four-wheel drive truck. Our family were Chevy people, but it seemed that most people had Fords. Dunny and I were parked in the Hardee's parking lot when a guy we had seen around from Auxvasse came pulling up. He had two hot chicks with him. They were drinking Jack Daniels. They were buzzing pretty good. They started to mouth off about how his Ford would pull the guts out of my Chevy. I kind of ignored them for a while, but they wouldn't let it go. Dunny finally said, "Let's go hook 'em then."

They said, "Okay. Meet us out of town on the Brown school gravel road." All our trucks had big tires and loud pipes.

I said to Dunny, "Man, I don't know about this. His truck looks badass."

"We'll just have to find out." It was snowing with about five or six inches already on the ground. We got to the gravel road and backed them up to each other. The girls were drunk and hollering and carrying on. With that much snow on the ground, it was bright out. We backed up until our back bumpers touched. Both of us would let our pipes sing. Dunny stayed in the truck with me, and one girl got out to say when to go. "Go" she hollered, and I stomped it. All four tires threw snow twenty feet in the air. Then *wham*, when the chain got tight, Dunny and I about went toward the windshield. All of a sudden, I started to grab hold and jerked the guts out of that Ford. Dunny and I hollered, "Yeah, take that!"

The girls said, "Oh no, the best out of three."

I said, "Give me a shot of that Jack."

She came up to my window. She had a wool cap and mittens on. She was hot. She smiled really pretty at Dunny and me. She gave me the bottle.

I said, "Before this night's through, you'll be getting in with us."

She smiled and said, "You think so?" Then she backed up and yelled, "Go." I had just put the bottle to my mouth, and *wham* the Jack Daniels went all over me and the other half went down my throat. I just stomped on the gas. Snow went everywhere. I like to think that's what two giant grizzly bears would sound like in a fight. Our pipes roared, but again, my truck started to grab. I jerked that Ford all over the place. Finally, the girls and the guy conceded victory. The girl said, "Pull over. We got another bottle." So we pulled over and wanted to sit for a minute. The girl with the Jack Daniels jumped in my truck with us. Man, she smelled good—a mix of perfume and whiskey. She was as pretty as a picture. Dunny and I were in love.

She said, "I'm from Auxvasse." We asked if she was in school.

"Yeah, I'm a junior."

Dunny said, "I am too." We tried our best to get her to go with us. Suddenly as we were talking, we could see some headlights coming down the road. We really didn't think it was anything until it got right up to us. It was a cop. Dunny said, "Damn, now what?"

The cop was calling in my license number. The Ford owner, he started his truck and hightailed it while the cop was on me. I said, "Well, this is what I'm going to do." I dropped the truck into gear and stomped it. Snow flew all over the cop car. My pipes roared like a lion. I was heading out of town. One thing we knew about the cops was they weren't from our town. They were usually young, and this was their first stop to a bigger city. The old cops usually let us go with a warning, but young ones had to pad their resumes. The young cops and really even a lot of people in town didn't know the gravel roads the way we did. We knew every gravel road and where it went. We could just about get to any town in Callaway County by gravel. I was flying down the gravel and the cop, he was trying to chase. Red lights and sirens were blasting. The girl, she was hollering, "Yeah, go, go, go."

Dunny was saying, "You are going to get caught and they are going to kill you." The problem I had with getting caught was I was probably going to get a DWI, plus everything else. I decided at least I'm not going to get a DWI. I hit a small gravel road that took us to the edge of town. We could hear cop sirens all over. No cars were out; it was snowing, and it was a weeknight at about 10:30 at night. We knew of a friend who had a trailer house in the country, so we got there and parked the truck in his barn. We banged on his door, and he had a police scanner on. He was listening to the cops say that it was my dad's truck, but there was no sign of the truck. It had disappeared. So I knew I'd have to turn myself in the next day. But for now, we stayed up most of the night drinking and smoking pot. The cute little girl stayed with us. We assured her she was in no danger. We laughed and carried on like nothing happened.

Chapter 34

The next day when it was real early, we got up from the couch. I woke the girl up and then Dunny said, "Well, you got to go and turn yourself in."

I said to my friend, "Can you give her a ride home and Dunny, can you go with me?"

They both said, "Okay." I drove into town and got to my house. No cops were there waiting, but Mom and Dad were waiting as soon as I came in.

My mom said, "They cops came here last night. They said they were going to arrest your dad if we don't bring you in." They weren't really mad, but I think more disappointed than anything. My dad and Dunny took me to the police station. I went up to the window and said, "I'm the one you're looking for." This young cop came and got me. They handcuffed me and took me back and put me in jail. There was an old cop named Nub, and he went to school with my dad. He came back and got me out of the jail cell. He said, "Hey, I know your family, and they are good people. So I'm going to help you out this time." After about four or five hours, they let me go. But I got charged with failure to stop for an emergency vehicle. That was all. I did have to go to court, but I was a juvenile. I was sixteen years old. They would postpone the court date all the way until summer, they said in case I got into some more trouble. On the way home, my dad told me he wasn't mad. He just said, "Boy, we don't have the money for lawyers and tickets. I'll help you this one time. After

128

that, you're going to be on your own." The funny thing is, I believed him. I had no right to waste his money. What I did was I became a smarter criminal. *The next time they won't have a chance to read my plates.* I didn't do anything wrong; I just wasn't smart about what I did. I thought this would help me if the giant and his crew came back and needed a driver.

Chapter 35

Mostly, Dunny drove for the rest of the winter. We partied a lot that winter. Usually, we'd go to a friend's house or a few hangout places. One such place was called Johnson's Inn. It was out of town about ten miles. It was near a nuclear plant that was being built. We'd go to the old beat-up-looking building and dance and sometimes a band would show up. We always tried to find music and girls. One night, we drove out to Johnson's Inn. We had heard a band was going to play so we were excited to go. We started to drink whiskey. We decided that the more soda we mixed with it the sicker it caused you to get. So we bought a fifth of whiskey each, then, one can of 7-Up to drink it with. Talk about getting drunk. That would do you in quickly. We picked up Tee and headed to the place. Dunny always drove, but Dunny couldn't handle whiskey. By the time we got there, Dunny had said he was going to have to stay in the truck for a while. Tee and I went on in and were having a pretty good time. We were toward the front of the building watching the band, and the door was at the back. One of our friends came up to us and said, "What's wrong with Dunny?"

We weren't real sure what he was getting at so we said, "Nothing that we know of. Why?"

Our buddy said, "Well, he's lying passed out in front of the door, and everybody is just stepping over him to get in."

We said, "Damn" and ran to see. Sure enough, Dunny was out cold in front of the door. Everyone was just stepping over him like a doormat. Tee and I picked him up and locked him in his truck. The problem was it was pretty cold, so we were afraid he might get frostbite. He never woke up the whole night. Drinking whiskey seemed to cause everyone to get rowdier than just drinking beer. So it was around 12:30 or so when a bad fight broke out. Several fights would start and then end. But one fight didn't. Two guys we knew got into a bad fight, and one guy got stabbed. He died right there in front of us. The cops had to come and tried to talk to us as witnesses, but we saw double ourselves. Then the cop started to act all bad and tough to everyone saying he was going to arrest all of us and catch us driving. So while he was running his mouth, one of my buddies snuck over to his car and let the air out of his tires. When he got in to leave, he drove a little way to get out of the driveway. Then, he realized something was wrong and got out and looked at his tires. They were flat. We all circled around him and just busted out laughing. He was so mad he had to call for backup. Not one of us liked cops. The younger ones were full of themselves. We actually liked the bad guys better. At least you knew what to expect from the bad guys. Sort of an eye for an eye kind of attitude. That's why I believed we found ourselves drawn to the giant and the suit man. They weren't just acting tough; they were tough. The guy that got stabbed, I'm sorry to say that he had it coming to him. He was a troublemaker, and I've seen him on several occasions beat up on his girlfriend. Truth be told, my buddy who stabbed him was probably trying to help the same girl. Even so, they arrested him, and they hauled him off. He went to prison for manslaughter. He claimed it was self-defense, but the cops thought all of us night people were guilty of something. We told Dunny the whole story, and all he could say was, "I'm not drinking whiskey anymore. I'll take a few shots of moonshine every once in a while, but that's it." To Dunny's credit, I don't recall that he ever did drink whiskey again.

Chapter 36

Finally, spring had arrived; we thought it would never get here. Everyone knows that spring brings new life to the outside world. Well, spring brought new life to the night people as well. The hot cars and trucks would ride through town, windows down, with music playing, and cigarette smoke boiling out from every window. The girls would start showing more of their body as the temperature would rise. Longer days and warmer nights, that was what the people of the night needed. If I hated school in the winter, I couldn't stand the idea of going to class in the springtime. I just didn't go to school. I went to work at the body shop and then worked at the gas station at night. One really warm spring weekend in late April, I went out to Hilltop Liquor. Dunny took me out there. We had decided we were going to go hang out with a group of really close friends from Mokane. They bought some small cabins at the Lake of the Ozarks. These cabins were really old and were used by the loggers and workers who built the magnificent Bagnell Dam. The guys said the cabins were haunted and at night you found yourself doing all kinds of strange things. That's all they had to say, and Dunny and I were in. Dunny pulled in really slowly, and we were listening to some Eagles music. Of course, I looked down at the now abandoned trailer of my desires—still no sign of any life. In my gut, I felt like any day now I would see them back in town. I ran into the liquor store and banged the door and cowbell on purpose. Here came Uncle Charlie. He came around with a mean look then stopped when he saw it was me.

"Well, if it ain't my shithead drinking buddy. What's got you all worked up?"

"It's springtime, and we are going to hang down at the Lake of the Ozarks."

"I guess then you heard who's back in town?"

That really got my attention.

He said, "Yep, Jesse and DW and those girls they run with."

My heart began to pound as if I had just finished running two miles. I could only imagine what was in store for this summer. It was to turn out to be another summer that I hoped I would never forget. I couldn't think in any clear way. I said, "Can I get a twelve pack, some ice, and two packs of cigarettes?" Uncle Charlie said, "That's five bucks." He looked at me like, "Ain't you going to say something more?" but I was speechless. I got in the truck and told Dunny they were back. I'm not sure how he felt. I think he was hoping they'd never be seen there again. For me, it was like a fire that had gone out, but there were still some coals burning. All that was needed was to add some fresh wood to the fire, and the blaze would come back. But before we were to head out toward the Lake of the Ozarks, we decided to drive down to the clay pit.

We drove on down to the pit. It had been a long winter for the clay pit as well. We didn't go to the pit as much in the winter, I'd say maybe only once or twice since November. Dunny and I loved that clay pit. It was, to us, the same feeling we had if we were in our own bedroom. We felt safe and comfortable at the pit. We eased down the gravel road, and we were listening to AC/DC's "Gone Shootin." Life was good. We were laughing and joking about when Dunny passed out in the front door and when I got thrown in jail. We were also saying that there was no way we were going to be seniors and virgins. We both felt that we could get kicked out of any man club around if somehow we didn't get to go all the way with some girl. We discussed some of the girls that may be easy to get and decided it was our one mission in life. We got to the top of the clay pit and stopped. We both looked down the hill to the familiar turquoise water. The water was calm and every so often you would see a little ripple from a fish skimming the water for bugs. I could see in my mind the band party night. I thought this is what we would have looked like from above. You had to be sure that the road was good enough to go down, or else you would not be able to get up the hill to leave. Many times, after a rain or even a thawing of the snow, the clay would be so slippery you couldn't even walk on it.

We saw a few puddles, but the road itself looked okay. We eased ourselves down the hill hoping that we were right in our thinking, and it was okay to try to go down. As we slid and bounced our way down the hill, I could only think about what I was going to feel like when I saw Lisa. I had rehearsed in my mind a thousand lines and even thought of a thousand scenarios I could have with her. Then I wondered, *If they were in town, then where were they?* I saw no evidence of them at the trailer house. I saw no evidence of new suped-up cars cruising through town. The best evidence would be the rumor of soapers in town. We got to our spot and got out of the truck. It was a warm evening. Birds were carrying on; the pond frogs were starting to get louder. Sometimes, they would get so loud you could hardly hear yourself think. Dunny said to me, "Man, this is nice. I wish time would stop right now."

I said, "I know, this is a piece of heaven." Dunny and I joked and laughed the whole night. We drank our beer and smoked our pot and cigarettes. We enjoyed a lot of music. We decided we better not drive so we just slept in the truck. We would go to the lake in the morning.

Chapter 37

I woke to the sound of all kinds of birds singing. It sounded like a choir singing, the cardinals and orioles; the bluebirds and turtledoves would go back and forth, and then the whippoorwills would come in and steal the show. A thin layer of fog was all around. The sun was trying to shine through the eastern sky, which was full of large dark gray clouds, but pink and orange spots came through the dark gray. In the western sky, it was still dark. It was, I thought, God's own version of a homemade quilt in the sky. But I could hear a rumble of thunder that was off in the distance from the southwest. The bad storms came from the southwest. I shoved Dunny and said, "Dunny, wake up. We've got a storm coming. I can hear the thunder." Funny thing about storms; if you pay close attention to the signs, you can tell how bad a storm might turn up. I was good at reading Mother Nature, but not so good at reading people. A talent that I would soon need to develop if I wanted to get through the trouble that was soon to turn up. Dunny jumped up, started the truck, slammed it into gear, and spun our way up the hill to the top of the clay pit. Then, we sat and watched as the storm headed toward us. We always wanted to see a tornado, so when a storm would come, we didn't take cover, we ran to it. We were too dumb to be scared. The thrill of seeing a tornado was hypnotizing, even when we knew death could be part of the encounter. The storm quickly blew by us. It wasn't a tornado, just a spring shower.

Dunny said, "Well, let's go home, and I'll cook some breakfast. Then let's go to those haunted cabins at the Lake of Ozarks." We got on the highway, and as we went by the trailer house, sure enough, a white Charger was parked in front of it.

Dunny looked over with me at the trailer and saw it too. Dunny said, "Let it go for now. Those guys want us to come see their cabins and fish and drink, and that's what we are going to do."

"Yeah. . . you're right. . . You're always right. . ." So we stopped to fix Junior some breakfast and pack a clean shirt. Junior was waiting like always at the kitchen table. When we walked in, he said, "You two shitheads ain't got even enough sense to get out of the way of the storm. Do ya?"

I said, "Man, one day I got to see a tornado."

"You all ain't got a lick of sense."

Then he shook his head and lit a cigarette. Dunny and I explained to him that we were going out to the Lake of Ozarks for the night, but we'd be back around noon the next day, and we'd play some cards when we got back. The promise of a good card game usually put a smile on Junior's face. But let me tell you, he never forgot that promise.

Chapter 38

The ride down was amazing. The trees were starting to get a faint color of green and redbuds and dogwoods filled in between the mighty oak and hickory trees. The Ozark Mountains were everywhere as far as you could see. I felt good, some sort of pure feeling. I felt I could use this night to come up with a plan. But it was going to be hard because the players were just then coming to the table. None of the cards had been dealt yet. We circled and weaved deep into the Ozark Mountains; it almost seemed like we were going back in time. Then we turned onto a gravel road, and we went even deeper into the woods and mountains. Every so often, I would notice a small cloud of smoke in the woods. I'm saying they were moonshiners. Finally, we came to a small clearing, and four or five small cabins were tucked into the side of a shelf rock hill. The guys were out standing by a small campfire. We parked.

I hollered, "Damn, this place is awesome."

Dunny looked around and then back at me and smiled from ear to ear. We both knew we were in heaven. For a brief minute, I had forgotten about the bad guys. But Lisa, I never could get her out of my mind, nor did I want too.

We made our way to the group, and they had our day and night planned out for us. We would fish for crappie all day and early evening we would start to eat and drink until we passed out. My friends would tell me, "We have to warn you, this place is haunted, and you will feel the ghosts of workers past at the party tonight." *Now, how cool is this going to be? Dunny felt the same way.* So we gathered up our fishing poles and hit the lake. Man, let me tell you, life could not get any better. We laughed and fished and told stories. Now, there ain't no way that God wasn't allowing me to see and feel what heaven would be like. My grandmother and the Preacher, this must be what they understood about God. Still, though, I knew my day, and my crossroads deal was about to come, and the devil knew it too.

We decided to call it good for the day of fishing, and by everyone's account, it was considered a good day. My lake friends were excellent cooks, and the feast we were about to have could not be bought in any restaurant. When we got to the camp, the fire was going, and they had a wood duck stew with rice and vegetables. Of course, fresh fish and fried potato cakes, and one guy even managed to cook a cake on the campfire. Then, while we ate, we passed around a fresh bottle of Ozark moonshine. Everyone would watch and laugh really loudly as the person who swallowed the fire and would growl and howl at the sky. We sang rock and roll songs that we knew, and soon the sun began to set. The night was calm, almost windless. The whippoorwills began to sound off and back and forth to each other. The night was here, and the ghosts of workers past were with us. They weren't evil; they were night people as well. We drank and smoked and laughed as loudly and hard as ever I had in my life. I almost could see the ghosts drinking with us, and I could see them sitting by the fire with us. The moonshine was doing a dance in my mind, and that familiar spinning was constant. I tried to think about the giant and the suit man. But mostly I thought about Lisa and what I would say if we talked again. It was really late, and people started to pass out one by one. I didn't want the night to end; I never want the nights to end even to this day. Dunny was asleep in the truck, and I finally joined him. The whole world was spinning. I looked over at the campfire, and I could see the ghosts of workers past standing around drinking and smoking roll your own cigarettes. I could see their dirty teeth as they would smile and pass the jug around. I was amazed because even though they were dead, they were laughing and appeared to be having endless fun. I managed to pass out.

Chapter 39

The morning came, and all the birds were singing, but this time, I could hear the gobbling sound of wild turkeys. One great thing about springtime in Missouri, you can fish for crappie, go turkey hunting and find mushrooms all in one day. I reached over and pushed on Dunny to wake up.

"Hey, wake up. We need to get back."

Dunny rubbed his head and said, "Damn! What a night. I could stay here forever."

I agreed it was a night to be remembered. But I was ready to go back, and I was ready to go through all the situations and scenarios in my head. We said our goodbyes and thank yous, and we headed back.

Now, what? Should I go to the door, or should I wait to bump into them? My mind was racing a mile a minute. I had been waiting for almost a year to see Lisa. I didn't even know if she was with them. It was quiet as we rode to Dunny's house. I smoked cigarettes one right after another. I was finally ready to do what I planned in my mind. I worked around cars for a year, got into a car chase, and got away from the cops. My resume was built. I asked Dunny if we could go out that night after we played cards with Junior. I wanted just to cruise around town and observe the night people. We pulled into Dunny's driveway, went inside, and Junior was sitting at the kitchen table. He was smoking and had his small radio tuned to the country station. He said, "Well, if it ain't the James's gang" and then he smiled and laughed. "What have you two shitheads been doing all night?"

I said, "Ah, we've been running the damn streets. . . Oh no, we drank with some ghosts instead," then I smiled and laughed back at him. There finally comes a time when everyone who has been laughing at you needs to be laughed at. I found out that laughter healed almost any tough spot a person could find himself mixed up in. Even though I was dancing with the devil, I knew that finding humor in my life was as important as an emotion I could keep up with. We had breakfast and just hung out with Junior. We played cards and drank a shot of moonshine. We smoked a lot of cigarettes. I thought there had to be some favor in God's eyes with us just hanging out with an old man who was about to die. Dunny decided he needed to take a shower and then we would head out. I sat and talked to Junior while Dunny was in the shower. We talked about how he was in WWII at the Battle of the Bulge. He was in some bad stuff, but he lived through it. He was real skinny and sickly. I felt bad for him. *What does someone think about when they are coming up on the end of their life?* I was only seventeen. I couldn't imagine being old.

"Did you ever find any girls while you were over there?"

He looked at me, and it was like God breathed on him. "Did I find girls? Boy, I was eighteen years old. If I wasn't worrying about being shot, I was worrying about girls. All I thought about was beautiful girls." Then he said, "Damn, I miss those days," and it was like God's breath had left him. He sunk back into his chair, almost depressed.

"Sorry, Junior. I didn't mean to bring up a sore subject."

"Nah, boy, those days have come and gone. I've got a lot of what if's and if only's in my past. You boys need to live life to the fullest and don't have regrets. My biggest regret is I met a nice sweet lady in Germany. I can still see her smile in my mind. I was an American soldier. She was just a village girl. She was even lucky to be alive. We had an evening together that two people only dream about. Then I had to go. I never saw her again. I can still feel her touch, her hair in my hands. How could someone feel something so pure only for a few hours and yet it haunts you thirty-some years? If that was the true love everyone talks about, then how come it only lasted for a few hours?" He put his head down, and so did I. After a bit, he lifted his head up and said, "That's one cruel joke if you ask me. I wished that I had died that next day. I loved her that much. I don't know whatever happened to her. I don't know anything. That's the worst part. I wonder, *Did she even like me?* If so, does she think of me?" He put his head down and just shook it about. I reached over and put my hand on his shoulder and said, "Junior, I'm only seventeen years old and ain't been in no war, but I can tell you being seventeen and in love, whether it's thirty years ago or one hundred years ago or even today, it hurts the same and feels the same. Those haunting visions are cruel as hell. I have them myself. I don't believe that there's an answer we will ever be satisfied with."

The bathroom door opened up, and Dunny came out. A steam cloud came out with him. He had a comb and was combing his wet hair back. He said, "Junior, we're going to leave. I've made you a sandwich for later."

Junior put on his tough guy face, "Go on and get out of here." As we were leaving, I looked back at him. He just had his head down in despair. *Damn, that's got to be tough.*

Chapter 40

Dunny started up the truck, and we headed out. He had to put in a tape, The Rossington Collins Band's "Don't Misunderstood Me." We both lit cigarettes and listened to the song. It was a good song. Music or laughter is the key to a good night. Even with one or the other, you're guaranteed a fifty-fifty chance of a good night. We always laughed. I hardly remember a night without laughter. Dunny and I headed through town. A lot of people were out. I could hear loud pipes and music every time we stopped. Dunny saw Larry parked at Hardee's, so we pulled in beside him. We rolled up to Larry, and his window was down. Smoke boiled out of the window. I could hear his favorite band, Van Halen, on the radio.

Dunny said, "Hey, Larry, what's up tonight?"

Larry spoke with a cigarette in his mouth, "I ain't heard of anything. I did hear that some Quaaludes were going around town."

I said, "Ain't they the same as soapers?"

Larry said, "I think so. But I'm not exactly sure. You all want some if I can find them?"

Dunny said, "Why not?" Dunny and I knew exactly where those pills were coming from, but we just let Larry think he was in charge. The odd thing was, Larry was by himself and that didn't happen often. Even in the mornings before school, Larry always had a girl in his car. Dunny said, "Why you by yourself?"

Larry kind of smiled and said, "Not for long." A carload of girls just pulled in beside us. Two of the girls were the ones with the guy when we pulled each other's truck. The real cute one, her name was Sammie. She stuck her head out of the window and said, "Hey, I remember you boys. I figured you'd be in jail." Then she laughed and smiled at me. I said, "Nah, just got a slap on the wrist." She then talked to her girlfriends loud enough so we could hear, "These boys here sure know how to show a girl a good time." I think she was drunk already.

Dunny said, "Hey, let's go to the clay pit and party. We can't get down the hill, but we can stay on top, and nobody will bother us."

Sammie said, "You all got anything to drink?"

Dunny said, "No, but we can get it."

Then Sammie whispered to her girlfriends, turned toward us, and said, "Lead the way, boys." Then they all screamed like they had just met some rock stars.

Dunny and I were thinking this might be the end of our virginity. My heart was starting to race. I hadn't felt that racy feeling in a long time. Dunny led the way. It was about seven o'clock, so it would be dark soon. Dunny pulled into the liquor store, and the girls followed us. They were laughing and playing music. I got out and went in, but really slowly. Uncle Charlie didn't come through the beads. This time, it was the giant. DW was in the back. I could hear him talking to Uncle Charlie. I didn't make out any words; I just knew it was him. When Jesse saw me, he smiled and said, "Hey, what's up, man?"

I think he was honestly happy to see me. I said, "Ahh, nothing, been working at a body shop half a day and working at the sixty-six station at night."

Jesse said, "Damn, boy, there's better ways to make money. Come down to the trailer, and we can talk about that."

"Sure. Why not?"

I wanted to ask if the girls were with them, but I kept it cool. I said, "Can I get a case of beer, some ice, and two packs of Marlboro Reds?" Jesse hollered back to Charlie for a total. He had all the totals in his head. The cash register drawer was never closed. The money would be hanging out all the time. When I paid Jesse, he leaned over and said, "Look here, I have some pills called Quaaludes. They will flat kick your ass. I'll sell them to you for two bucks apiece."

I really couldn't say no. "Okay, give me six of them."

Jesse laughed really loudly and said, "Have a good trip."

I took the Quaaludes from him then paid him. I started to walk out when Jesse said, "Hey, I'm serious. If you want to make some real money, stop by the trailer Saturday about noon." I turned and smiled with worry. I said, "I'll see you about noon," then I opened the door, rang the cowbell and went toward the truck. Sammie jumped out and helped me with the beer. She rubbed up against me. I could smell perfume and whiskey. She smelled good and even looked as good as I had remembered. She smiled at me. I thought that she might like me. She was shorter than I was, but she tried to stand on her tiptoes to get closer to my face. Her smile was so nice. Her blondish-brown hair was long and straight. She had dark brown eyes. While we were putting the beer in the cooler, the other girls were watching us and giggling. *Damn, how good is this night going to get?*

We both said, "See ya there" at the same time. Dunny started the truck while I was jumping in. He backed out and said, "Damn, how hot are those girls?"

"I feel like we must be in heaven."

Dunny pulled forward, and I looked down at the trailer. I saw two girls leave the trailer and get in a black Firebird Camaro. I was pretty sure it was Missy and Lisa. They didn't see us. Dunny drove on toward the clay pit. The girls followed right behind. We pulled over, and the girls pulled up behind us. Dunny and I got out, opened the tailgate, pulled the cooler up to us, and handed out a beer to each of the girls. We put the super tuner on KSHE95 and started to make small talk. Everyone lit a cigarette at the same time. One girl spoke up and said, "Your Chevy truck was badass."

"How do you know it's just a stock truck. Nothing suped up on it."

"I was with my boyfriend that night you all hooked them up."

"Oh, I never really could see who was with him. I only could see Sammie."

"Yeah, he got real pissed after you beat him."

"Oh, well that will teach him to drive a Ford."

The girls started to sing a song by Ted Nugget, "Hey Baby." One of the lines in the song says, "Jump in the back of my Ford." Then they all laughed together.

I would go get a Ford right now if one of these girls would jump in the back with me. The night was clear and full of night noises. In between songs, you could hear whippoorwills sing, and the pond frogs were getting really loud. We drank and smoked some weed. Then, the later it got, the rowdier we got. We were dancing and flirting with each other until finally Sammie grabbed me and planted a kiss on me that should not be allowed between two people who had just met. How pure it is when young people start falling for each other, that connection that you can't explain, but you just know that it's going to end up with more than a kiss. I stopped everything I was doing, and we kissed again.

The girls all yelled, "Whooo," and laughed at me. I was shocked, but I was proud that someone liked me enough to kiss me. We let go of each other and took to dancing with someone else. Man, I'm telling you, this night was what every boy dreams about happening. Even if every boy didn't dream about it, I know I did, and so did Dunny. Dunny and I sat on the tailgate and watched the girls dancing and laughing. Not one girl had a bra on, just t-shirt and shorts. I looked over at Dunny; he had a smile from ear to ear. I'd say I had that same smile. It was about 11:30 or so when one of the girls said, "Hey, you all ever take a Quaalude?" Dunny and I said, "Not yet."

"My boyfriend gave me a couple to try."

Dunny said to me, "It's getting late. I have to drive home yet." Then he said, "Oh well, we can sleep here if we have to."

She handed out one to everybody, and we all ate them. The pill didn't quite hit as fast as a soaper, and it had the number 714 on it. But it was the same feeling. My head began to get cloudy, and everyone looked blurry to me. The girls kept on dancing to every song they heard. I sat down on the tailgate. My head was spinning like I'd drunk a case of beer. I felt good. I was not feeling any pain at all. Sammie came over and sat by me. She kissed me and hugged me. We crawled up in the bed of the truck, but then one of the other girls would pull her back, and they would start to dance again. We saw some headlights shining on the trees. The lights jiggled because of the car or truck hitting the potholes in the road. The lights got closer and came on us quicker than normal. The vehicle stopped suddenly and just shined its lights on us. A thick cloud of dust surrounded us. No one would get out. You could only see a silhouette of two people in a big sky blue Ford truck. One of the girls said, "Sonny, you son of a bitch, I said leave me alone." The truck revved up its pipes and eased closer to us.

Another girl yelled, "Get the hell out of here. Leave her alone." We were all in too bad of shape to make much sense out of what was happening. Dunny stood up and said, "Hey, turn off your lights." The truck eased up closer.

One girl threw a full beer and hit the windshield. Beer went all over his headlights and windshield. *Man, how on earth could this be happening? Who is this dude?* Then, I stood up next to Dunny. I figured we were about to get our asses kicked by somebody I didn't even know. I saw up in the trees more headlights coming toward us. Then, it pulled up to Dunny and I, and it was the white Charger. The giant got out and said, "Hey, so the party's here?" I don't think he knew we were in trouble. The driver side of the Charger opened; DW got out and lifted the seat so the two other people could get out. I could see her leaning to get out. I saw her. I had been waiting a whole year to see here. There she was. Nobody on earth was going to tell me she wasn't an angel—no way, not possible. She smiled and looked down at the ground. She had a beer in a cooler cup holder. Her hair was braided, and it almost was down to her belt. My head was spinning like a top. I tried to sober up and get a grip on myself. I just could not fight the Quaalude. It was kicking my ass. From my point of view, this was my best night, my worst night, and for all I could tell, maybe my last night on this earth.

I looked at her, wishing I was in better shape. One of the girls said, "Hey, this asshole won't leave us alone." The giant's demeanor changed instantly. He calmly walked up to the truck, and I could hear words being exchanged. Then, the truck revved up its pipes and turned around and rumbled off.

The giant said, "He thought he better leave." He laughed, and DW laughed with him. The girls were all bummed out. They said, "Thanks, mister. We better go."

The giant said, "Hey, come up the road. You all can crash there."

Chapter 41

My head was spinning so bad. All I could see were flashes of my brief life. I could see Lisa when I first met her—her smile and laugh. I could see Debbie and Kathy dancing and taking off their shirts. I could see Sammie who was as cute and perfect as a puppy. But when I saw Lisa, I thought for sure God had sent her as an angel. All the girls I had dreamed about and been close with, well, they were number 8s or 9s, but Lisa was a 10. I couldn't imagine a more perfect girl that God would have made. I simply couldn't believe that someone like that could have any interest in me. How or what I did to make her like me, I still don't know. But I knew I felt like Junior did in Germany. It was one brief brush with heaven that I could not let it pass me up. Even if it was for a moment. I needed to feel her touch, and I had to be with her or die trying. I thought over and over, *God, how pure of a thing was Sammie and her smiling at me when she'd yell "go" and the snow falling on her when I was pulling that Ford. How pure were Debbie and Kathy dancing naked in front of a sixteen-year-old boy. How pure was Lisa's smile when we were alone and saying she was mine. I couldn't explain, God, but I could feel God in those visions. Maybe it was the devil, but so be it.* I choose to say God is pure and those moments and those girls, they were as pure of anything I had known. My mind was gone from any normal way of thinking. That night was about to have to be put to rest. There was not a chance I was going to win the fight with this pill. Dunny, the girls, and the Charger all went up to Jesse's trailer. While Dunny was driving, I kept asking him, "Are you okay to drive?" Dunny couldn't speak. I began to fall in and out of sleep. We pulled into the driveway, and Dunny turned off the engine. I told Dunny I was going to stay in the truck. Dunny didn't say anything. He put his head down on the steering wheel. I could hear footsteps outside my door. I couldn't open my eyes to see who it was. I went out cold.

Chapter 42

I woke up. I had to blink my eyes a dozen times. My vision was blurred, but I felt good. My head didn't hurt at all. You would think that something as powerful as a Quaalude would make you feel bad. I guess that's why everyone liked them. It totally kicked your ass, but you felt no pain. *What smart person invented the Quaalude?* Some hippie dude that didn't like a hangover set out and discovered a pill that would get you drunk but with no hangover. I knew it was still early. The birds were carrying on. It was obvious the birds didn't party. The first sign of light and they were happy, playing, and singing. I didn't feel so good that I wanted to sing, but I felt good. I looked over to check on Dunny. He was still slumped over the steering wheel. I don't think he moved an inch all night. I pulled myself up straight to look out the windshield of the truck. The girls from Auxvasse, their car was parked in the yard. It was tucked in behind the white Charger and our truck. I guess they were hiding from the dudes in the Ford truck. I heard a noise behind our truck. I turned around; it was Uncle Charlie. He was cleaning up junk around his garage. He had slung open the old wooden garage door. I saw a midnight blue SS Chevelle. I thought that was the most perfect car in the world. I wasn't sure if I had ever seen it before. Charlie just went around it with a broom sweeping. Dunny and I were the only people aside from Charlie who were outside. I stared at everything. It was quiet. I wondered what time it was. I let Dunny sleep. As my mind began to get clearer, I started to piece together the night before. *Damn, another chance to finally go all the way with a girl just got away!* My head didn't hurt, but I had pain inside of me. I was just about to explode. I thought about my dad's stud colt. I figured maybe that's the only way. Maybe that's the difference between a boy and a man. Maybe you had to fight for the girl. Maybe you were supposed to break down the gate and fight a big stud horse, even if it killed you. *That's it.* Any real man would fight. I thought about the dudes in the Ford truck and how we were scared of them. But then Jesse came, and he wasn't afraid. He walked right up to them. He didn't even know if they had a gun or knife. The guys left, and all the girls thanked him like he was some kind of hero. Even DW was a badass. Could that be the way the guy gets the girl? Well, I was going to find out.

I poked on Dunny to wake him up. He moved a little. I shook him again.

"Dunny, wake up, you deadbeat."

He stirred a little. Then he said, "Damn, I don't know how I even drove up here. Those Quaaludes are badass."

"Maybe we should just take half of one next time."

"Nah, that was great."

"Do you think we should go inside?"

"We better wait until someone stirs."

I opened my door and got out. The sun felt so good on my body. I lit a cigarette. I said, "I'm going over to say hey to old Charlie." Dunny leaned back in the seat.

"I'm going to rest a little while longer." Then he closed his eyes. Dunny wasn't a lightweight when it came to partying. Many nights, we would stay up all night and watch the sun come up. I was good at it myself. I walked up the driveway toward Uncle Charlie. I could hear turtledoves hooting. I smoked my cigarette and waved a peace sign to Uncle Charlie. He waved back and smiled at me. I walked up to him, "Hey, what's up?"

"Ah, I need to clean this car up. She's going on a trip."

"Oh yeah, where are you going?"

"I ain't going nowhere, but this baby is sold."

"Damn, that's about the most perfect car I've ever seen."

"Yep, now you see what we do. It's hard not to love this!"

I looked at him a little confused. I wasn't sure if he was admitting he was a car thief or if he was admitting he was a great mechanic. Then he said, "So you want in?"

"I'm in."

"Okay, once you're in this world. . . well, you ain't gettin' out." Then he turned around and said, "You want to hear her running?"

"Yep."

He got in with the door still open. He barely touched the key and *whoop* it started. It sat there and purred *whoop. . . whoop. . . whoop.*" He let off the engine and let her idle. I was in a state of awesomeness. The amount of power I felt coming off that car was like the thunderstorm we had heard a couple of days before. Uncle Charlie said, "I got to go on inside and open up. You come back around noon, and we'll talk." He was more serious than I had seen him. I said, "I'll be here." I turned, and he shut off the car. I walked back toward the truck and trailer. But then I thought Old Charlie just made the first play in this game. I didn't know what cards he was holding, but I knew he was at the table, or maybe he was the dealer. Either way, the game had started.

Chapter 43

I lit a cigarette. I'm not sure I fully knew what I had just got myself into. I knew that it was time for me to kick down the gate and get out of the cage. I was ready to fight for something that I cared about. I got in the truck, and Dunny was awake. He said, "Damn, what the hell kind of car was that?"

"That was a badass car. You should have been next to her. She just about took the breath out of me."

"It sounded sweet from here."

The trailer house door opened slowly and squeaked. I looked toward the front door. Sammie was coming out, and her friends were behind her. Sammie looked as fresh as the spring morning. She looked good even after sleeping all night. She was smiling. Her friends got in their car, but she came over to me. Man, she looked even nicer in the daylight. She put her hands out to give me a hug. I put my hands out and gave her a hug. She stood on her toes and said in my ear, "I want to see you again sometime soon." Then she kissed me on the cheek. I felt like there was no way this just happened to me. She let go of me and walked toward her friends, and at the same time, she looked back and smiled. Dunny said, "Damn it, boy, your luck is about to change. I can feel it."

"You think so? I sure hope so."

The girls drove off waving and laughing at Dunny and I. I looked back at the trailer house, and I saw the corner of a curtain move just a little. About that time, the door opened again. I could see it was Jesse and DW coming out at the same time. Jesse said, "Ah, man it feels good out here." It was only about eight o'clock in the morning. I heard people inside the trailer moving around. I could hear dishes being moved out of the kitchen sink from the window. I looked at the window. It was Lisa. She looked good and calm as usual. I could see her eyes look at me. I looked at her. I wanted her so bad. I just wanted her.

Jesse said, "We got to go for a few hours. But you be here around noon." Then he and DW got in the white Charger and slowly drove off. They stopped at Charlie's garage for a minute. Then they drove off. I looked at Dunny, and he said, "Wait a minute. Let's go before you get us killed."

"Just give me a minute."

He rolled his eyes and slumped back in the seat. I went up on the porch and inside without even knocking. I could hear the shower running. I wasn't sure who was in it, though. I walked back toward the kitchen, and from the bedroom, Lisa came out. She was pulling on her t-shirt like she had decided to change from one to another. It was tie-dyed in purple and blues. She wasn't startled or anything. She smiled really pretty at me. The water was running from the bathroom shower. She came right up to me and hugged me. She was as perfect of a human being as I had ever laid my eyes on. She squeezed me tight. She leaned back to look up at me and said, "Man, I missed you. I thought about you every day I was gone. I thought you'd be in love with some girl by now."

"Yeah, I'm in love all right, but not with some girl. I'm in love with you. I didn't know what happened or where you were."

"I know; it's best you don't know."

"It's too late. I'm in. I'm coming back at noon."

"You need to stay away from this. It will ruin your life. You could get killed."

"I don't care. I can't take all this mystery shit."

She wasn't going to say anymore. I knew she wanted me to be part of all this or she'd never had messed with me. She kissed me for a long time, then said, "I want to finish that song and dance with you."

"Name the time and place."

The water shut off from the bathroom.

"Don't worry; they'll be going to Auxvasse tonight. I'll see you when you come back."

We kissed again. Then I left. I left slowly, but inside my mind, I was floating on air. When I got to the truck, Dunny said, "Man, you look like you just seen a ghost."

"Nope, I didn't see no ghost. I saw an angel, though."

Dunny just shook his head and started the truck. Dunny was the best friend a person could have. He was always trying to find the good in things, but he just couldn't see an angle where I didn't wind up dead or hurt. I told him I just didn't care. I told him about his dad's story in Germany. I told him I was willing to do something wrong to get something right.

He said, "Listen, you have to tell me what you're about to do."

"I will. I don't know until I see them this afternoon. But I don't want you to be involved, so I'll come here by myself."

"No, I'll bring you here; then I'll leave. You tell them I had some running to do."

I couldn't believe Dunny would help me that much, and yet I wasn't surprised. After all, we were best friends, and I'd say closer than any brothers could be. We pulled out and headed to Dunny's house.

Chapter 44

We pulled up to Dunny's house. We went in, and Junior was sitting at the kitchen table. There was an empty bottle of whiskey and a .22 pistol on the table. Dunny stopped so suddenly that I ran into him.

He said, "Junior, what's wrong?"

"I feel like shit. I'm dying, and I'm all alone in this house."

He reached over and grabbed the pistol.

"Hey, hey, put that down. You ain't shooting yourself."

"Stay back."

He shot the gun right above our heads into the ceiling. We stopped. We both weren't sure if the other had been hit.

Dunny said, "Damn, Junior, you almost hit one of us."

"I'd hit you if I was trying. Now get back." I really wasn't sure what to do except one thing. I knew I had to stay calm.

Dunny said, "Now put that down. I'm coming over toward you." Junior just dropped the pistol on the ground;. . . then he cried. It wasn't like he was crying like crazy; it was just tears with no noise. We eased our way to the table, and Dunny picked up the gun. I sat down. I said, "Damn, Junior. What brought all this on?"

"I feel like shit. I'm old and dying. I look back on my life, and I say so this is it? Is this all that I have to show for being born to this earth?"

"Surely you got some good out of being on this earth."

"Ain't got shit! I don't see any way possible of a good outcome."

Well, at seventeen years old, that was some heavy stuff to be dealing with. I'm not sure I knew what to make of it. In a way, I knew getting old had to be painful, but I never really thought it would be so painful that you'd want to die. The only reason I wanted to live was I didn't want to die a virgin. I hadn't amounted to much of anything yet, good or bad. I felt his pain, though. I really think he wished that he would have stayed in Germany. I think some regrets he had early in his life was coming back to haunt him.

Dunny said, "I'm going to make some breakfast. Then I got to go for a few hours, but I'll be back."

I knew he was referring to dropping me off at the trailer house. We ate breakfast, but not much was said: I tried to bring a positive light to the room, so did Dunny. Junior just wasn't having much to do with us. We got ready to leave, and I put my hand on Junior's shoulder. I didn't say anything. He didn't say anything either. Dunny said, "I'll be back in twenty minutes." We got in the truck, and Dunny's face was red with anger. He said, "He pulls this shit all the time. He gets drunk and starts to think about the war. The VA calls it battle fatigue. I call it bullshit." Then he turned the radio on and lit a cigarette. It was ZZ Top, "*A Fool for Your Stockings.*" It sounded good.

Chapter 45

It wasn't quite noon, but Dunny still pulled on up to the trailer house. The white Charger was there. Dunny left the truck running. I got out and went to the door. They said, "Come on in," so I motioned for Dunny to leave. I didn't have any idea how long or what we were going to talk about. I figured I could use their telephone to call Dunny when we got done. When I sat on the couch, it was quiet. A radio was on but really low volume. *Did every decision I've ever made bring me to this point? If I would rewind my life, then go forward, could I see a crossroad or even several crossroads, points that had I gone the opposite way than I did, would I still be right here?*

Then Junior's voice popped into my mind, "The what if's will haunt you when you get my age."

I heard someone walk up onto the porch. They came inside. It was Uncle Charlie. He had a Mason jar of clear liquid. I looked at him as he looked at me. He walked over to the kitchen table and pulled up a chair. When he sat down, he leaned back and said to Lisa, "Bring me some glasses, please." She moved without hesitation. I sensed that something was different. I realized old Uncle Charlie was the boss. He wasn't just a player; he was the dealer. He had played me the whole time. He was sizing me up, but I'm not sure he really figured out I was sizing them up. Not him, I thought he was just the uncle of some bad people. He poured us a shot of moonshine. Lisa stood back near the kitchen sink. Missy stood by Jesse. She always stood by Jesse. Charlie said, "Come up to the table, boy, and have a drink." I had heard those words before, but I was scared of them this time. *Calm, be calm.* I got up and sat down at the table, picked up my shot and tipped it back. The fire went down to my guts. Silence. Then everyone busted out laughing. I held back any expression. Uncle Charlie said to me, "Now, here's the deal. So far you ain't did nothing wrong. Hell, you don't even know anything about us. I'm going to pour us another shot. If you chose, you could leave right now. No harm done. But if you drink it with us, then you're in and there ain't no way of getting out. Not one person in this room is innocent. Any one of us can go away for a long time."

They looked at me. I looked at them. I looked at the shot glass. I looked at Lisa. She had no expression, only a stare. I couldn't tell if she wanted me to join them or if she had played me as the mark. I thought the what ifs would haunt me. This was a crossroad. They'd probably kill me either way. I grabbed the shot and slammed it back. They didn't know I had plans myself. They didn't know, but I just figured out who was in the game; now, I knew who was at the table. Jesse went, "Hey," then he laughed really loudly. DW laughed. Missy laughed. Charlie laughed. Lisa, she smiled and turned her head.

Jesse said, "All right, here's the deal. That beautiful blue car in the garage, it's sold. We got a rich buyer back in Greensboro. We can get thirty-five thousand dollars once it's delivered to a garage up in the mountains of North Carolina. You are going to drive this baby. You're going to take Lisa with you; drop her off in Hampton. She's going to pick up another car to bring it back here. After you drop her off, she'll give you the directions to the garage. You take the car to the garage and park it. In the garage, a man will give you thirty-five thousand dollars in cash. Stay the night in this motel. Lisa will pick you up the next morning, and then you come back. We get the money. I give you five hundred dollars for driving a car to North Carolina and back. If you get caught, we will find you and kill you. If you don't come back, we will kill your friend, and then when we find you, we will kill you. There's only one way this ends up good for you. . . Don't get caught and come back."

"When do we go?"

"Right now. You got an hour to clean up, and then you're out of here."

I wished that I had time to clear my head. But really it was best this way. My family wouldn't think much about me being gone for a few days. I usually stayed with Dunny and would call or check in every so often. Everyone got up from the table. DW leaned over, and he said, "Don't get caught," then he smiled at me. Talk about your crossroads. I just came to one. But I knew I wasn't going to get caught. I hadn't been caught yet. Lisa said, "There's the shower. I got you a clean t-shirt." Well, this is it. This was my play. I just called in this real life poker game. Now, was when everyone at the table would try to figure out what kind of hand the other player had. Well, I knew my hand, and I knew I was the joker, it was a matter of the ace, Lisa, who held her. I know now why Lisa was so calm. I was thinking she and me in that car by ourselves overnight. If I was going to die, then at least it was going to be with her.

I got out of the shower and toweled off. I opened the door, and Lisa was standing in the hall with just a towel on. She said, "I need to take a shower before we go." She smiled at me. Man, she was perfect before. Now, looking at her in a towel, my heart started to thump, and I got real short of breath. She knew that I was about to explode. She laughed and brushed up against me to get in the shower. I walked into the kitchen. Everyone was outside except Uncle Charlie. He had gone back to his liquor store. I walked out on the front porch; the screen door slammed behind me. Jesse smiled, "Hey, okay, come here. I got more to tell you. First of all, Lisa has done this a hundred times. She knows the roads, the turns, everything. Right before you change into another state, you'll need to pull over and change the plates. It looks less suspicious when you have plates that match the state. Here's three hundred dollars for gas. Don't stop to eat. Eat when you get gas, get some crackers or chips, but don't stop. No matter what, do not let that car out of your sight. You let Lisa go in and pay for the gas. If we can steal a car, other people can steal a car. When you get to the garage, take all the plates off and bring them back to the car that Lisa will be driving. Then he stopped and took a breath, "Oh yeah, don't forget to get paid."

Then they all laughed really loudly. He turned and said, "One more thing. A gun is in the glovebox. If the man doesn't pay, you point the gun right between his eyes, and then you tell him you will kill him."

I said, "The man is supposed to pay, right?" Jesse said, "He's always paid. You won't have any trouble."

We all lit a cigarette. Well, I'm not stealing a car. All I'm doing is driving one, so really I'm okay with this. I just felt uneasy about the killing part.

Lisa walked out. Her hair was wet and braided. She had a wide red, white, and blue headband on her head. She had a small purse. She walked toward us, and we all walked to the car. Jesse got into the car and started it up. *Whoop. . . whoop.* I felt the serious power the car had when it was just idling. Jesse got out and said, "Have a good trip. We'll see you here in about thirty hours from now." Lisa walked around and got in the car.

Here I go. I jumped in. The power of the car was enormous. I touched the gas and it roared. Jesse said, "Easy." Then I put my foot on the brake and put her in gear. It clunked and jumped. I could only imagine what a horse jockey felt like on top of a thoroughbred in the shoot waiting for the gate to open. I could imagine the horses grunting and snorting. I could imagine their hearts beating and pounding. Then I could imagine for a brief second of silence, when everything stops and all time is suspended. Then, the gate swings open, and they're off—dirt and dust and the rhythmic pounding of the horses running. Pure and raw power that only the jockey gets to experience. I pressed the gas and eased my way to the highway. Dust clouds were boiling out around the car as I eased her to the pavement, turning onto the highway. The speed limit was fifty-five, so I kept her between fifty-five and sixty. We were off. . . The gate had opened. I looked over at Lisa, and she smiled. Her hair was blowing around. I know why she braided her hair and wore a headband. We made it to Kingdom City and turned onto I-70 and headed east to St. Louis. The sun was behind us. I felt the power of the car. The 454 horsepower engine at fifty-five miles per hour sounded like a purring cat. I figured it was like a joyride around the track for my thoroughbred horse. We rolled up our windows and began to relax. All I had to do was not get pulled over. I didn't know these roads, so outrunning the cops wasn't going to work. Lisa said, "Once we get through St. Louis, we're going to take all backroads. It's good roads and less traffic. Just keep it at the speed limit."

"Sounds good. I need a cigarette."

She pushed in the cigarette lighter and lit a cigarette for me, then lit one for herself. She reached over and put it in my mouth for me. I was thinking about how much trouble I would be in if I got caught. I really thought there would be plenty of peopled lined up to kill me, like Dunny, my mom, and God only knows who else. Then I thought about God and my grandmother and the preacher. I decided that it was too late to be having all this holy thinking. I did say a prayer for God not to let me get caught. But my second prayer was, don't let this night end. I thought only about Lisa and me on this thirty-hour trip. I was sure that we could find a way to relax somewhere. She turned on the radio, and we smiled and looked at each other, then said, "When we get through St. Louis, I'll tell you everything you want to know."

I nodded my head okay. Then she slid all the way next to me in the seat, and she put her arm around me. I felt like I was a king. I had this badass car and a badass girl. Jesse and DW knew that if any cop saw us, they would just think we were teenagers out for a drive. It worked because we saw a few cops and not one of them paid much attention to us. I could tell Lisa had made this trip before. She knew every lane I should be in long before any turns I would make. She knew what gas station to stop at for gas. Gas was about seventy-five cents a gallon. The car got about twelve miles to the gallon. It was about a seven-hundred-mile trip we had. I figured a twenty-gallon tank, so I thought we'd stop about four times to fuel up and get any supplies. One thing was for sure. I didn't drink any liquor or smoke any weed. This trip was all business. I did think about the five hundred dollars I'd make when we got back.

She said, "When we get through east St. Louis, they'll be a rest stop before Illinois. Pull in there so we can go to the bathroom and change the plates." She was serious, but even when she was acting serious, she was calm and still the prettiest girl I'd ever seen. I remember a movie I had seen about Bonnie and Clyde, how they were outlaws madly in love. There must be an added rush to love when you throw in the outlaw factor. Maybe it's because your heart is already pounding and your senses have peaked. Throw in love and attraction with all that adrenaline, and you got a very explosive situation. I have to admit; I know what Clyde must have been feeling. I thought I'd die for all this right now. When we got to the rest stop, I pulled the car in toward the bathrooms. I slowed her down, and she just idled down and purred. People would look at us but not out of suspicion. They looked out of envy. The guys would look at the car and the girl. I know they thought I was the luckiest man on the earth. Hell, I thought I was the luckiest man, so I know they did too. I pulled to a stop and just let it idle for a minute. *Whoop. . . whoop . . .* Then, I turned her off. I imagined how a racehorse would run one lap then walk one lap to cool down, never just stopping instantly, but rather a gradual cool down. Jesse told me to keep my eyes on all the gauges at all times, and when I stopped, always check under the hood. Check the oil, the belts, look for anything that may have loosened up. Lisa knew all about cars, so we both looked the car over. We checked the tires; we did an inspection that any NASCAR pit crew would have done. I went to the bathroom, but it was a fast trip. I didn't want to be away from either the car or her. I felt I was the protector. I felt changed. I wasn't scared anymore; I wanted to protect and guard Lisa and the car. I felt strong inside and full of confidence, and I felt lucky to be experiencing this moment. I knew that *now*, this moment, was the only moment that counted. I thought just enjoy the "now" and don't worry about the "what ifs." A flood of optimism filled me.

Chapter 46

Lisa was sitting in the car. She had already moved over to be next to me. I came out of the bathroom filled with a new outlook. I wasn't going to find myself old and sitting at a kitchen table ready to blow off my head. If this was my Germany experience, I was going to take it. I don't care if I die today, I will take the chance, and I'll have no regrets. When I got in the car, I thought, if Larry could see me now, he would be smiling, maybe even envious. I started her up. *Whoop. . . whoop. . . whoop.* She jumped forward just a little. You had to keep your foot on the break, or she would take off. I backed out, then in forward, then I eased her on toward the highway. Everything seemed to be in slow motion. We got on the highway and headed on toward the Kentucky lines.

It was about 3:30 in the afternoon. We would drive until dark. After dark, the cops begin to watch the cars more. We would have to stop and sleep in the car. No way we could leave the car even for a minute. There was an all business type of feeling coming from Lisa. She was focused and knew every move we needed to make. But as I began to expect, she was calm and cool. We finally began to get to the remote backroads that I was anxious to reach. She was changing the radio station. When she finally settled on one, a song by Fleetwood Mac, "You Make Lovin' Fun" came on and then she just sat back and took a deep breath. She knew all the words and sang them to me. When the song ended, she turned, smiled at me and said, "Okay. We should be good for a while. I'll tell you anything you want to know.

I'm not going to have you wondering about me, and I want you to know that I love you."

What the hell did she just say? She loved me? How on earth could a seventeen-year-old virgin boy get a twenty-one-year-old girl to love him? Not just any girl, but the girlfriend of a guy that most considered a murderer. Naturally, that was my first question. I said, "Anything." She nodded her head yes.

"Well, I've been trying to figure out if you really like DW, and you're just playing me or if I'm maybe someone you really like?" She smiled and moved her ponytail to the opposite side of me. "Okay, where we are taking this car is my hometown. We've lived in the mountains of Tennessee for generations. It's the most beautiful place on earth. My family makes a hard living off of timber. But we make a better living off of moonshine and chopping cars. I have three older brothers and three younger sisters. DW came to know one of my brothers because of the Vietnam War. They were in some bad shit together in that war. My brother was always a fighter. I wasn't surprised that he was a badass in the war. He came back with all kinds of medals, but it seemed like only half of his mind would come back with him. He and DW and Jesse watched out for each other over there. While they were out on some mission, they were coming up with a plan to get back home. My brother told DW and Jesse about how you could chop a car into many parts, then put it back together, and it would be almost impossible to figure out that the car was stolen. They all decided to come back here and get in the game. They got out in 1970 and showed up at our house. I told you we lived in the Appalachian Mountains. It seems like we don't have any neighbors, but when you start to look around, we have garages and shops all spread out with different neighbors. Not one garage does it all. Instead, one garage does one part of the job. One garage builds the motor; one does the paint, one does the transmission, one does the carburetors, and so on. This way, a lot of families make money— money that we need to live on. It really all started way back in the moonshine and prohibition days. Our cars had to be able to outrun the cops. We knew all the dirt backroads, and we built cars for just that purpose. We don't run liquor and outrun the cops today, though. We outsmart the cops, and we sell the cars."

"Someone always wants these cars." I wanted to talk, but Lisa was on a roll, so I just listened. "If someone wants a car, they talk to someone in Greensboro, North Carolina. That someone, I don't know who, would get in touch with my brother. My brother would start the process and in about two weeks, they'd have a car ready. This setup works as good as any factory in Detroit. My brother and DW and Jesse are the ones that took this operation and made it big. It took hooking up with some big muscle guy from Chicago and other cities. Every so often, some real fancy, well-dressed dudes would come to our house. They'd all meet in the garage. Then they'd leave. One night, one of my other brothers was listening in on the meeting, and DW caught him. DW beat him about half to death. My family was pissed at DW, but DW talked his way out of it. DW is a smooth talker. Well, all my brothers would just as soon fight you than look at you. So he wasn't going to let DW off the hook. He decided he was going to kill DW." She stopped talking for a moment and said, "We'll need to get in this lane and stop at the next gas station."

My head was trying to keep up. I had waited a year for these answers, and now I was memorizing her every word. The car just purred along. I imagined how if the car had 454 horsepower, we were only using about ten of them. Then I really fell in love with the car. I knew the car, and Lisa were the same to me. I knew it had been built from scratch. It was a perfect machine. In a way, it was an evolution of mechanical lessons learned. The car was a horse, a thoroughbred horse and a champion at that. I slowed her down and turned into the next gas station. Now, I wondered if even the gas stations that we stopped at were part of the assembly line. I pulled up to the pumps and let her idle for a minute. Wherever I pulled into, everyone would stop and look at us. I was proud. I was very proud. This car was a perfect machine. I didn't feel I was stealing anything. I felt I was delivering a gift. I really couldn't say that this car was stolen; it was created. Maybe from parts that were stolen, but the car itself wasn't stolen. It was to be a prize to some rich person. I began to realize why Jesse warned me about coming back. I think he knew I had fallen in love with the machine and Lisa. I think he was wise to think that. But there was no chance I wasn't going to do what he wanted. Too many people counted on me to come back, and I know Lisa was going back. I shut off the engine. It was like the air all around the car was at rest. People turned back to what they were doing. Lisa jumped out and went inside to pay. I pumped the gas, but I also watched her. She was getting us some Mountain Dews, peanut butter crackers, chips, and a Slim Jim. She came out and just smiled at me. I felt lucky to have her with me. I felt enchanted by her presence. It was about six o'clock.

She said, "We are about halfway. We can drive to the next rest stop and then change the plates to Kentucky."

I asked her, "Should we go to the bathroom here, or would we stop again?"

She said, "You'll need to do everything here because we'll be on some backroads, and there ain't many places to stop."

I ran around the back to use the bathroom. It was locked. I had to go inside and get a key. I could see Lisa as she was sitting in the car. I hurried up and did my business. I got back in, and she was sitting and waiting, drinking a cold Mountain Dew and eating chips.

I said, "Okay."

"Just keep heading east."

When she said that, I heard the words, "Head East." That was one of Dunny and my favorite bands. They had a song "Never Been Any Reason." It was a great song. I touched the key and *whopp. . . whopp. . . whopp.* The car fired right up and jumped. The air all around us moved. People all around us stopped and looked. *Damn, this has to be heaven.* I eased her onto the road, and we settled back into our trip. I'd say there's not enough money on earth to buy these moments that Lisa and I were having. I think we both began to feel that this was a moment that people dreamed about. I think we both felt something very special because everything we did had a purpose. I knew that the next stop would be our resting spot. We had blankets in the trunk, and we would sleep in the car. Where that was, I was not sure, but I figured it was already determined.

Once Lisa felt we were in a good spot on the road, she began to tell me more of her story. Before she could talk, I said, "I don't need to know anymore if you don't want to tell me."

"No, I want you to know who I am and what I am. I really have feelings for you. I want you to have me."

I almost choked. *This can't be happening to me.* She started telling me, "DW shouldn't have beaten my brother the way he did. That set in motion a chain of events that's happening, even now. They say when a person goes to prison, the only thing they learn is how to be a better criminal. Well, they sent my brother, Jesse and DW to Vietnam to kill people, and all that did was make them better killers when they came back. My brother used to go hunting in the mountains with friends. When he came back, he never went hunting again. He'd say, 'Once you hunted a man that is hunting you, it's unfair to hunt any animal.' Both my brother and Jesse didn't like killing people, but DW liked it. I think he snapped that night he caught my brother sneaking around the garage. I think he's still in Vietnam. But my dad and all my brothers knew DW would turn on them if he got a chance to save his own neck. They knew DW would kill anyone if he could get away with it. That all happened in 1971 when I was about thirteen years old. That next spring in 1972, my middle brother came up missing. He ain't been found yet. Everyone knew DW had to have something to do with it. It's just that DW wasn't around here much at that time. We think maybe my brother went looking for him. My brother says DW was in jail then and tries to change the subject when it comes up, but he thinks DW had something to do with it or knowledge of it."

Chapter 47

The car just purred on down the road. I listened to Lisa tell her story. I wasn't surprised to hear DW was messed up in the head. I was surprised at how calm Lisa was when she was telling the story. If someone had beaten me or my brother, or Dunny, I have to admit, I would spend the rest of my life getting even. Now, I wanted to kill DW myself. Only one thing, I wasn't a killer. So I decided to listen to Lisa tell me more. She continued, "I'm the oldest girl in our family, and all my brothers are older than me. My dad figured that DW would expect trouble from any of my brothers. But he figured DW wouldn't expect it from one of his girls. DW, he's a good-looking, smooth-talking guy. He thinks all the girls love him. I'd say most girls do love him but not me. I hate him, and one day he'll know it was me that took him down. I'm going to see him go down one day. My dad said I was going to be the one that makes it happen. So that was my mission once I hit eighteen years old. I've been on it ever since. I have a good plan. I'd act like I liked him and get real close. That even meant that I would have to sleep with him. That's not anything I'm proud of or enjoy. I did it only when I had to. I was really good with excuses. Plus, DW's married and got women everywhere. The car business was good. We figured out that Jesse was from central Missouri and that we'd get our cars there. Then, we could go in all four directions to get it to a buyer. There's a set route in every direction we follow. We have been doing it for years. The only problem we have is the drivers. They can't seem to remain calm enough if they get in trouble. You saw that happen one night at the clay pit, and you also saw DW putting a gun to a guy's head. Our drivers either drank too much or smoked too much, or they looked like bad guys. So when Jesse saw you in the liquor store, he thought of a different type of driver. He thought of you. He said the cops wouldn't think much about a teenager. But when I saw you that first time, I thought of you as a good guy, someone I'd like to be with on a date, someone to go to the movies with and to dance with. Those are things I've never even done with a boy. My life has been this planned out scheme to make something right for my family. I was good with all of it, that is, until I saw you." She stopped talking for a minute. I kept my eyes on the road, my foot on the gas. The car never missed a beat. It was as if the car was on this springtime joyride. We were getting close to our rest stop, so I figured I would say just a few things that were on my mind.

"Hey, Lisa, I don't know how this all turns out. I ain't sure I can see even much past the next hour or even the next minute. But what I can see is you. I ain't never been all the way with any girl. I really ain't been much past first base with too many girls. The night at the liquor store, your smile and just how you looked at me, stopped me dead in my tracks. I began to dream about you from that time on. Then, when you came up to me at the clay pit and hugged me, and we danced, well, I was praying to God that he let our paths cross again. I'm not going to let anything stop me now. We are here, and right now is all that matters. I'll take you on a hundred dates and to a hundred dances. I'll be with you forever. We can figure out a way to get DW together."

She elbowed me in the gut and smiled and laughed at the same time. Then she said, "Get ready. In about a mile, the rest stop is around the corner." We both smiled and looked deep into each other's eyes. The rest stop was near. We stopped right before Paducah, Kentucky. The rest stop was empty, so we idled right in next to the bathroom. Lisa jumped out and went to the bathroom. I turned off the car and waited for her to come out. She jumped inside and opened the glovebox. A pistol was in there.

She said, "An empty rest stop is the worst kind. One thing to always remember, a rest stop is never empty."

Damn, they've thought of everything. I said, "I'll hurry, but honk the horn if something is up."

"I won't honk the horn if someone messes with me." Then she showed me the gun. I ran in fast, did my business, and ran back out. She just busted out laughing at me. We both inspected the car and found her in top shape. I imagined this trip was but a brisk spring training run. I felt the car wanted to open up, but that would be a mistake that most drivers made. Just because you have the power, you didn't have to use it, a lesson that most powerful people would do good to follow. My job was to deliver the car, and I was focused on that. I jumped back in, and Lisa jumped in and slid over almost on top of me. We both looked at each other—then kissed. It was really the first time we kissed on this trip. We were both so focused on our mission that we really hadn't been close enough to be with ourselves. We hugged. She felt so good, and she smelled so good. We slowly let go of each other and turned back to the front of the car.

She said, "Okay, we are going to drive to a little town called Eddyville, Kentucky. The network begins in Eddyville. We will have a garage to pull her into. We will have to sleep in the car."

How am I going to sleep with her next to me?

"We will sleep until the first sign of day and then we will go. When we get to the garage, we'll check the car out. A friend owns the garage, and he's a top mechanic. He'll check out everything while we shower and eat. This is all part of the network. Everyone has a part, and everyone makes good money. But no one can be tied to the whole operation. If one thing goes down, another one takes its place. I hit the engine and again she hit, *Whopp. . . whoppp. . . whoppp.* I eased her back onto the road, and we settled into some music and talked about dreams we had. Eddyville was only a couple of hours away. It would be around seven o'clock at night. The car purred on; it was doing its part. The sunset was behind us. If we hadn't been doing something wrong, I'd swear we were doing something right.

Chapter 48

We rolled into Eddyville; it was quiet and not much different than most small towns.

She said, "Take a right at the stop sign. Then head out of town." I turned on the small road that would take us out of town. We went back into the brush. It reminded me of the backroads in Callaway County. I was amazed at how much of this was thought out. How many years did it take to perfect this network? I was proud to be part of it. I just didn't like the idea of killing anybody. She had me turn here and turn there until finally, I didn't know which way to turn. She would laugh at me and elbow me to pay attention. Finally, in the middle of, I'd say nowhere, she said, "We're here."

We pulled up to a small, white, well-kept house. Smoke was coming out of the chimney. The garage was off a little way from the house. It looked like a small barn, one that cows and horses would be in. She said, "Pull up to the garage," and pointed at it. The car acted like it knew where to go. I got her to the door and just let the car idle for a minute. The rumble of the engine filled the woods. Then I shut her off. There was silence, the kind of silence that I had only heard at the clay pit. Like those nights Dunny and I would stay out all night and sleep in the truck. I heard a whippoorwill next to us. The night was full of lightning bugs. I stayed in the car. Lisa got out and went to the front porch, and someone came out. They knew we were here; they had been expecting us. I'm sure that Jesse had called and checked in with them. Lisa came back and said, "You can get out, but stay close to the car. Stay close to the gun. You never know when someone gets greedy."

Damn, why ruin a good thing?

She went in the house, and I could see her sitting at the table with the family. I saw some kids. I'd say they were grandkids. The man looked pretty old to have young kids. I was getting a little anxious when Lisa and the man came out. They both walked toward me and the car. I remember Lisa saying "an empty rest stop was a dangerous rest stop." I knew why she said to stay with the car. She knew where we were, but she wasn't sure it was safe. They got right up to me, and Lisa said, "It's okay." The man said to put it in neutral, and we could push her in. I wasn't sure why we were going to push her in until he opened the door. He said, "Okay, push her in." Lisa and I pushed, and he helped. He said to make sure it stopped over the carpet.

"I don't want any oil on my floor."

We stopped it where he wanted. He shut the door. I looked around, and it looked like more of a hospital operating room than any garage I'd seen. There were engines all over on hoists, on hangers, on stands. It was a dust-free, smoke-free place. No smoking signs were everywhere. All I could do was look.

Lisa looked over at me and said, "You look like you've seen a ghost." Then she and the man laughed at me. I said, "Damn, what a place."

He said, "Dust is an enemy to an engine. Dust gets in and creates all kinds of trouble. That's why we pushed her in. Now, let's look her over. You all can go in the backroom and clean up."

I said, "Lisa, you go first. I'll stay here with the car."

She looked at me with a "Now you're getting it" look. She opened up the trunk and grabbed a small bag of soap and stuff, then said, "I'll just be a minute." The man went over the car like a doctor. He went under her and inside her. He slammed down the hood and said, "She's as perfect as the day I built her." I thought, I had looked at God himself. I was in awe. I said, "How could you ever build such a machine? Better yet, how could you ever let a machine like this get away?"

"There's always another car. I make them for other people to enjoy."

"How come you make them this way? Why not do it a way that won't get you put in jail."

"This way pays better. Look around you. All I got takes money. Besides, who says what I do is illegal?"

"Sorry, mister, I didn't mean to judge you. I just know that this car has to be the most perfect car ever made. Anyone that can make this car should be a king."

The man just smiled. I could tell he was proud of his cars. The bathroom door opened, and Lisa came out. She had taken a quick shower, and her hair was wet. She was as beautiful as the sunset behind us. I looked at her and stared. I couldn't take my eyes off her. She said, "Would you like to get in the shower really quick?"

"Yeah that would be good." As I walked by her, she punched me then laughed at me. I went inside and took my shower. *God, there ain't no way I'm going to live through all this.* If this car deal doesn't kill me, this Lisa thing will. I'm about to die being next to her. I was not sure if God liked me right now, but I still thought I better ask for his help.

When I came out, there was only one light on under a bench. Lisa was in the car and had a blanket spread out over the backseat. She had some crackers, some chips, and a Mountain Dew. I stumbled over a car dolly and looked in the car. There she was, smiling that perfect smile. She said, "Come on, we need to rest tonight. But when we get to Hampton, I'll show you how much I love you." Now, how on earth was I supposed to rest? My heart was just about to jump out of my chest. I was there with the most beautiful girl in the whole wide world. I was not sure God heard me clearly. She just laughed and punched me. She knew she had me like a bridled horse. She could lead me anywhere. That's a dangerous thing, to have that kind of power over a boy. But like our car, just because you got power, don't mean you got to use it. We kissed and hugged and snuggled. Soon, Lisa fell asleep. I know it may sound creepy, but I watched her sleep for quite a while. I don't know how, but she was even more beautiful in her sleep. I laid back and stared at the ceiling of the car.

I thought about Dunny. We hadn't spent too many nights apart. I thought about my mom and dad. I figured if all this didn't kill me, then they would. I just couldn't get past Junior wanting to kill himself. I felt so sorry for him. There's no way I was going to let that be me. I got to this moment. This *now* in my life. Every decision I'd made had put me right there. I looked over at Lisa sleeping, and I thought this ain't so bad. I've been in worse spots. This ain't so bad. If I die now, I'll die on top. I dozed off, then fell asleep.

Chapter 49

I woke up to a loud crash and boom. It was a spring storm. I was always told that thunder was God letting you know he's still the boss. It wasn't light yet. It was close to sunrise. I hugged Lisa, and she stirred slowly. I asked her, "How can you sleep that good?" She smiled that perfect smile. I said, "Should we go or wait awhile?"

"Wait; storms can get bad on these roads. It will pass and then we can go." We snuggled and kissed and fooled around while the storm was carrying on. I loved her more and more. I never wanted this to end. I could not imagine how this was going to turn out. I just begged God to fix all this and to get Lisa and me home safely. We finally heard the storm pass. It was almost daylight. I asked Lisa, "What next?"

"We are going to go along the Kentucky, Tennessee, border until we hit Middleborough. We will stop and change the plates to Tennessee. Then go south to Hampton. When in Hampton, we'll go to another garage like this, and we'll get our money. I'll call my dad, and he will come and get us."

"Damn, that sounds simple enough."

She punched me in the gut, and said, "You're supposed to go to a motel and stay until I pick you up in the morning, but you're going home with me. I want you to meet my family. We will stay there for the night and leave at daybreak. We will have to drive all the way through without stopping to get back in time."

"Damn, is that all?"

She punched me again in the gut. I really didn't mean to make light of our situation, but it did seem to make her laugh. We got up and went to the bathroom. I opened the door, and we rolled her out. It seemed like the car didn't sleep much either. I shut the door on the shop, locked it from the inside, and came out the side door. Lisa was sitting in the middle right next to me. I touched the key and *whopp. . . whopp*, she fired up. Damn, I loved that sound. It was raw power. It felt like the air was sucked out of everything within twenty feet of the car. I put it in reverse and backed out really easily. The rain had caused some mud puddles. I didn't want to spin or splash anything on her. We eased out and headed toward Tennessee. I have to admit; I was a little nervous about meeting her family.

We followed the Kentucky/Tennessee line and then stopped as planned in Middleboro. Again, the rest areas were empty. It wasn't really a typical rest stop, more like a scenic view type of stop. We both talked about how good it would be to get to her house. It had been a month or so since she had been home. I tried to get her to describe it to me, but she said, "You'll just have to see it to believe it." My heart was pounding again. I figured I must calm down. I was still on a mission. Lisa began to tell me more about DW and her family.

"You know, I was pretty young when my brother came back from Vietnam. But I remember he took a while to relax. My mom and dad would have to tell him the war was not here. He really is a good person. We just do as a family what we can to make it. It's mostly illegal, we all know. There's just not many choices; there's the coal mines or timber. There's even less of a choice for girls. Girls pretty much get married and have kids. I don't see much of a future for myself."

"I don't worry that far ahead. Maybe I should, but I can't see that far. Dunny and I, our only worry was not to die a virgin and where the next party was. So far, we are doing good on the partying part." I stopped, and we both looked at each other with big smiles. Then, she elbowed me in the gut. We had talked enough that the trip to Middleboro seemed short. It was about nine o'clock in the morning. She gave me directions so we could stop, get fuel, and change our plates to Tennessee. It would only be a few hours to her house.

She said we should be there by noon or 1:00. The car never missed a beat. I just purred along. Lisa never really changed her outlook on the mission. She was always calm and knew every move to make. I could tell we were getting close though because she talked about some places on their land that she wanted to show me. I was really looking forward to a time we could both relax. I think she was too. Pretty quickly, we entered into the scenic part of Tennessee. I could see the Great Smokey Mountains. The sun was getting higher in the sky, but the mountains were staying in line with it. We drove by a massive blue water lake called Cherokee Reservoir.

She said DW would tell her, "If you ever wanted to hide a body, this would be the place." I think all of Lisa's family believed her brother was somewhere in that reservoir. If there was any one thing that was always in the back of our minds, it was DW.

I said, "Let's forget about DW for the next few hours. I just want to see where you are from. I want to know all about you and your family."

She smiled really pretty like and hugged me. I really was in love with her. I'm not sure I had any real idea of love. I figured this must be what love was like, just spending time together on a scenic drive enjoying the awesome views. She would lay her head on my shoulder. I wanted to pull over and kick back, but we were almost to Hampton. We rolled into town around noon. It was alive with people, but it was small, about half the size of my town. She had me turn and go alongside a nice creek; then we headed out of town. The car was steady, but what was funny was people didn't look at us like everywhere else. Well, they did look, just not stare. We turned on a road. The sign said no outlet. We were completely engulfed in trees. It reminded me of Dark Hollow Road we would drive on at home. We went up and all the way to the end of the road that turned into her driveway. The car was idling slowly. It sounded so good pulling up to the southern two-story farm house.

"Pull her over by the barn."

I was trying to remain calm. A dog came wagging its tail. I turned the car off. We both took a breath. I think for the first time, I caught her being a little nervous. She said, "Now you can leave the car. My brother will take it the rest of the way. He will bring back our car to take back to Jesse."

I wasn't sure I could part with the car. It was a machine, but man, it was priceless. I hoped whoever got her understood what a rare machine they had bought. She hit me and said, "Come on, get out." I opened the door and got out, and she slipped out right behind me. We started to walk, and she grabbed my hand to hold. The door swung open, and three girls came running out. They were yelling her name. Her two brothers and her dad came out but stayed on the porch. Then her mom came out. The whole family was good-looking. No one looked poor or worn out. I could tell they were blessed with good health. She stopped and kneeled down on one knee as her sisters came to hug her. She was so happy. I felt it from her, the heavy burden she carried. But she was as strong as this mountain they lived on. The brothers came toward us; they both smiled and hugged her with a big bear hug.

"SL, these are my brother James and John."

I reached out to shake their hands. The eldest brother, James took my hand and pulled me right up to him and gave me a big bear hug.

"So this is the man my little sister was talking about all winter."

I was proud to know them. He grabbed us both and walked us to the house. I felt like I was one of the family. We got onto the porch, and I said, "Sir, it's a pleasure to know you and your family, but the biggest pleasure has been meeting Lisa."

He smiled and then I said hello to her mom. I could see Lisa in her mom. I was thinking her mom was a looker in her day.

Her dad said, "Come on inside. We have lunch ready."

I went inside, and I saw a picture of Jesus. I saw a Bible on the fireplace mantel. I was surprised they were Baptist. I knew my grandmother was a Baptist and drinking was a big sin. I had thought they made moonshine and stole cars for a living. I thought I might ask Lisa about that sometime. But really, I didn't care one way or another. How was I supposed to judge anyone? We sat down and had a good lunch of sandwiches and salad. I told Lisa it was better than her lunch of Mountain Dew and crackers. She elbowed me in the gut. It was getting to be around 1:30 in the afternoon. James said, "So come and show me your car," and looked right at me.

"Okay."

We both excused ourselves and went outside to the car.

"She's a prize car. I'm envious of the person who gets her."

He smiled and said, "Yep, the cars we build are the best that money can buy. It's hard not to get too attached to them. Just remember, there's always more cars, but there's only one of us."

I shook my head yes.

"I'll take her on up the road, and I'll get you the money. Most of the time, I don't see the drivers. Usually, we have them go right to the garage that buys them. But Lisa said she was bringing you here. I know one thing. I haven't seen Lisa act the way she does around you. She's not the same girl since she met you."

I was happy to hear she was thinking of me that whole time.

"Sir, I'm not so sure that we were meant to meet that day, but I know my life has changed because I have met her. I was so afraid that I was being used as a mark for a scam."

"Trust me, you ain't no mark. Better go on back inside."

He got in the car, rolled the window down, and said, "What until you see what I'm bringing back for you." Then he smiled, laughed, and touched the key; and that familiar sound came from the car.

Chapter 50

I went back toward the house. I looked around, and I was surrounded by trees—old trees and old forest with a house and barn stuck right in the middle. The trees were thick and green. I felt like I was under an umbrella made by God. The trees put off so much oxygen that a thin layer of white cloud stayed at the treetop level. I felt I was in heaven or at least heaven had to have trees. As I walked back, I thought about God, and I wondered if God really did watch out for us and over us. I thought God might have a better way of understanding us than we do him. How come just about everything I did was wrong? Yet, how could this place, these people, and Lisa seem so right? I knew no man could measure up to God's standards. I wondered what's the use in trying to. I figured there were evil people, and there was a devil carrying on, but how could what I was feeling for Lisa be so wrong? Better yet, I'm not sure that I even cared if God did care. Lisa and her family went to church, believed in God, but they made moonshine and built black market cars. When I looked over the situation, I decided to let it be. We are all sinners in God's eyes. When the day comes, I guess I'll have to be a man and confess and beg to be forgiven. I went up the steps. I could hear a lot of laughter. I wiped my feet and put my hands over my hair to make it lay down. Then I went inside; I looked over at the table, and Lisa's little sisters were giggling and laughing and whispering about me. Lisa was smiling and laughing with them. Man, she was beautiful. It almost hurt to look at her. I was the luckiest guy in the world. This girl liked me, even better yet, she loved me. I went over and sat at the table. I didn't know what to say or do. They all just kept looking at me. Lisa got up and came over to me.

"Come on. I'll show you the bathroom, and I'll show you the couch."

Then they all busted out laughing. I really didn't know I was that funny. She grabbed my hand and pulled me toward the hallway.

"Here's the bathroom. You may as well take a shower and change your clothes."

"Only one problem. I ain't got no clean clothes to put on."

She laughed. "Oh, I'll find you a change and mom can wash yours."

So I went in and took a shower; when I got out, a folded set of clothes were sitting on the sink. I got dressed. I felt clean. I walked out toward the kitchen, and Lisa must have been in her room. Her mom was at the kitchen sink. I remember Lisa standing at the kitchen sink at Jesse's trailer. I walked up and asked had she seen Lisa.

"She's in her room. She wants to take you up the mountain and show you some places we have."

"Man, that would be nice."

"Lisa's never really had a serious boyfriend before."

"I can't understand why."

Her mom laughed and smiled. She said, "I don't believe I've ever seen her act this way. It's nice to see her act like a lady."

"Ma'am, she ain't anything but a lady."

She laughed at me again. Then she said, "You know what I mean, don't you?"

"Yes ma'am. I think I have it worse than she does."

She laughed again. She said, "Well, you're welcome here in our home for as long as you like."

"Thank you, ma'am, and you're welcome in my home as well."

That was stupid.

Lisa came down the steps, and I almost died. I'm saying even the clocks stopped ticking because it felt like time had stopped, kind of like when you can hear it ticking then silence. If ever there was a time for a picture, it was right now. She had on blue jeans and a plain white t-shirt. She had her hair woven in some sort of weave that models wear. She had a headband on like native Americans would wear. I had never seen a more perfect girl. She smiled at me. That's one thing I always liked about her; she always smiled. Her mom was watching me look at her, and she knew that Lisa was my whole world. Lisa came down the steps fast and said, "Hey, come on, I'm going to show you some really cool places on the mountain." She grabbed my hand and pulled me outside.

"Hold on. I need to fix my shirt."

"Come on. We ain't got much time."

We jogged up to the edge of the forest. Now, I've climbed some hills in my day, but I haven't ever climbed a mountain. Not even Larry could say he'd done this with a girl. We went into the woods and up a little way, and there was a clearing in the trees. We walked up to the clearing, and I could see mountains and streams in every direction.

Man, how small am I? I don't even amount to a speck on this earth.

I grabbed Lisa's hand, and we stood together. I was speechless. No wonder Lisa was as calm as she was. If only I could escape up to this mountaintop whenever I had a thought or worry. I needed one of these mountaintops to go to in my life. I thought back to my Sunday school days when God sent Moses to the mountaintop. I never really thought much about that story. But now I think I understood why. God wanted Moses to see how small he was and how big God was. It's funny how when you can get above something how easy it is to see. The saying, "You can't see the forest because of the tree"—well, I was looking at the opposite. I couldn't see the trees because of the forest. A flood of thoughts and emotions took over my mind.

"Come on, I want to show you a waterfall, and then I want to show you a tree house that's been in our family for as long as I can remember."

She pulled me onto a small trail that led into the trees. As we got closer, I could hear the sound of the waterfall. As we walked, we laughed and joked and were relaxed. It felt good to relax and not be worried about anything but ourselves. We reached a rock ledge, and a mist of water was rising out of the forest floor. The sound wasn't loud but had a steady, calming noise. We went down to the rock ledge to a clear pool of water that looked deep and cold.

"It's not warm enough to swim, is it?"

"I don't know."

She grabbed me to push me in but held me so I didn't. Then she said, "It has to be the hottest day of the year to swim in this pool of water."

Damn, I was sure wanting to take a swim with her.

"Come on, this is something you'll really enjoy."

We went up the mountain as far as we could go. We come upon a perfect tree house. I was in awe. All my life, I wanted a tree house.

"It started out as a lookout to observe the mountains and its trails. I'd say because of the moonshine business. But I'm not really sure. My dad and brothers started to make it into this tree house for all of us."

I went up to it. It had a rope bridge you climbed to get up to the deck. The deck wrapped around a covered roof. The deck went to extend out over a rock ledge, and you felt like it would take forever to fall to the bottom. Trees were under us all the way down. I was again in a trance. This whole place had a feeling of greatness. I told her how lucky she was to grow up on this mountain. She smiled and said, "I know I'm lucky, but not because of this mountain." There was a small radio that had to be hand cranked for power. She reached over and cranked it then put in her favorite song. It was Tom Petty's "Breakdown," the song she was playing when we were in the back-yard of Jesse's trailer. She began the song, and we held each other. I knew I wasn't going to be a virgin anymore. We spent the next hour on the deck floor under an old blanket that was stored in a locker. We held each other like this was our last day on earth. I had hoped and wished for this moment for at least the last five years. I didn't care if I died right then; I felt my life was complete. I wished for time to stop. We stayed there as long as we could. Then she said, "We have to get back, it'll be dark soon."

I watched her. I had seen her naked only briefly. This time, I took in and memorized her whole body. It was perfect in every way. She got dressed really slowly. I got dressed with her. I looked at the mountain view and the sun that was trying to set. I knew we were about to enter a time that may cost us our lives. We knew we had each other. That was only a taste of what we wanted. I knew we were both still at the poker table, but I had the ace and the joker and she did too.

We walked up the path and headed to her house. It was starting to get dark. The forest was a lot darker right at sunset. The noises of the forest started up like someone flipped a switch. The lightning bugs were everywhere. Lisa's sisters were running around trying to catch them. They ran and laughed. Lisa and I joined in with them. Laughter filled the mountain air. It seemed so innocent. Before too long, the whole family was on the porch. They had a pitcher of sweet tea on the porch table and were sitting around in wicker chairs. For this brief time, no one had any worries at all; all we had was that moment. Lisa and I took a minute and sat together on the steps. We watched and listened to all the noises. She laid her head on my shoulder. I said, "Man, I could stay right here forever."

She smiled and said, "Me too."

I knew now why Jesse said, "If you don't come back."

He knew I'd fall in love and start to think differently. Young people who fall in love don't always think rationally. We both knew we had to go back. We both knew we had to face the devil. I was ready. Lisa's brother James got up and said, "Come over here. I want to show you something. Lisa, you need to come with us."

We both jumped up and followed him toward the barn. When we got close to the door, he said, "You'll be taking this back to Jessie and Charlie." He opened the door and hit the lights. It was a chocolate brown '71 SS Chevelle. I thought they weren't kidding when they said there would be another car. He said, "The money is in the glovebox next to the gun. Here's some money for your gas. Jesse will pay you for the drive."

Then he gave me the keys. Lisa and I looked at the car. She had been through too many trips to get nervous. But I was nervous. This was a nonstop trip. We would have to leave before sun up. We turned off the lights and locked the barn door, then walked back toward the house. Her mom was telling everyone to come in and eat.

We all gathered around the table. They said a prayer and I said my own silent prayer. I asked God to bless this family, and if he could see any way to get Lisa and me out of the jam we were in. I had begun to realize I needed God in my life and that the only true way to beat the devil was to let God do it for you. But it would take the rest of the summer before I really realized how much I needed his help. I sat down next to Lisa. We were happy to be there together. We passed the food around. You could hear the silverware scraping the dishes and glasses of sweet tea would jingle with ice cubes. About every ten minutes or so, Lisa would elbow me in the gut and laugh when I jumped. She was a little ornery. We all laughed, and they told stories on each other. It was a good time. As we finished, the girls all cleared the table, and they cleaned the dishes. The men went outside and talked, but not about anything that would raise your eyebrow. I really only listened to them talk. My mind was on the trip back and, of course, my encounter with DW and the prowling lion. I was also thinking about Dunny. I'm sure he was worried sick. I figured I hadn't been gone long enough for my mom and dad to catch me. They knew I was usually staying with Dunny. But most of all, I was thinking about the time Lisa and I had spent at the tree house. I didn't know what a girl thought about her first time, but I know what I thought about it, the way two people become one, the way when you feel each other's energy, the gift of being intimate and totally free with someone. I thought it would be a milestone event. But instead, it became a private memory for only me. I didn't want anyone to know what we did or what I felt. That was our own private memory. I wanted to guard Lisa and me. I was going to get back and help Lisa settle the score. Lisa came out on the porch. She looked good. She always looked good. We grabbed hands and walked out to the edge of the woods. She smiled at me, but she looked worried. She said, "I don't think I can go back. I can't be with DW now. I don't want to be with anyone but you."

I didn't have any words.

"Say something." She was starting to cry, just a little bit.

"I'll go back on my own. But I just got you back, and now I can't stand to think we will be apart."

She cried and put her head on my chest. I said, "Can you at least write down every turn, and how do I leave the car when I get fuel?"

She laughed and said, "Lock it and always park it close to the door."

"How do I go to the bathroom?"

"You'll figure it out, and my brother won't kill you if something happens."

Now I got worried. The "what ifs" came into my head like a flood. Then I stopped myself. "What about you and me?"

"I'll be here waiting for you to come back to me."

Damn, that's all I had to hear. She wiped her eyes. We walked back to the porch.

Her brother said, "Damn, have you all seen a ghost?"

"No, we ain't yet, but I'm about to."

Then he knew what I was talking about. He said, "Let's go look the car over really quickly." We walked to the barn. Lisa went inside. He said, "Listen, DW is a bad dude. Jesse's a good guy. You just don't want to mess with him. Those boys and I have been in some bad shit, some stuff I can't talk about, but DW, he will kill you in a minute. We ain't sure of how many people he's killed. He's a time bomb ready to go off. I'd say you should make up a story. Say Lisa got really sick. He'll know, but it will take him a while to scheme up a plan. Hell, he's likely to come back here. I'll have to kill him if he does. But as soon as you get there, I want you to call here. Lisa is crazy about you. We have to end this thing with DW."

Chapter 51

I was proud to be considered part of the family. The car was sitting there like it was listening to every word. He looked at the car and said, "She's a prize, a spectacular prize." Then I shut off the light. We walked inside the house. James had a wife and kids so he told everyone goodbye, and me goodbye. I could see the younger girls looking at me. I looked at them, and they laughed. Lisa came down the steps. She had a pillow and a blanket. She said, "The couch is your bed," and laughed. All the girls laughed. She came down, and we went back outside. She said, "Listen to me, you will have to leave around five o'clock in the morning. That should put you home around 5:00 or 6:00 at night. Jesse will be waiting. When you get back there, be ready because they'll want to party. If DW or anyone offers pills, take them and just spit them out when no one is looking. Be ready for anything, especially the next few days."

"I'm going to have to go home sometime or my mom and dad, they'll kill me. Plus, I think I'd like to leave earlier than five."

"Okay, I'll wake you up at 3:30 so you can take a shower."

We hugged with no words. She squeezed me hard. She wouldn't let go. She stood back and said, "Please come back. If you come back, we'll settle up all our past problems and start over."

We went inside, and she turned out all the lights. They left the bathroom light on but cracked the door. We kissed and hugged, and she went up the steps. I covered myself, but there was not much chance I would sleep. My mind wandered through all the events of my life. It wondered through all the people in my life. *How did I get here?* Once again, one of the crossroads came up on me. I thought about the stories of a man meeting the devil at a crossroads to make a deal, a deal that usually involved a wager against his soul. Was that the kind of crossroads where I was? I felt like it must be. What? My soul to rid Lisa's family of DW? Could I make that deal? I would find out soon enough. I drifted off into a light sleep. I had no more shut my eyes when I felt an angel was waking me up.

"SL, get up! Get up," she said in a whisper. "Go take a shower and I'll get your clothes." I rubbed my eyes and grabbed her. We hugged and squeezed each other.

"Damn, you look good."

Of course, she punched me in the gut. She had a glow about her, more so than normal. I went and took a fast shower; some could call it a whore's shower. I got out. I was in a hurry. Lisa had made me a sandwich and chips. She gave me a letter to read when I got to a safe rest spot. She gave me another piece of paper. It had every mile marker, every lane change, every turn signal from here to home. In big letters, it said, "Follow these instructions."

We walked slowly to the car. We were both sad and worried.

"What about the noise when I start her up?"

She laughed, "The sound of a car up here doesn't' even wake up our dogs." The garage part of the barn was as clean as any hospital room. She hit the light, and the car was waiting, like a thoroughbred horse, ready for a race. It was only fitting that this weekend was the Kentucky Derby. We kissed and hugged like this could be our last. I tried to remember everything—her smell, her touch, her smile, her laugh. I tried to remember her. I let go; she was crying. I hit the key and *whopp, whopp*—454 horses stood to attention. We kissed from inside the car. I had to go.

Chapter 52

I pulled out and eased on forward. I wanted to stop, but we both knew I had to go. I touched the breaks. She was crying just a little and waved me to get. . . so I did. I made my way through town and got to the open road outside of Hampton. Her road instructions were different from the way we came to Hampton. It had me on all the interstate highways, going through Lexington and then West through Louisville, then through Illinois and St. Louis, then home. I got a little ways and then it hit me. I cried like I hadn't cried since I was a little boy. I wasn't real sure why I cried so hard, but I did. I could only see flashes of her and I, and her smile was branded in my mind. I really went over our special day in the tree house. The time we spent was something people dream and wish for, a love that was as pure as anything on this earth. I kept seeing us rolling around in slow motion. She then me, we both shaped each other. I drove on and followed every word she wrote down. I turned at every lane she said. I did exactly what she said. I looked over at the letter; it was on the seat where she would be sitting. I remember seeing girls sit next to Larry in his car. I couldn't wait until a girl would do that with me. The car was amazing; it was spectacular. I never thought that a car could replace the blue one, but really, why did it need to? It purred right along. I turned on the radio. It was The J. Geils Band's "Detroit Breakdown." I turned it up loud. I drove and kept driving. Finally, I had to stop. I knew she had already planned for the place to stop, so I looked for it. It was a sixty-six gas station in a small town. I pulled in really slowly. The car just idled down. I got close to the door. I sat for a few minutes while she idled. Man, she sounded good. Words can't describe the sound she was making. Finally, I turned her off. The air around us took a break. I went in to pay, and a nice-looking but older man said, "Man, that's a sweet ride."

"Yep."

Then he said, "James left you this note."

I was taken aback for a minute.

"Yeah, James is looking out for you. You're going to slingshot all the way home."

I grabbed the note and looked at the man. He just laughed at me. I paid for the gas, but the man said, "Nope, we got the gas, young man." I ran and jumped back in the car. I ripped open the note. It said, "SL, don't worry about being stopped by the cops. This is your car. It's a gift to you and Lisa. She said how much you loved that blue car. I love my sister. She loves you, so come back. Tell Jesse I'll get him another car when he sends you back."

I cried. How could anyone give a shit for someone they really only just met? But I guess really he had met me for a year. I just hadn't been there in person. I looked up at the gas store owner; he smiled and tipped his hat to me. I touched the key and *whopp. . . whopp*; the horse stood up. I eased her out to the road and headed north to Lexington. The weather was good. I cruised on. I came upon Lexington, and the instructions told me where to stop. I found the small gas station. I idled into a spot next to the door. I got out and ran inside. A lady came out and said, "What do you need? That's a nice car." I was counting out some money then stopped and looked up. She smiled and said, "Get what you need. It's already been taken care of." I was so amazed that the network had already heard. The word was going before me. I smiled and said, "Thanks, ma'am."

"Don't thank me, thank James."

I filled her up, and all I could do was think about Lisa. She had planned all this. How amazing was this girl? What did I do to deserve this? I jumped in the car. The lady smiled and laughed at me. I touched the key, *whopp. . . whopp*. I eased her on out to the highway. I sat back and let the car do all the work. I could only think about what was going on. I would need to meet DW and that day was coming fast. I wasn't protected from that day. But I was calm. The purring engine had that effect on me. I was coming to Louisville. I was going to rest and then read the letter. The instructions said to find a small gas station on the east side of Louisville. I looked for it and saw a sign that led me to it. This time, I went in and looked around. I saw a really old man come to the cash register.

The network may not reach this far. I said, "Sir, I need to fill her up."

"That's a nice car. James said you'd be here."

Damn, how could this be? I saw in the window a sign that said, "Place your bets on the Kentucky Derby this weekend."

What the hell? I'll place my bet.

I looked at all the names. I didn't know one horse from another, but one name caught my eye. It was "Spectacular Bid." That sounded good, so I placed my bet. I gave it to the man. I put my mom and dad's name and address on it, laid down two hundred dollars and then told the old man to place my bet. He shook his head and said, "You got it, sonny." Then I got on the road. My car was acting like it was on a Sunday cruise. I finally reached a rest stop. I grabbed the letter so fast and held it. I wasn't sure if I could open it. It smelled like Lisa. I opened it. I could see her when I saw the letters. It said, "SL, you will be protected this whole trip. Everyone in the network knows about you. No one had ever done what you've done. Most drivers either steal the car or take the money. You were the mark. But now you've passed our test. Everyone needed to know if someone could do the job of driving our cars. I told everyone last winter about you. I knew when I saw you that you were the one. The real problem began when I started to love you. I couldn't do the job anymore. All I know is I love you. I will wait until I see you again. I'm yours. Please come back to me. Love, Lisa."

I dropped my head on the steering wheel. I wanted to cry, but I didn't. I didn't want to be a mark. I did what I did because of Lisa. The chance of being with her was the only thing I cared about. I didn't know of a network. But the more I thought about it, the more I liked it. I began to think about the trip down there. Lisa always went in and paid. We always stopped at certain stops. It looked like she knew them. This network was widespread. I didn't realize I was in love with the daughter of the head of the network. Damn, funny how things work out. I knew I needed to get back. I started her up and headed west. I had to get home. I knew of only one thing, and that was to get home. I hit St. Louis at about 3:30 in the afternoon. I figured the final stop would be after I went through St. Louis.

Surely the next stop they won't know about me and my trip back.

I rolled into a little town off of I-70 called Mineola. I let the car idle into the station. The car felt good and strong. I was ready to stop and take a break. I stopped and turned off the car. An older man walked out from the garage part of the station. I could hear the slight sound of a radio and a Hank Williams song; "Let's Turn Back the Years" was playing. I walked in, and a cowbell rang at the top of the door. I knew that sound, and I was anxious to see everyone back home. The man said, "That's a nice car." We both looked into each other's eyes.

"Yep."

"Fill her up, young man. It's been taken care of."

I couldn't believe it, but I should have by now. The network truly was spread out in all directions.

"Sir, do you build cars?"

"I've been building cars since the fifties. That's the only thing I'm good at."

"Has this network been around that long?"

"Longer than me. It goes all the way back to the prohibition days. They'd have to run liquor and needed cars that would outrun the cops. There's roads and stops from the east coast to the south, and to the north. It's a well-kept secret. That's a secret you'll die for. James and his family go way back to almost the beginning of the network."

"Damn! Well, thanks, mister. I'll maybe see you again."

"Oh, you'll see me."

He tipped his hat and smiled and laughed really loudly. I got in the car and turned the key. *Whopp, whopp, whopp.* She fired up, taking all the air in around us. I eased on back to the road. The road was a small version of Hampton, Tennessee, down through some hills and over a creek. Eventually, I was led back to I-70. I was thinking about the network, and I thought when I see Lisa again, I'd like to know how it all began. I was only about thirty minutes from Jesse and the trailer. I was nervous on the inside, but I was relaxed on the outside. I wondered who would be there waiting.

Chapter 53

I pulled into the trailer park. The car was idling, but a dust cloud was circling all around me. I looked over at Hilltop Liquor and then looked down at the trailer house. It was about 5:30 in the afternoon. I saw cars, the white Charger, and Dunny's truck. Man, it felt good to be home. I was excited to see Dunny. I eased the car down to the trailer and let it idle before I turned it off. It sounded good. The car knew it was home. While I was letting it idle, Dunny came out, lit a cigarette, and walked toward me. I shut the car off. All the air around me relaxed, and the dust cloud drifted off.

Dunny said, "I'm going to kill you," then he grabbed me, and we hugged and laughed. He said, "You son of a bitch, where have you been? Larry and Junior and even Tee have been asking about you. Then I had to lie to your mom and say you've been with me. Damn, I ought to kick your ass."

I stood there and took my tongue lashing. I said, "Hold on, I'll tell you what I can. But before anything else, I got to get rid of this money." I showed him a fat envelope of cash. His eyes lit up like he saw a giant birthday cake. Jesse came out and yelled "Hey" really loud and laughed really hard.

He said, "Damn boy, what took you so long?" Then he laughed and came toward me.

Dunny said, "Jesse has told me a little bit but not all. After you didn't call me, I got worried and just came back here. All they would tell me was you left with Lisa. Where did you all go?"

"I'll tell you later."

Jesse and I met at about the edge of his yard. He grabbed me and gave me a big bear hug. He was proud of me, I could tell. He said, "Damn it, boy, you did it." And then he hugged me again and again. I gave him the envelope of cash. He yelled, "Hey, everybody, let's drink." I just realized I hadn't drunk or smoked pot since I left. I never really even missed it. My mind was so caught up with the mission and being with Lisa that I didn't need it. Jesse said, "Come on up to the porch." I was ready for a drink. Dunny and I went toward the porch, and the door came open. It was DW. He was smiling but looking past me. I could tell he was looking for Lisa. He got a confused look on his face then said, "Hey, man, you did it. Where's Lisa?"

I quickly said, "She got really sick toward the end of our trip, so I had to take her to her house. They took her to the doctor, and I left before they got back." He acted like he believed me. That was my first bluff in the poker game of real life we were playing. I'm sure he got right on the phone and called James. So Jesse came out with some moonshine and poured a few shots. We sat around and smoked and drank. Jesse laughed a lot. He'd say, "Man, wait until I see Uncle Charlie."

The funny thing is, Uncle Charlie knew just about every step that I had made. The network was telling him every time I stopped. I didn't know, but the stops were more like checkpoints. The network had a line of communication. DW got up from the porch, went in and got on the phone. He was calling some veterinarian in Auxvasse. I really couldn't hear much about the conversation. But I did hear something about Quaaludes. Jesse was waiting for Uncle Charlie to come over.

Jesse said, "How did the car act?"

"Ah man, it was the baddest car on the road. Everyone looked at us. It purred like a cat."

He smiled. "Tell that to Uncle Charlie. He loves to hear about the engine."

I felt lucky to know Jesse and Uncle Charlie. I still could not get my head around the idea that what I did was illegal. Quite the opposite, I felt lucky to have met these guys; well, everyone but DW. Jesse looked at the brown car and said, "That's a good-looking car." I stopped everything I was doing and looked right at him. He smiled because he knew what those words meant. It was code for "It's a network car." I said, "Yep."

He said, "James, said that's not for sale. He said Charlie was to store it for you. Then when you go back to bring it back to him." I acted like I didn't know any of that information.

"Oh, I'm going back?"

Jesse said, "You know you're going back." He busted out laughing. Dunny was lost to most of our conversation. DW came out and said, "I got to go to Auxvasse." He got in his car and left. He seemed really agitated over something. Dunny and I would soon find out why.

It was getting late, and I was buzzed. Dunny said, "Hey, Jesse, we got to go. My dad's been really sick."

Jesse said, "Hey, man, I'll see you boys later."

One thing I noticed was Missy wasn't around anywhere. Usually, she was right by Jesse at all times. Dunny and I got to the truck. We played some good music by Black Foot, "I got a line in you." I was relaxed and feeling no pain. I told Dunny I had to stay with him so we could talk.

He said, "You're going to call your mom."

"Oh yeah; I better do that."

Dunny looked over at me and said, "Damn, boy, what have you been doing? I can't imagine what you've been up to."

"I'll tell you later, and I'm not sure you'll believe me."

Chapter 54

We got to Dunny's house, and I went inside. Junior was sitting at the table with his head down. I said, "Hey, Junior." He looked up and said, "Well, if it ain't my favorite shithead." He managed to smile.

"How's it going?"

"I feel like shit." He put his head back down and smoked his cigarette.

Dunny said, "Man, call your mom."

I called my mom and told her I was going to stay one more night at Dunny's, but I'd be home the next day.

She said, "You need to come home sometimes. I'm not sure what you're out doing half the time."

I assured her I was with Dunny just hanging out. Dunny had made soup the night before. We all sat at the table and ate soup. Junior would look at me and shake his head. Dunny told Junior we were going out for a little while. Junior shook his head. I thought we were staying at his house, but I could tell Dunny needed to hear my story. We got in the truck and decided we would take a ride down Dark Hollow. I wanted to see anything that resembled Hampton, Tennessee. It was around nine o'clock at night so the road would be dark. But the headlights from the truck lit up the hills and the creek. I began to tell Dunny of my mission, which really was an adventure. I didn't tell him about the network. I only told him about the badass car and, of course, I talked about Lisa. I had tried so hard to memorize every minute we had together, even though it was only twenty-four hours or so. I told him the car was the most awesome machine ever.

He said, "Man, how lucky are you?"

I loved Lisa, but when you put Lisa in that car, well, there is no way that a boy should have lived from that experience. Dunny said, "Come on, tell me more. What about the girl?"

"Well, the only way I can describe her to you is this way. You know how when you hear a badass song for the first time? Then that's all you think of. You hear the song in your head. You sing it. You hum it all day long. You have that song in your head. Well, that's Lisa. She's in my head. I can't imagine what heaven would be like without her in it. She's the most perfect person on this planet. I see her in everything I do. I see her in every song I hear. I know now what it means to become one. When pure love makes love, it becomes one. I could feel her heart beating with mine. It was the best feeling I've ever had in my life. Words can't explain the feeling. I thought It would be this high-five, 'brag to your buddy' type of thing, but it's not. It's the most private moment two people have with each other. You never want it to end, and you can never get enough of it. I think I'm going to die without her."

Dunny said, "Damn," then he was silent. We drove for a little while with no words. The night was good. Dunny and I always had good nights together. A best friend, if you have one, is closer than family. I'd die for Dunny; he'd die for me. We drove on; we smoked some pot, and we laughed and talked about our times at the clay pit.

"Man, I thought you were dead. You never called. I finally went to Jesse's trailer. I told them I needed to know where you went. They said you would be back in a day, but I didn't believe them. I hate that damn DW. He's no good. I told them I was coming back the next day and waiting for you. If you didn't turn up then, I was going to the police. That didn't seem to bother Jesse, but DW got really weird acting. He said if I even thought about the law, he'd make me disappear. I looked him straight in the eye and said bring it on. I was mad as hell and really worried."

"Dunny, they wouldn't even let me change my damn clothes. They said I had to go that minute. I'm sorry because you're my best friend. But I just thought about the girl and the money. I didn't really know what was going to happen. But, man, it was worth everything. I love that girl. I'd just as soon die right now than to think I won't ever see her again."

Dunny shook his head. "Damn, that must be good stuff."

"How the hell am I supposed to know it was good or not? It was my first time. But what I think I do know is I just want to be with her for the rest of my life."

"Damn, boy."

We turned around and went back through the dark hollow. I told Dunny about the mountains and the waterfall and the tree house. I told him about the mist that was at the top of the trees, and about their house and her family, her brother and little sisters. I told him how they prayed and believed in God. Dunny was listening to every word like he was trying to memorize everything I was saying. We decided it was late, and we should go home. I told Dunny I needed to sleep and that I was used to a couch. We just laughed.

Chapter 55

I woke up on Dunny's couch. Junior was looking at me. Dunny said, "Come on, it's a school day."

"Shit, I ain't going to school no more. I'm done."

"Man, there's only two weeks left until summer break."

"I don't care. I got a job already."

"Fine, stay here. I'm going to school."

He got in the truck and left. I stayed on the couch until noon. I was crashing badly. The whole week's experience had caught up with me. Finally, I got up and went to the kitchen table with Junior. He laughed at me. I shook my head and said, "Damn."

He laughed and said, "What's wrong? Too much to drink?"

"Something like that. No, really I had a Germany experience."

That got his attention.

"I decided I wasn't going to let love pass me by. I decided I was going to take the chance you didn't."

He put his head down.

"I saw how it hurt you. Actually, I see how it hurts you even now. Man, I don't want that to happen to me. I met this girl a year ago, and she's my heaven, my dream come true. We slept together. Now, I'm haunted by that night. I see it repeat in my mind. The events, everything. It won't get out of my head."

"Boy, that's no ghost. That's love. Love is a spirit just as much as hate or anything else. But love comes from God, from heaven. True love comes from heaven. Don't let anyone tell you differently. I saw true love. I felt it in Germany. The Germans were killing Jews, and I saw a Jewish girl. She looked evil in the eyes and overcame. I'm sure they killed her. I should have taken her and saved her, but I'm sure they killed her. I didn't have the balls to die for her. I loved her so much."

He put his head down. I knew what had haunted him. He should have died with her. I don't know how he met her. I don't know if he made love to her. I'd say he had to have, but I know that he lived and she probably died, and that guilt was eating him alive. I told him I was not going to let Lisa die. I'd die first. No way that I'd stand by and let her die. We both sat in silence, thinking about our lives.

Dunny came home from school, and he took me home. I hated being home. I loved my family, but I hated being home. Nothing was going on at home. Everything was going on in the streets. The nightlife was my life. The streets were my home. I had to be out at night. Dunny called me up to come and get me. My mom said, "Do you know anything about this check for three hundred dollars and a reservation for a motel in Louisville, Kentucky?" That was because I chose the winner of the Derby. I got a room reserved in our name for life.

"What?"

"Did you all bet on the Derby or something?"

"No."

"I think this must be a mistake. I'll call them."

"No, it ain't no mistake. I'll call them."

"How do you know about the Kentucky Derby?"

"It's a long story. I'm going to stay with Dunny."

She shook her head and said, "I hope you know what you're doing."

"I know, Mom." I heard the truck pull up and said, "Mom, I got to go" and ran outside. My mom did only what she could do when a boy has to run. She prayed that God would get me through it. Only a prayer to God could help. Sometimes, a prayer to God is all a parent has. Dunny was in the truck waiting on me. He had a cigarette in his mouth. I jumped in the truck and said, "What's up?"

"I got some bad news to tell you."

I wasn't sure what he was going to say. "Jesse, they say someone has shot and killed him." My heart stopped. I wasn't really sure how to feel. I wasn't sure if it was even true.

Dunny said, "Last night after we left, I guess Jesse went out to find Missy. Well, he found her all right. She was seeing someone else. I think it was that guy from Auxvasse, but I ain't sure. I think it was the guy in the Ford who you pulled the guts out of, plus, I think it was the same guy who was shining his headlights at us when we were at the clay pit with those girls. Either way, she was seeing someone. I guess Jesse went after them at some house across town. I figured we would drive by and see the house."

We drove to the house on the edge of the city limits. I could see several cop cars parked in the street. The red flashing lights bounced off the trees, the houses, the cars, and many people that had gathered. Dunny tried to get close, but the road was blocked off, so he pulled over and we sat in the truck. I began to wonder who the guy was. I first thought DW must have done it. But they were such good friends; I couldn't believe that was a possibility. Every so often someone would walk by us, and we'd ask, "What happened?" They'd say that someone was killed while breaking into the house. My mind raced back and forth. I thought of how big Jesse was and what it'd take to kill him. I could picture him the first time we met him. He was a giant. He looked like the leader of Hells Angels. I knew he wasn't scared of anything, so I think that may have played into his death.

I told Dunny, "Come on, let's go to Jesse's trailer. Maybe we can find out something there."

Dunny started up the truck, and we went through town. A lot of cars were out and about. There was a buzz in the air. We saw Larry parked in the Hardee's parking lot. Dunny pulled beside Larry's car. He was smoking a cigarette.

Larry said, "Hey, what's up?"

Dunny said, "Did you hear about Jesse?"

"Yep, I've caught bits of the news. I've been listening to the scanner."

"What have you heard?"

"All I heard so far was Jesse found out Missy was meeting some dude on the side. I guess the guy is from Auxvasse. I'm not sure who the guy is, though. I guess it had been going on from last year. It's just that they've been gone until last week. So I figured she must have tried to meet up with the dude as soon as they got back here. I know Jesse was crazy jealous. I heard he followed her yesterday to a house in Fulton."

I remembered Missy wasn't with Jesse when I got to their trailer. I guess she was with the dude even then. Larry continued, "Well, later on, last night, I guess Jesse came to the house they were in and kicked the door down. He went into a rage and chased after the guy. I guess the guy had a gun. It was a .22. He shot Jesse right in the heart; killed him on the spot. Missy went into a nervous breakdown. She saw the whole thing. Now, they say some big and important people will be coming to town. That dude who killed him was afraid for his life. So he went out of town and then he killed himself, shot himself in the head. They found him in a big four-wheel drive truck on a gravel road outside of Auxvasse."

I said, "What kind of truck?"

Larry said, "I heard it was a light blue Ford. I've seen him around town before, I think." I wondered could that really have been the same guy at the clay pit that night Jesse ran someone off from us? It's funny how so many events tie themselves together, how one thing leads to another until you find yourself at a crossroad with the devil trying to make a deal. I guess the devil won this time. My mind was flooded with memories of Jesse. When it was said and done, he was my friend. *How could he make it through the jungles of Vietnam and then die here in a rundown house, shot down not by an enemy sniper, but a hippie?* I guess when the devil calls in for the debt to be paid, our time is up. I thought about Lisa; I just wished I was with her, hanging out in the mountains of Hampton, Tennessee, catching lightning bugs with her sisters. I was really feeling tired of the nightlife. It is fun to party and listen to music with Dunny and try to chase girls, but there is an evil side to the nightlife. I was only seventeen, but I had seen stabbings, fights, stealing, and now the murder of a friend.

I said, "Dunny, let's go to Jesse's trailer." Larry had pretty much quit talking; in fact, that's the most I've ever heard him say at one time. Dunny started the truck, and we headed toward the Hilltop Liquor trailer park. I figured I would start by going in to see Uncle Charlie, but I was a minor, so I had to be careful when hanging around a liquor store. When we got close to the trailer park, I could see a lot of cars coming and going. The place was full of cars I hadn't seen before. But one car was missing; it was the white Charger. I wondered who would get the white Charger. I hoped that DW wouldn't get it. We tried to get to the trailer, but there was no way. Too many people were gathering at the trailer. I said, "Dunny, let's just go on to the clay pit."

"Yeah, I'd say we better stay away from here."

I just wanted to relax, and the clay pit was the only place I could think of. Dunny and I got to the pit and parked. We turned on the radio and got out to sit on the tailgate. We talked about Jesse and how much he'd be missed. We saw the headlights of a car or truck coming toward us. It was taking its time. It got up to us and stopped. It was Sammie and her girlfriend. They were crying. They had only barely met Jesse, but they liked him. I guess when I was gone, they had partied with Jesse trying to find me. Jesse never would tell them where I went. The girls got out and stood by us. They wanted to know what had happened.

The girl with Sammie said, "That was the guy who wouldn't leave us alone last weekend."

I said, "I was wondering if that was him."

Sammie smiled at me; she was very pretty. She said, "Where were you last weekend? We looked all over for you."

"Yeah, I had to go out of town for a few days."

She looked at me, confused. She didn't say anything much after that. I think she may have figured something was up with me. I liked her, a lot. I loved Lisa, though. Guys act all tough and stuff around their friends, but I realized now when true love hits you, you'll go down for the ten count. There's not a guy in the world who will admit that they are whipped by true love, but every guy knows the truth. True love will lead a guy around like a bridle on a horse. We told the girls all that we knew. They decided they should go. I could have had Sammie stay, but I couldn't do that. That was the kind of guy DW was with women; I had a girl now. They left, and we decided we should go ourselves.

Chapter 56

The following days were crazy around town. The motels were all full. It looked like a mob boss had died. There were a lot of out of town plates. My interest picked up when I saw a plate from Tennessee. I never could catch anyone in the car, but it was a black Cadillac. We kept looking and driving by the motel where it was parked. Finally, I saw it was James. I had Dunny drive up to him. I jumped out, "Hey, James!" He stopped and looked to see it was me. He lit up and grabbed me. "Hey, man," he said in a really excited way.

I said, "So that's a bad deal with Jesse."

He dropped his head and said, "I never expected to be burying Jesse. He was the last person I thought would die. He went through so much bad stuff in Vietnam; I thought he was untouchable."

"Yeah, now what?"

He knew I was talking about DW. "Listen, come by here in the morning before the funeral. I'm going back after the service."

"How's Lisa?"

"Ah, man, she's lost without you. That girl is floating on air since you two met. I've never seen her happier. You have to come back as soon as you can."

"I'd be there today. I'm going to work out something; then I'm going to come back."

"I know you are. That's what I need to talk to you about. I'll see you then." Then he bear-hugged me. I jumped back into the truck and Dunny said, "Who was that?" I told him that was Lisa's brother.

He was confused. I said, "I'll tell you some more about why I was gone, but not until he leaves." Dunny shook his head. We decided to go see Uncle Charlie. While on our way, I thought about the real-life poker game I was in. So now one of the players was out of the game, and the cards he held went with him. That left DW, Lisa and me. The time to place our bets was near. The time to face the prowling lion had come.

But on the way to Uncle Charlie's, we decided to drive by the house where Jesse was killed. It had police tape all around it. A big X was on the door and said "Don't enter." We drove by it really slowly. It was hard to look at. I could only imagine the terror that went on in that house. We went on by the house and headed toward the Hilltop Liquor store. We pulled in, and I did see the white Charger, but it was in Uncle Charlie's garage. Dunny and I both got out and went inside. I opened the door slowly so as not to bang the door against the cowbell. Uncle Charlie came out from the back room as he always did. I looked straight at him. I hadn't seen him since I had been back. He managed to smile at me.

"Hey, Charlie, how's it going?"

"Ah, not too good, but I'll get over it."

"Damn, that's messed up. What happened? Is it true how it all happened?"

"What did you hear?" I told him what we had heard.

"Yep, that's all about right, except one thing. The boy that shot him didn't commit suicide in his truck. Some guys came here that night from Chicago and chased that boy down because he was with the police for a while. They had to wait for him. Then they caught up with him and put one in his head. He was in his truck, though." Dunny was silent. I'm not sure Dunny knew what all Jesse and Charlie were tied up in. Dunny looked at me, and he looked like he had seen a ghost.

I said, "Well, I suppose the guy had it coming to him. *The devil must have collected on two debts that night.* I was caught off guard by his comment myself. I said, "The funeral is tomorrow at one o'clock, right?"

"Yep, I'm going to drive the Charger right behind him. He will be buried in the Veteran's Memorial Garden."

"Dunny and I will be in line with you. Is anyone at his trailer?"

"Nope. I locked it up. I don't know where DW is or Missy. I'm sure they are with friends. He did leave this envelope for you." It was thick and had a small note with it. I put it in my back pocket to read later on. Dunny stared at the envelope. I said, "Charlie, you need anything from me?"

He said, "Nope, just read the note, then come see me after the funeral."

Dunny and I left. We got in the truck, and Dunny said, "Boy, you're mixed up in all this, ain't you?"

"I'll tell you what I can. Let's go on down to the clay pit and I'll tell you."

Dunny put it in gear and headed out toward the pit. He put on some Rolling Stones, "Symphony for the Devil" and then looked right at me. I said, "I know, but it ain't like that." We parked at the top and looked down to see if it was clear to go to the water. Dunny eased the truck down to the water's edge to our favorite spot. We parked, and got out. Dunny had some pot to smoke. We lit it up and passed it back and forth. We made small talk, but Dunny said, "Okay, so let's have it." I told Dunny of the car delivery, of Jesse and Charlie paying me five hundred dollars. He about died when I told him of the five hundred dollars. That may as well have been five thousand dollars for that was a lot of money. I told him about Lisa and the network. He was in disbelief.

He said, "Okay, if all that's true, what's in that letter?"

"Okay, let's see." I opened it, and it was five hundred dollars in fifty-dollar bills. It had a note that said, "Hey, man, you're a real badass. I knew when I saw you I liked you. There's more of this when you're ready. Thanks, Jesse."

Dunny was silent. Dunny said, "So you can get five hundred dollars a delivery?" I didn't want him to think it was quite that easy.

"Yeah, but it's intense as hell. You're on the edge the whole time, worrying about being pulled over by the cops."

Dunny put his head down in deep thought.

"Damn, boy, I'm not sure what to think. You're living a crazy life. I almost don't believe the shit you do. I don't know why you have to live on the edge so bad."

"I ain't sure myself. I think most of it comes from wanting to be with girls. I love my family, my friends, and I even love to party, but once Lisa touched me, once I saw her for the first time, it's like a magnet pulling me to her. She even left last winter, and all I thought about was her. Everywhere we would go, I'd look for her—in the store, at the gas station, everywhere. I know that seems crazy, but I didn't sit out one day and plan all this to happen. Life happens. I know now life just happens. When you find someone like that, are you just supposed to ignore it? Fight off your obvious feelings? It could be the one chance for that once-in-a-lifetime person. Everyone says I'm too young to see the future, that this love is wrong because we are so young. So I know what, why don't I just let this feeling pass so I can live the rest of my life wondering why I let it pass? So I can find myself sitting at a kitchen table trying to blow my head off or maybe get shot in a jealous rage? Maybe I am young, but trust me, I can see the future. I can see it both ways. The way I see it is I'm going to choose the future with her. I'll have to see how that plays out because, without her, I'm already seeing how that's playing out."

Dunny remained silent. Then he said, "Damn, why didn't you just say so?" We busted out laughing. The rest of the night, we laughed and enjoyed our friendship. We listened to a Son House song called "Preachin' Blues."

We talked more about our lives. I said, "You know what I can't figure out is how come it seems like you are always in a fight, you find someone you really like, but then you have to fight off those feelings. You're either too young or too old or too something. Junior told me one night that when you're in war, you're most alive when you're close to dying. When the next moment may be your last. But ever since he came back from the war, he wished he was dead. Now, he spends every day fighting off killing himself. I just don't know what I'm supposed to make of this life so far. I got this big giant hole in me when I'm away from her. Everyone says, "Well, that's not love, you're too young to know. Know what? I can tell you what I do

210

know: it sure ain't a feeling of hate. So if it ain't love, then what is it? Loving her is the one thing I don't have to fight. I fight everybody else telling me it ain't love. Funny thing about all this stuff is she loves me back as much as I love her."

Dunny said, "Man, I hope I find what you have found! I can really see true love in your two." We laughed more and thought on the subject of love. But we came to the conclusion that really to search and find someone you can't live without was what everyone is searching for whether they accept it or not. The night got late, so we picked up and went home. The funeral was in the morning.

Chapter 57

I woke up in a strange place. It was my own bed. I had to make sure I wasn't dreaming. In fact, my mom would tease me that a stranger was in my room the night before. My mom said, "I still don't understand why I kept getting notices from these motels in Louisville, Kentucky. They all say I hope to see you next year at the Derby." I would laugh to myself. I'd say, "Ah, Mom, they just got your name from all those sweepstakes things you send off for."

She shook her head and said, "I guess so."

I was really looking forward to the day that I could introduce her to Lisa. I said, "Mom, I got to go to a funeral today." She looked really confused.

"I don't know anybody who died. Whose funeral?"

"It's a guy I work for at the body shop. I actually worked for him and his uncle. I'd sweep their garage." She was trying to get ready for work and was putting on makeup.

"Oh, I didn't know you did that too. I'm not really sure what you have to wear."

"Ah, I will figure something out."

She and my sister left, and my dad was also gone. I dug through my clothes. I found a black t-shirt and some black jeans. I found a pair of black shoes. I called Dunny to come to get me, but I told him I needed to go back to the motel where James was staying. Dunny came and got me. He wanted to ask more questions but didn't. It was about nine o'clock in the morning. Dunny looked good. He was dressed in black. He had washed the truck. He dropped me off at the motel. I said, "Can you come back in about an hour?"

He said, "Yeah, but the last time you said that you disappeared." We laughed, and I assured him I'd be right there. I walked up to the room and banged on the door. It was a clear, crisp, spring morning. The birds were carrying on and singing and playing around. I looked over in a tree and saw a bright red cardinal. He was as red as I had ever seen. I remember my grandmother telling me the male bird was the most colorful because that's how he attracted his mate. *What do humans do?* I guess we fight each other for a mate. If not, I wouldn't be going to this funeral today. James opened his door. He grabbed me and pulled me in with a giant bear hug. That was another question I had. I had only met this man two or three times, yet, I'm as much family to him as his own brothers. That is more of a sign of true love. Someone accepts me that easily only on the words of his sister. He was dressed in black. He had on his war medals that he got in Vietnam. He said, "Man, come in and sit down. I got to get right to it with you. I know Jesse's death throws a wrench in everything, but we can't carry on with our past. DW's got to go away, but I don't think he will without a fight. He's my war buddy, but he's messed up. I've had to shoot dogs I loved, but when they got messed up and mean, I couldn't have them around my family or me. Now you, on the other hand, you're my family. You're as much a part of us as our own flesh and blood. I'm going to bring you into the business. When you get back to Hampton, I'll let you in. Just remember, you're part of us and the network."

I sat and listened, then said, "I ain't sure what you mean exactly, but I think I do. But mostly, I got to get back to her. My sole mission now is to get back to Lisa."

"Well, that's easy. She's at home and she ain't going nowhere. DW is going to get out of hand without Jesse around. I say, keep your eye on him."

Here we go again. I got to fight something. Now, I'd have to fight DW. I heard Dunny pull up.

James said, "Your ride is here. I'll be in touch. This is our address. Write me, write Lisa. We'll write back. You can even call me collect if you want. And remember, that's a good-looking car." Then he laughed and hugged me again. I walked out of the room. I was floored by all the stuff that was happening to me. I just knew the one thing in all this mess was my love for Lisa. That's mushy and sappy, but it was true.

Dunny was smoking a cigarette. He said, "What's up now?"

I said, "You're driving, but I think we got to go see Uncle Charlie really quickly now."

Dunny shook his head but didn't say anything. Then Dunny said, "We need to leave Charlie alone." He said to look him up that night after the funeral.

"Yeah, you're right. I guess we can just hit the gravel until it's time."

"Yeah, you need to tell me more. I don't think you're telling me everything." We rode to Dark Hollow gravel road. Dunny said, "Okay, tell me more."

"Dunny, they think I need to go to work with them. I want to work with them. I just ain't sure how to go about it."

"What about your life here? Your friends and family?"

"Well, I ain't dying, I'm just moving. You can come and visit."

"Well, I hope so, but we got time to worry about that later, right?"

"Oh yeah, I got to deal with DW sometime."

We stewed and thought of plans, but none sounded too good. Dunny said, "We better go. It's time."

We got to the funeral home an hour before it was to start. The line was all the way out in the street. It was full of gangsters and army buddies, black Cadillac's everywhere you would turn and look.

Dunny said, "Shit, would you look at this?" Most of the people we didn't know. Some we did. We saw Larry with Debbie and Kathy. I saw James, and he waved. He was with some war buddies. I saw a lot of hippies and dudes with long hair and long beards. I saw the hearse and the white Charger was parked behind it. I was just looking around when I heard a nice sound, a sound I would never forget. It was my blue SS Chevelle. It was at the stoplight. There's no mistaken it was my car. It had North Carolina plates on it. It sounded good. I wanted to see who got it. I watched it idle by, and everyone watched it. I knew that feeling. It parked up the street. A nice-looking, well-dressed old man got out of it. He had a nice looking, very well-dressed old woman with him. They both had gray hair.

Well, the car is in good hands.

The old couple came up to the line and stood a little behind us. I kept looking at them. They were friendly looking. Finally, I walked back and said, "That's a nice car." The women didn't say anything. She did smile. But the man stopped smiling, and he looked right into my eyes and said, "Yep. I just got her last week. The people that brought her to me are the best." He smiled. I shook his hand; we both knew. He said after I was walking away, "That car is a pure thoroughbred champion. The person who had it before me knew how to treat a car."

I smiled and nodded. I got back in line. We moved up slowly until finally, we got to the casket. Jesse was laid out in blue jeans and a black leather jacket and a white t-shirt. His medals were pinned on the jacket. They cut his beard shorter. I'm not sure why. He still looked big, but not as big lying down. He was pale. I missed his big, loud laugh. I never thought Dunny and I would become such good friends with him, considering how we started off. The cops never looked into this death much. The rumor was the cops were glad he was dead and they were secretly watching who was attending the funeral. I thought that sounded like the cops. I finally could see Missy at the front of the place. She was crying. I'm not sure why; she was seeing other dudes. I really couldn't figure out what she saw in the scroungy dudes. I don't think Jesse was a Christian guy. Nevertheless, a preacher did speak. I'd heard the same words from other preachers, how our time on earth is temporary, but time with God is eternal. I think that goes without saying, but I guess you need to say that sort of thing like that at a funeral. The preacher talked about faith in God and trying to live according to his will and testament. *Someday, I should get baptized; you never know when your number will be called. Is that how it goes; somehow, there's this big wheel they spin in heaven, and when it stops spinning on that person, then you're done? Is there any reason to how people die?* I figured I better keep on living then. The preacher ended up with a prayer and asked for anyone to come forward and say something. I wondered why at funerals people get up and say nice things to a dead person? Shouldn't you have said those nice things to the person while they were alive? Several people stood up and told stores. Mostly, his war buddies talked.

I knew Jesse was a badass, but he was good to me. We all stood and walked out shaking hands with people we knew. Dunny and I got in the truck. Dunny said, "I thought they'd never shut up. I need a cigarette." I saw James; he nodded to me that he was going to leave. He didn't want DW to know that I knew him. DW was there, but it looked like he was only there in his body. I think his mind was still in Vietnam. He hung around Missy and was shaking people's hands. He had another woman with him. I'd never seen her before. I would say it was his wife. From the truck, we watched DW and the people we knew. Dunny said, "I'm staying in the truck until they leave." Finally, we left for the graveyard. The line of cars was a mile long. Cops had to stop traffic. I bet they hated that. They buried Jesse. I thought that's what we are reduced to, we live our life, they say some nice things, drive you through town, then say some more nice things, and then bury you. Then, pretty quickly after that, you're forgotten. So how much you love someone in all your time on this earth, then it is up to you. Because, when you're dead, the love you have experienced is dead too. I have to admit; I was ready to get on with something more uplifting. I didn't go see Charlie that night. I waited for a few days.

Chapter 58

A few days had passed. I decided it was time to go see Uncle Charlie. I borrowed my dad's truck and went to see him. I wasn't sure how he'd be or what he wanted to talk to me about, but I thought it was time to find out. I went through the front door even though the sign said "Closed." He never locked it during the day. The cowbell rang. He came to the front. He looked good. I think he knew we all lived on the edge of life. He said, "Hey, boy."

"Hey how's it going?"

"Ah, just going through Jesse's stuff down at the trailer. Well, more like junk than stuff." He laughed. It sounded good to hear people laugh. It seems that laughter was always good medicine. I went back in the kitchen with him. He poured me a shot of apple crisp. The country music station was playing a Johnny Cash song, "There Ain't No Good Chain Gang," on his radio. We sat down, and I slammed it back. Still, the fire went all the way to my toes. I guess it wasn't as funny now. He smiled, but that was all.

I said, "You still taking care of that chocolate SS?"

"Oh yeah. That's a nice car." I'll never get those words out of my head. I looked at him, and we both laughed. The real truth of the fact was "it was a nice, really nice car."

He said, "That's what we need to talk about. I'm not so old that I'm giving up on life, but I want you to learn Jesse's part in this, and we can keep on making money. Your cut will be more than five hundred dollars, though. But when I'm done, I want you to have all of my part in this as well."

"I ain't sure what I can do right now. I ain't but seventeen. But I'm in. I just got a lot of things to get settled."

"Listen, now 95 percent of the network is legal. There are still a few guys that actually steal stuff for the cars. But now we are as about as legal as any business. The problem is, we deal in cash and the government hates cash. They can't tax what they don't see. So you could have ten thousand dollars in cash and not be able to spend it. That's why you need a business to hide your money in." I was listening, but it was a little too deep for me. I said, "I don't have a business that I know of."

He laughed really loudly and said, "I know. James and I are going to show you."

"Well, as long as you and James show me, but I've got to get back to my girl."

"You will. That's all up to you. You're going to have to tell your parents and friends something. And it needs to be the truth about a real business and not the network."

He stopped and poured us another shot. We slammed them at the same time. He said, "Come here back in the garage. I'm going to show you something." He lifted the hood of my car and painted in small letters was VFN in cursive lettering. That stands for "Valley Forge Network." These are the network points of origin. This car started out in Valley Forge, Tennessee. This is James's network; he deals in Chevelle only. Each network deals in their own specialty. Come here." He popped the hood to the white Charger. It had "CCN" that stood for Callaway County Network. This is mine and Jesse's network."

"But you had me take a Chevelle to Tennessee."

"The network is all over the US, and we all store or keep each other's cars for each other from time to time. We just only build the cars we specialize in. You can only be really good at one thing in this life. Find that out as early as you can."

My head was full of deep stuff. I really was just wanting to be a kid again. I wasn't sure I was ready for all this knowledge.

"Charlie, before I can do anything, I got to get rid of DW."

"Yeah, I know. He's bad news. See, he likes to sell drugs and that's going to get you caught. Drug money is a really hard business. Too many will rat you out when they get caught. Then the cops will be watching you. We don't want anyone to know we exist. The network is a ghost. There're only fifteen network points of origin. But there's a hundred garages and gas stations that assist for a cut. Way back in the twenties, this was started, and at the top of it, only a few know who is at the top. Our biggest enemy is Detroit. Detroit wants all the cars and all the money. The Teamsters union and stuff so we stay really low key, and we don't make a lot of noise. Usually, people who buy our cars are doctors, lawyers, and big shit rich people. They just want a car, a badass car. And we provide it to them."

I wasn't sure what to say. I just said, "Okay. I'm in." I never really knew what I was going to do when I grew up anyway. "So what's next?"

"For now, go on about your usual business. You'll be here next Friday buying beer. Just act normal."

"Okay, that is easy enough. Well, I got to go for now. I'll see you then."

I got in my dad's truck and put my head down on the steering wheel. My head was buzzing. But I thought if this gets me back to Lisa, then so be it. I gathered myself and drove home. When they said to lay low, they weren't kidding. It was the end of May, and school was over, not that it really mattered to me. I didn't go anyway. Lisa and I talked through a few letters. We missed each other so bad. She said she had a big surprise for me when I came back. That just about drove me crazy wondering what it could be.

Chapter 59

Dunny called me up at the gas station I was working and said, "Hey, man, I'll pick you up. Let's go to the clay pit. There's an end of school party out there."

"Great, come and get me."

I was in a hurry for my night of work to end. At about nine o'clock, the phone rang, and I answered. The voice said, "Put your hands over your eyes and guess who." I just about died. My heart started to pound, and I got really short of breath.

"Lisa, I can't believe it's you. Man, I have missed you more than you can imagine. I relive every moment we've had over and over. Is that crazy or what? How did you get this phone number?"

"Charlie knew it. I just wanted to surprise you."

"Speaking of surprises, what is my surprise? I can't wait."

She laughed. Man, I waited so long to hear her laugh. God only knows how incredible that moment was to me.

"Okay, but then it won't be a surprise."

"I don't care."

"Well, we are inviting everyone in the whole town to our house. We're going to have a dance. And you're my date."

"You're kidding. When?"

"It's going to be at the end of the summer. So you better get your act together and get here."

"The devil himself couldn't stop me from getting there."

We laughed and told each other about our undying love. But then, we had to say goodbye. I was sad. Dunny was coming at ten o'clock to get me, so that was a good thing. All I could think of was when I could hold her again. I was in deep pain. I wasn't sure what I could do to help myself. But I did know this much; if I ever got back to her, I was not going to leave her ever again. I washed down the station bays and got ready to close. I had my back turned, and the bell rang to get someone some gas. I turned, and it was DW in a car with two girls. I got really nervous. I went up to the driver's side, and he said, "Hey, boy." He was really nice, but I knew he was a fake. He said, "Fill her up. And look what I got" and showed me a bag of Quaaludes. "You'll be needing some of these for your next party."

"I won't need that many." I washed his windshield. I looked inside the car, and I saw a briefcase that he had opened up for me to see on purpose. It had two guns inside of it. Then he said, "Wonder how Lisa has been doing?" He looked right at me.

"I don't know."

"I bet you don't know. Sometime, you and I need to have a little talk."

I got mad, but on the inside, "Yeah, I'd say we do. That's fifteen bucks on the gas."

He paid with a twenty and said, "Keep it. You look like you need it. We'll be coming back through town; we got to go to Jefferson City and see a man. I need to have a talk with him too." He smiled really broadly, and the girls laughed loudly. Then he drove off. Now, DW just played his hand, and I knew he didn't have the ace, and he knew I did. I didn't even need to bluff because I held the ace and the joker. But like so many poker games, the loser will accuse the winner of cheating, and the guns are brought out. As I went over the game in my head, I went in and locked up and waited for Dunny.

Dunny pulled up a little past ten. He was smoking a cigarette. Man, I was glad to see him. It seems at my worst times, Dunny would show up. I jumped in the truck and lit a cigarette. He had some good music on, some ZZ Top. We liked ZZ Top. A song named "Beer Drinkers and Hell Raisers." He said, "Man, you look like you saw a ghost."

"I did; it was DW. He knows about Lisa and me."

"Well, then bring it on. It's time to settle this score once and for all."

I was surprised; Dunny was usually laid back. But I could tell you one thing about best friends; you really shouldn't mess with them. I've been through a lot of stuff in only seventeen years, and a best friend is worth more than gold. We decided that if DW wanted to play, we could play too. Dunny had beer on ice, and he had the cigarettes. We were set to go to the clay pit. That was our home. No one messed with the pit. It was kind of fun to see Dunny involved in my life. I really didn't know he cared that much. We grew up together, but still, I was the one that was always helping him. We headed out to the clay pit, but we hit the gravel roads to get there. We popped some beer tops and even smoked some pot. We jammed to some good music. We put on the Eagles' "One of These Nights." We sang that song as loud as we could. It sounded so good. I thought about Lisa and all of the fun we had so far, but I just wanted "one of those nights." Dunny and I laughed and sang out loud all the way to the clay pit. We came through what we called the back way. But as we got close, we could see flashing red lights. The red flashing lights bounced off the sky, the water, the trees—the whole place was full of red flashing lights. There weren't any night people there. We stopped and turned back. We were drinking so any cop that we saw would arrest us. Dunny and I weren't sure what to do so we headed out on other gravel roads and then went back through town. We came upon Larry sitting in Hardee's parking lot. Larry was just sitting there, stoned. He had Ruby with him. We pulled beside him. Larry was smoking a cigarette.

Dunny said, "Hey, Larry."

"Hey."

"Man, what's going on at the clay pit?"

"The scanner said they found a body floating in it. But they think it was murder. They said it was believed to be a veterinarian from Auxvasse." Dunny and I looked at each other. The only doctor we knew of was the one that DW was blackmailing for drugs. If it was that same doctor, we knew who did it. There wasn't a doubt. But we didn't talk to the cops, so we figured we would wait and see.

Larry said, "Not much more to say. They act like it's a big murder investigation. They plan to bring in special state investigators. You boys know anything about this, you better run."

I said, "I only know a little and ain't none of it fact."

"I don't care. They'll be asking around."

"Damn, that's not good."

Dunny said, "Well, we better get out of here." He started the truck, and we figured it would be best if we went to his house. Damn, we were all pumped to go party at the clay pit. Now, the damn cops would be watching everyone who goes there. So we went to Dunny's. It was only about 11:00 or so. Junior was awake. We brought the cooler in and played cards with him most all night. He was happy to have us.

Chapter 60

We stayed up almost all night playing cards. We smoked a lot of cigarettes; the house stayed full of smoke. So what happens in a good game of poker is the dealer calls the game and names the joker as wild, then deals the cards. As the dealer deals, the players study their cards, but, more importantly, you study each other without giving anything away about the hand your holding. When the dealer asks if you want to throw any away and get new ones, then the real game has started. Then the bets and bluffs take on the outcome of the game. I'm sure now I was in the bet and bluff part of the game with DW. But one sure thing I had learned in my few short years of life was to slow down the moment, slow it down—so slow that it almost stops.

I woke up on the couch. Junior was staring at me. He laughed. Then he said, 'You ain't as tough as you think you are."

"Why is that?"

"Shit, you boys went down. I could have played all night."

"I know, but you got a few years on us."

Dunny got up and cooked bacon and eggs. Man, it smelled so good and tasted even better. We told Junior we had to go out for a while and find out about a murder at the clay pit.

"You boys best stay out of stuff like that."

But we couldn't; we knew who did it. We decided to go out and see what was going on. We drove out toward the clay pit. It was daylight so we figured there wouldn't be much going on. We stopped at the Hilltop liquor store first. I ran in and hit the door hard. The

224

cowbell rang hard. Charlie came around with a pissed-off look then saw it was me.

"Boy, what did I tell you about hitting that door so hard?"

"Sorry. Did you hear about the body in the clay pit?"

"Yeah, I've been hearing it on the scanner."

"Charlie you know who done it. It was DW."

"Boy, you need to steer clear of this mess."

"I know, I ain't talking to no cops, but that's that doctor DW was blackmailing."

"I know it was, but that damn DW, he's smooth. He'll have this blamed on you, me, Jesse, anyone but him. We need to stay away. I'm telling you, if you ever want to see Lisa again, you'll stay away."

That stopped me dead in my tracks. No way I was not going to see her again. The only problem was, she was with him a lot during the times they would go to the doctor. But she never really went there; he always went alone to see the doctor. But he was a snake. He'd say or do anything to save his hide. A few weeks went by, and I was really scared that the prowling lion was going to pounce. But I never saw or heard from DW. It was an unsettling kind of silence. But then one day, Dunny called me and told me that DW finally was arrested. DW was a real slithery snake. He lied all the way to jail. I was glad he was in jail. I never really had that talk he wanted to have, but still, the cops never had a whole lot. It was a weak case. So he was going to get out. When he got out, he was on the prowl, trying to get anyone to take the fall. It turns out that while in jail he tried to get one of his buddies to kill one of the guys he knew that could tie him to the doctor. I thought he would have pinned that on Lisa had she stayed. Maybe God was looking out for her. It was a scheme that only DW could hatch. He stole someone's checkbook out of their car. He then wrote a forged subscription and paid for it with the stolen checks. They had him, they thought. He decided to kill the doctor and put him in the clay pit. He got out of jail somehow. So he and his girlfriend figured to take any witness they knew of and kill0 them and float them in the Missouri River. They were trapped. Finally, DW got himself caught. He told one lie too many. He went to jail, and now he sits on death row. He's still lying to this day. I decided I needed to visit him one day. I figured we needed to have that talk. I went through all the gates to see him. I took five cards in with me. He sat down, and I picked up the phone and looked at him.

"DW, the devil always collects his debt. You went to the cross-road. Now it's time to pay. Then I held up one card at time, and I said, "This ace is Jessie, this ace is Charlie, this ace is James, this ace, well this ace is Lisa, and the joker, well, that's me. I put all five cards up to the glass."

Then I said, "You just got played by a kid. . . You lose. . ." Then I hung up. He screamed at the glass, and he hit it. I smiled at him and nodded my head. This was one time when you use all the power you have. He was so mad. The guards came and took him away. I walked out of the prison. Dunny was waiting for me. I got in and said, "It's over. It's finally over." The sun was out, and we felt so good. We headed home. All I could think about was Roster Cogburn with the reins of his horse in his mouth and saying come and get it to the bad guys.

Dunny put in AC/DC's "Highway to Hell" and we cruised. It was a good day. DW was going to hell and I was going to Tennessee. All I knew was I didn't do anything. Somehow, God worked me out of that impossible mess. But, I'd say it was for a reason I would later find out. DW hung himself with all his lies and trickery. Charlie was right. The drug scene, it's too much trouble. They say, give a criminal some rope, and he will hang himself. I knew with Jesse gone, DW would hang himself. He did.

Chapter 61

The town started to heal itself. The hard drugs slowly dried up. I'm not sure if all the hard drugs could be blamed on DW, but we knew he was to blame for a good part of them. After DW was arrested, he would start a long battle of appeals in the courts. Dunny and all of us night people went back to our routines. With the murder solved at the clay pit, we slowly went back there to hang out and party. The summer was coming to an end, and there was a rumor of another summer-ending party. Dunny and I were all pumped up about it. In the back of my mind, I was thinking of leaving. Even though I didn't really go to school much, somehow I managed to get a few credits. I went to the guidance counselor and asked him what I had to do to get a GED. He found some book I could study, and there was a test I could take. I took the test and passed. Dunny looked forward to being a senior, but I looked forward to leaving. I wanted to go be with Lisa. I never really spoke of my leaving with Dunny, but I did tell my mom and dad. I told them I had a job and a place to stay. I had met a girl who was everything any guy could ask for. My parents didn't' really have any objection. For one, I never really was home anyway, but I really think they were my age when they met, and I think somehow they understood what young teenage love was like. Also, I think they thought I was lucky to be alive. The nightlife has its share of troubles. I had seen it up close and personal. But it also had its share of fun. Dunny and I laughed more than we ever cried. We laughed hard and long. If there was one thing I learned from my teenage years, always laugh at yourself more than you laugh at others. My mind flashes are always full of memories of people in my life laughing. I even remember the sounds of their laughs. I never actually saw the preacher guy that summer. I know he went to school to be a missionary. I did listen to his words. I told myself when I got to Tennessee that I was going to get baptized. I went and visited my grandmother often the rest of that summer. I knew she'd be the one I'd miss the most. She made me a quilt. It had many circles on it. I think she called it wedding band. I still have that quilt. I don't have my grandmother. A few years later, she went to heaven. I'm saying that she was the one who saved me. She prayed for God to protect me. My grandmother was as pure as they come. I doubt she ever even drove to a crossroad, much less made a deal. I'd go and sit with Junior in his kitchen. He never really ever recovered from his "what ifs." The war was bad, but not choosing love was what killed him. He got sicker and sicker and now he's in heaven. I never actually saw Larry again. Once I left, and the times we could come back, but I never would see him anywhere.

Now, Tee, he's still around and as good as ever. He always steered clear of the bad stuff. He's got kids now. But as sad as leaving was, I knew of the one happiness that I was going to. I wasn't going to be a guy who missed out on true love. I saw that bumper sticker that said, "God is love." Well, I guess that summed it up.

Chapter 62

The day came when I was to head out. I had called Lisa and gave her all the details. She, of course, gave me a list of points where to stop. I was going to do a slingshot. It's where you drive to a specific point, and then you don't stop until you get to your destination. I got up really early that morning. I packed all my t-shirts and blue jeans, socks, and shoes. I went down the steps. My dad, mom and sister were waiting for me to come down. I never really thought I would cry, but I did. We all did. I cried really hard. I never really knew why I didn't stay home much. I just hated being at home. I never hated my family. I just hated being home. We hugged and hugged until Dunny drove up the driveway. I loaded my stuff, and my family stood on the porch. I told Dunny I needed to make some rounds to tell everyone goodbye. He took me to my grandmother's, then to see Junior and finally to see Tee. I cried at every stop except in front of Tee; I couldn't let him see me cry. Instead, we punched each other and laughed really loudly. Still, I didn't think leaving would be so hard. The idea of seeing someone for maybe the last time hit me hard. I was always good about living for the now, but I found myself hoping and looking toward the future. Finally, Dunny took me to Hilltop Liquor. He parked his truck. He didn't even remember what my car looked like. I had described it to him, but words could not do it justice. I went up to the door, and I hit it as hard as I could, and that cowbell rang as loud as ever.

Here came Charlie, who said, "Boy." Then he and I busted out and laughed really hard.

"Charlie, I can't take no shot today. I'm driving."

"I know, maybe another time."

Charlie and Dunny followed me out back to the garage. There she was. My car, my gift. Dunny said, "Damn, now that's a nice car." Charlie and I stopped and looked at Dunny. He didn't know what those words could mean. He lit a cigarette. I said, "Hey, let's take her out and go to the clay pit and back. You can drive." Dunny's eyes got wide as a baseball.

Charlie said, "Why not, it's your car!" Dunny got in her and touched the key, *whopp. . . whopp. . .*"

It was like we woke a sleeping bear. Dunny said, "Damn, this is a nice car."

I said, "Yep." He pulled her out slowly. A dust cloud circled around us, and we went to the clay pit. I had some ZZ Top in the super tuner. It was the song "Waitin' for the Bus." It sounded good. We jammed, and Dunny smiled the biggest smiled I'd ever seen. The raw power of 454 horses is something only a person can feel. No way can one describe it. The car was glad to be out of its stall. Like a thoroughbred horse, it was meant to run. We drove to the pit and stopped. We got out and talked. I told Dunny that he'd be totally taken care of. He didn't know what I was talking about. My plans were, I'd give him Uncle Charlie's network when the time came. He would be set up for life selling beer and cars. He'd be in heaven. We knew it was time to go. I had to walk over and look down at the clay pit. I knew it was always going to be here, but somehow it would be different. I looked down at our spot, and a car was there. Some teenagers had made a fire and slept in their car all night. Then I saw flashes of Dunny and me hanging out. Worrying about girls and dreaming of the day we wouldn't be virgins. I saw ghosts of the band night and parties. I saw ghosts of Jesse and the girls and even DW. I thought a hundred years from now, kids will come here to party, and Dunny and I, our ghosts, will be like the ghosts down at the Lake of the Ozarks. We will join them and laugh and drink into the night.

I saw Lisa and her smile and her and I dancing. I started to cry. I thought I was done crying.

Dunny came up to me, and we both hugged and cried really hard. I think we laughed because we were crying. Dunny said, "Come on, let's go." We turned away from the pit and got in the car. I know those spirits are there even today. Dunny hit the key, and we left. For me, that was the last time I ever went to the clay pit. A few years later, someone bought it and mounded up all of the entrances to it. You can only see it if you are trespassing on it. I've thought about asking the owner if I could just look at it one more time, but I never did ask. We got back to the Hilltop and Dunny's truck. We got out. I told Charlie I was leaving. I didn't know that would be the last time I would get to talk to Charlie. Later on that year, he got sick, but he didn't die. He just couldn't move around all that good. He would drop letters to me, but we never spoke in person again except we did talk on the telephone.

Dunny said, "Well, this is it, for now at least."

"For now. I'll call you as soon as I get there. And I want you to come and stay with me sometime."

"We'll see. I can't leave Junior alone right now."

"I know."

We hugged really hard, and I got in the car and slowly drove off. I could see Dunny standing and watching me and the car. He lit up a cigarette; so did I. I was off. I turned the radio to KSHE95 the song "It's a Long Way There" by The Little River Band came on. I cranked it, and it sounded good. I went toward Kingdom City, took a right on I-70, and I was going to Hampton, Tennessee. But this time, it wasn't a race. This time, it was for my own future and my own happiness. A lot of thoughts went through my head. I was a young teenager. I drank a lot; I smoked a lot, and I partied a lot— enjoyed many all-night adventures. I'm not sure if I'm supposed to feel bad for those things or not. I know I didn't hurt anyone and I know I had to run, like a champion thoroughbred horse; it was just in my blood to run. I still even today have a free spirit inside me. As I stopped at my spots, no one would take any money for the gas I got. Every stop was planned out. I could tell someone had already taken care of the trip; all I had to do was drive. Drive is what I did. The sun was in front of me when I started and would be sitting when I finished. Though in a way, aren't we all protected and aren't our routes planned by God?

The same way, Lisa would warn me only to stop at the planned stops; it's when I strayed from the courses that I was in the most danger. Even the planned routes we take have their obstacles, so maybe it's the stops along the way that get us in trouble. Maybe we should pay more attention the stops along the road we are on than the road itself.

Chapter 63

My mind was full of images from my short life. I relived all my life while driving. Most of the time, I would laugh out loud. Sometimes, I would cry. The emotions of this day were hypersensitive. I rolled into Hampton. It was about seven o'clock in the evening. I made the turn to take me through the town. I used my blinkers and followed the speed limit. But a cop came up on me and hit his lights. I was nervous. I wasn't really sure that I had done anything wrong. But like my mom would say to me, "If you weren't doing something wrong now, then she figured it was for something I got away with earlier." I stayed in the car, and the cop came up to me.

"Sir, can I see your license?"

I showed him my card. I worried if he ran the plates that it would be in James' name.

"Sir, what did I do wrong?"

He handed back my card then said, "That's a nice car." I wasn't sure, so I looked right at him. He had a really serious look. Then he smiled and said, "Follow me; I'll give you an escort." He then laughed as loud as Jesse would have. It turns out; he was a relative of Lisa's. I put my head down on the steering wheel, took a deep breath and mumbled "shit." The cop led me to the drive then peeled off. He tipped his hat to me as he left.

I drove up the drive, not really sure how I would act. I was ready to be home. The trip was long and emotional. The lightning bugs had started to come out, and the whippoorwills were sounding off. The peeper frogs were going off. The cicadas were loud. Life was everywhere. I could see the porchlight and people were in the yard and on the porch. The car purred its way up the driveway. I stopped. I could see her. She was calmly walking toward me. Everyone was watching her and me. I turned the car off. I was fighting off crying. I had waited so long for this moment. I opened up the door, and she met me right there. I cried like a baby, and she did too. We couldn't let go of each other. I was never going to let go of her. We kissed and hugged. Our tears mixed together.

Finally, she spoke, "I have saved the best surprise for now," and she looked down at her stomach. She had a baby bump.

"Oh my god. How long did you know, and why didn't you tell me?"

"I knew that day. I could feel it."

"That's got to mean something. I was a virgin and then a dad all in one day."

She punched me in the gut, and we began to laugh. Finally, the crying was over with; I would much rather laugh than cry. We walked up to the family, and everyone hugged me. The young girls would look at me and whisper and laugh. I asked Lisa to marry me right then, and everyone cheered and clapped. Her mom cried. James and the other brother sat back and relaxed. We all knew her brother's death was settled. It was Saturday, and Lisa said, "Sunday, we'll go to church and talk to the preacher."

"Can't we just get married tomorrow?"

She punched me and said, "Oh, no, we are going to have a dance right here." We are going to turn this party we're having into our wedding day."

That's exactly what we did. I got my family and Dunny to come. He couldn't bring Junior: he was too sick. But he sent me a brand new deck of cards. Dunny was my best man. Tee came with Dunny, and he was a groomsman. It was a wedding to be proud of. Lisa wore blue jeans and a white t-shirt. She had on a thick red, white, and blue headband and one big woven ponytail. I couldn't take my eyes off her. I wore the same, except I didn't have a ponytail. We laughed and danced all into the late night. God had blessed me beyond my wildest dreams. I told God I was going to get baptized when all this was settled. The following Sunday, Lisa and I both went forward at the church. The preacher took us to the coldest stream in Hampton. We were man and wife and now baptized. I have thanked God every day since. But I soon discovered that just because we were baptized and married, the prowling lion didn't give up on us, and there were still crossroads, and empty rest stops in front us. But, that is a story for another day. . .

Chapter 64

We have been married now; it's been thirty-five years. Lisa was in the yard. I was sitting on our front porch in Hampton. A great Santana song came on my radio "The Game of Love." I began to daydream about the famous horse that won the Kentucky Derby in 1979, "Spectacular Bid." I remember seeing his picture in a lot of magazines and even on the cover of *Sports Illustrated* magazine. I remember he had an aura about him and that I couldn't help but feel his spirit and desire to win. I love all horses, but the thoroughbred is the one I really can connect with; I felt as if "Spectacular Bid" and I were connected in the spirit world and were racing and both of us had to win. I watched him race on video at the Florida Derby. He stumbled out of the gate, then ran into the fence and then went all the way outside and around to win. It was as if nothing was going to deny him the finish line. I thought that was just like my own life race, to get to Hampton, my life race to get to Lisa in my car it was "my spectacular bid." Even the colors of blue and black that were on his saddle blanket were the same as my SS Chevelle. As I daydreamed and stared out into the yard, Lisa was playing in the yard with the grandkids. She was running around. Funny, how we are in our fifties now, but when I look at her, I still see her as twenty-one, and I still can't take my eyes off her. I still see us at that clay pit. I can still see us walking to the tree house and playing Tom Petty's song "Breakdown." I can see her smile, and I can hear her laughing. How lucky was I to find and marry my first and only love? How lucky was I to even be alive;

my guess is, more than luck, it was a grandmother's prayer and, of course, the ability to laugh a lot with good friends. My mind flashes always end up with my friends and me laughing and the wonderful sound of a cowbell and of the whippoorwills sounding the signal that the night has arrived.

My granddaughter came running up on the porch to me, and she heard a noise come from my cell phone. It sounded like a cowbell hitting a door.

She said, "What was that noise, Pops?"

I said, "Oh, that's my text alert from someone."

I looked at it, and it was a text message from Dunny. Dunny was now the proud owner and sole manager of the Hilltop Liquor store and trailer court and also the Callaway County Network. I looked at the text, and it said, "You still got that nice car?"

I looked up and was watching Lisa play, and she smiled at me. I texted him back, "Yep. . ."

That is my story. . . my spectacular bid and it sounded good.

About the Author

The author still lives in Callaway County Missouri. He follows all the major horse races but has a great interest in the Kentucky Derby. He is a fan of classical rock music of the 1970s and is particularly interested in classical cars from the 1970s as well.

CPSIA information can be obtained
at www.ICGtesting.com
Printed in the USA
LVOW03s1126250517
535774LV00035B/1202/P